The Don's Tale

A Mary Jo Thibodaux Novel

Thomas R. Lawrence

Also by Thomas R. Lawrence:

Delta Days, Tales of the Mississippi Delta

Cow College, Tales of Mississippi State College

will d...a life in science

My Magic Year

Jake's Revenge

The Queen's Captain

Wu's Byte

A Good Tale Well Told

Front Porch Press, LLC
Publishers
4881 Canada Road
Lakeland, Tennessee 38002

Front Porch Press Logo Is a Registered
Trademark of
Front Porch Press, LLC

Library of Congress Cataloging-in-Publication Data
ISBN Print 978-0-9978114-3-8
ISBN E-Book 978-0-9978114-4-5

ACKNOWLEDGMENTS

Special Thanks to the Following:

My companion, Clista Haley, for providing her support, encouragement, and honest feedback throughout my writing.

Tim Patton, photographer extraordinaire, for the *About the Author* image.

My copy editor, Maggie Lee, for her final edits of the book.

My business partner, Deborah Fagan Carpenter, for performing the first edits, providing the cover art and design, formatting the book, and executing all production.

For My Children,

Sam, John, and Mary

INTRODUCTION

Tom Lawrence embraced many passions, and, in Mary Jo Thibodaux, he created a character who is fully engaged in all of them. Sadly, Tom didn't live long enough to bring all of his concepts for the adventurous, strong-willed protagonist to fruition, but in *The Don's Tale* he gives his audience a comprehensive look at most of what she embodies.

In *Jake's Revenge,* readers were introduced to the charmed Mobile, Alabama, life of retired army counterintelligence officer, Mary Jo Thibodaux. In that first book of the series, she's revealed to be not only a successful engineer and a skilled investigator, but also an expert at managing physical confrontation. *Wu's Byte* presented a slightly more cerebral and organizational side of Mary Jo, with just a glimpse of the warrior she is at her core. In *The Don's Tale,* a beautiful, sexy, competent, deadly combatant takes center stage.

All of Tom's books make it abundantly clear that he was a food lover, an enthusiastic traveler, and a soldier at heart, and *The Don's Tale* is no exception. Mary Jo Thibodaux is thoroughly wined and dined in France and Italy, and Tom's love of travel and his command of observation and detail allow the reader to experience the magic of Paris, the beauty of Rome, and the intrigue of Corsica. In addition, *The Don's Tale* provides the opportunity for would-be warriors — like Tom — to live vicariously through the escapades of the heroine.

I continue to grieve the loss of my friend Tom Lawrence, and I also mourn the sad fact that he won't be able to further develop his writing passion and his captivating character, Mary Jo Thibodaux. *The Don's Tale* is a fitting end to the three-book series, however, as readers share a life-altering journey with the "take no prisoners" leading lady.

— Deborah Fagan Carpenter

ONE

ERNESTO CAPRIATI SNUGGLED in the wool blanket and turned toward the crackling fire. Outside, rain and wind beat against the windows of his study. One of Corsica's rare winter storms had descended from Northern Europe with Viking fury, but Capriati knew that it would blow itself out and the warm, sunny Corsican December would return. He was drifting to sleep when a sharp knock came from his study door. He put on his glasses and called out, "Prego, entra."

The massive ironclad door swung open, and a grizzled, small, gray-haired man came in and stood silently in front of Capriati. After an extended silence, Capriati said in Italian, "Jeppe, may I assume you are here for some purpose?"

"Si, Don Ernesto, I am."

"Do you care to share with me?"

"Si, Don Ernesto, I do."

"Today?"

"Si, there is a visitor to see you."

"Does this visitor have a name?"

"Si, he is Antonio Vincentia."

"Well, show the man in!"

The little gnome said, "Si, il mio Don," and disappeared through the door.

Capriati smiled to himself and thought, "Jeppe has been at my side since I can remember. He taught me nearly everything I know about leading people, but he still can be as irritating as ever."

Jeppe returned and held the door as a trim man of about 30 entered the room. The visitor had a full head of jet-black hair and the weathered, chiseled face of a seaman. He entered the den and said in Corsu, the Corsican dialect spoken by many of the older families on the island, "Good morning, Don Ernesto. I apologize for interrupting you, but I felt it was important."

"Good morning to you, Antonio. You are always welcome in my home. What can I do for you?"

"I'm afraid I bear disturbing news. One of our ships was attacked and boarded last night; it was left adrift, with all of the crew dead!"

"Who was the captain?"

"Giovanni Brusca."

"And he was killed along with his crew?"

"Si, il mio Don."

Capriati closed his eyes and was silent for a long moment. "Do we know who did this?"

"Not yet, but we will soon. I just received the news from the Italian naval officer who discovered the drifting ship."

"Was the cargo taken?"

"I don't know. The ship is being towed into the naval base at Genoa, and I plan to go see for myself."

"Good, when can you leave?"

"The ship is scheduled to arrive this afternoon. I'd like to be there when it makes port."

"Antonio, if the weather clears, take the helicopter. If not, use our hydrofoil."

"Si. I'll give you a report as soon as I know something."

"In the meantime, be sure that all of our other ships are alerted to the danger and that they take proper precautions."

"This has already been done. I'll find out who is behind this, Don Ernesto, and I'll do it quickly. Now, if you'll excuse me, I need to get ready to go to Genoa."

"Of course, Antonio, and be sure to take care of yourself. You might be their next target."

"Si. I will call as soon as I can."

Antonio turned and left the room, and, immediately, Jeppe came in, walked to the fire, and stood, warming his back. Finally, he spoke. "We both know who is responsible for these treacherous acts."

"Si, Jeppe, I believe we do. It's got to be those Castellanos from Sardinia. The bastards have been nibbling around the edges of our business for the past five years."

"Si, mio Don. Nibbling is one thing, but now they've taken a big bite. What do you plan to do?"

"First, I am going to call the family of my captain and express my deepest sympathy."

"That is a good thing. You might also mention the pension they will receive, and someone should do the same for the dead crewmen."

"Will you see to that?"

"Si, then what?"

"What is your advice, Jeppe?"

"We must be patient. The Castellanos will be prepared for us to react hastily. I suggest that we wait until they drop their guard and then strike them hard. In the meantime, we must see that our ships are well armed and prepared to defend themselves."

"I agree. Let us assign a guard detail to each vessel and provide them with enough firepower to resist a boarding party — something like 20mm cannons and RPGs, along with fully automatic rifles. I doubt the Castellanos will have anything more substantial."

"Mio Don, these things are inevitable in our business. Where there are great rewards, there will always be those who want to take it for themselves. As our cousins in America like to say, 'It's time to go to the mattresses.'"

"Yes, indeed, it seems to be that time. I regret that this must come during Natale when all of my boys are coming home."

"Do you want me to let them know?"

"No, Jeppe. Let's hope that the Castellanos will wait until the Anno Nuevo to make their next move. I don't want to drag the boys into this. Do we know when they will be arriving?"

"Si, Paulo and his family will be here three days before Natale. Giovanni will be here the next day, and Maurice and his lady friend will arrive at the same time. Paulo has been promoted to Chief Inspector and has taken the whole month off before reporting to Marseilles for his new posting. The entire NATO headquarters closes for Natale, and Giovanni will be coming here after a family vacation in Marrakesh. Jean's ship will be in port in India for Natale, and he will fly in in time."

"Well, again, let's hope this business with the Castellanos will wait until they have come and gone."

"Yes, let's hope. But I fear it won't," Jeppe said under his breath.

TWO

MARY JO THIBODAUX SAT in her office, sipping her third cup of coffee and thinking how lucky she was. "Mobile's a beautiful city in a part of the world I adore. I have a lovely home, a thriving business, and all of the toys I ever dreamed of having. I'm about to leave on a trip to Paris with a wonderful man who loves me and who wants to make me happy. I wonder what I've done to deserve such good fortune."

Mary Jo smiled to herself when she thought about going to Paris with Maurice Lebeaux. He was currently the head of security at the Dalhousie Merchant Bank in Mobile, and she had worked closely with him on several projects earlier in the year. Maurice grew up in Corsica and was (as Maurice had recently revealed to Mary Jo) the oldest son of a Mafia Don. There had been a misunderstanding with the Italian Navy over the contents of one of the Don's ships, and Maurice had accepted an enlistment in the French Foreign Legion, rather than a stint in an Italian prison.

After retiring from the Legion, Maurice had joined a French security firm and was later recruited by the Dalhousie's Bordeaux office. He had quickly been promoted to head of security for North America. The relationship between Mary Jo and Maurice had become intimate after a world of shared interests and mutual physical attraction had overcome any professional reluctance they might have experienced. The trip to Paris and the subsequent trip to Corsica to meet Maurice's family would be their first opportunity to spend extended time alone. They were both looking forward to it.

Thinking about meeting Maurice's Corsican family triggered thoughts of Mary Jo's own family. As she sipped her coffee, Mary Jo reflected on her youth in south Louisiana. Her parents had been killed in an auto accident when she was five, and her mother's sister and her husband had taken Mary Jo in and raised her as their own. She loved her Aunt Claudette and Uncle Carmine, and she was very close to their son, her cousin, Andy. They had hunted and fished the entire Atchafalaya Basin together, and they'd both been talented athletes.

At New Iberia high school, Mary Jo had been a top student and had made the state championship as a sprinter. She finished six out of six in the finals, behind five exceptionally fast girls, but her times and her grades had been sufficient to land her a full ride to run track at LSU.

In Baton Rouge, Mary Jo carried a full load in Civil Engineering, lettered four years in track, and was named a Distinguished Military Student in Army ROTC. She graduated cum laude and received her commission as a 2nd lieutenant in the infantry. Mary Jo found the order and discipline of the military appealing, and she planned to make it a career. She applied for jump school and was accepted, but was turned down for Ranger training, due to her gender.

Mary Jo quickly realized that the peacetime army bored her, and she needed to find a way to get closer to the action. She attracted the attention of army intelligence, and, after extensive testing and interviewing, she was accepted and sent to Fort Huachuca, Arizona, for training. Mary Jo demonstrated such skill in both the classroom and the field that she was chosen for counterintelligence and assigned to the 902nd Military Intelligence Group at Fort Meade, Maryland.

One of Mary Jo's first solo missions was working with a Navy SEAL team in Afghanistan. She was wounded during the assignment and received the Silver Star for gallantry in that action. After recovering from her injuries, she rejoined her unit and ran independent operations all over the world.

While Mary Jo sat in her courtyard, letting the memories flow through her mind, her cell phone began to play "Hold That Tiger," the LSU fight song. She checked the caller ID and saw "Maurice Lebeaux" on the screen. She smiled to herself and answered in Cajun French, "Mon Cher, laissez les bon temps roulette."

"Oh no, Mary Jo! *Please* tell me you won't try that out in Paris," he replied, stifling a laugh.

"You're one to talk. Your French sounds like a Corsican peasant."

"At least it's close to modern French. That stuff y'all speak in south Louisiana is like Chaucerian English," Maurice responded.

"Well, hopefully, one of us will be able to order dinner. I'm glad you called. I need to run a couple of things by you about our trip. Got a minute?"

"Sure, what's up?"

"The first thing is nonnegotiable. I'm paying for this whole thing from start to finish. I've got more money than I'll ever spend, so I won't accept any arguments, okay?"

"I'm perfectly willing to go Dutch. I'm not exactly broke. I know your grandfather's settlement with the oil companies set you up for life, but don't forget that my father is a major Mafia figure in Corsica."

Mary Jo thought, "I know he's right. His father is probably a billionaire, and I need to go easy on his male ego."

Mary Jo said, "Okay, Dutch it is. Now, for the second thing. I'd like for us to take my plane. I know it's not designed to fly the Atlantic, but I've figured out a route that will be safe. It'll take a couple of days, but it might be fun to do it."

"Mary Jo, I respect your flying skills, and I enjoy flying with you, but wouldn't it be a lot easier to go commercial?"

"I don't know about easier. It would certainly be faster, but I have another reason to take my plane. I want to trade it in while we're in Europe."

"Yes, go on."

"There's a dealer in Paris who has a Cessna Citation CJ4 that is bigger, is faster, and has almost twice the range of my Mustang, and it can get in and out of the same small airports. I've cut an exceptional deal; thus, we can fly it while we're in Europe, *and*, with its extended range, we can get home much faster."

"I don't see why not. It'll make getting to Corsica to see my folks a lot easier. Can we still leave in time to spend Christmas with my family?"

"No problem. If we leave next Monday, we'll have some time in Paris before we go to Corsica for Christmas."

"Alright then. I'll let Emile know that I'll be taking a month off, starting next Monday. Since we'll be using my family's flat in Paris, we won't have to worry about hotel reservations, so we can be flexible."

"Speaking of Emile," Mary Jo said, "I need to give him a call…so we're agreed? We leave next Monday on my plane, and we split the whole trip down the middle?"

"Agreed. Now, if I'm going to be gone for a month, I need to get back to work. See you tonight?"

"Yes. Plan on coming over for dinner."

"Great! What's Laurie fixing?"

"Why? Will that determine whether or not you're coming?"

"No, but I like to know anyway."

"Well, call her and ask. I gotta go work on our flight plan.

Before Mary Jo started on the flight plan, she placed a call to Emile Dalhousie.

A pleasant female voice answered, "Good morning, Mary Jo. How can I help you?"

"Morning, Melissa. Is Emile available?"

"He's just finishing a conference call. He should be off in a minute or two. Do you want me to have him call you?"

"No, just put me on hold till he can pick up. If I leave the line, I'll call back."

"Okay. He'll only be a moment."

The on-hold music started, and Mary Jo placed the phone in its cradle and punched the speaker button to wait for Emile. Mary Jo's mind went back to when she first encountered the Dalhousie firm. She had just been released from the army hospital in San Antonio and had been promoted to senior agent. Shortly after arriving at Ft. Meade, there was a letter from a law firm in Houston informing her that the class-action suit her Thibodaux great-grandfather had joined in 1928, accusing a group of oil companies of obtaining fraudulent mineral leases on the small family farm, had finally been settled. As the only heir of Aldo Thibodaux, Sr., Mary Jo had been awarded $41,989,776 as her share of the settlement.

The letter, of course, had stunned Mary Jo. She had received $250,000 in life insurance when her parents had been killed, and it was put in a trust for her care and education. The full track scholarship to LSU paid for most of her college costs, and the bulk of the insurance money had been released to her when she reached age 25. This nest egg, along with her salary as an army officer, had allowed her to live comfortably. Now, she was faced with what in the hell to do with nearly 42-million dollars.

Mary Jo mentioned her problem to Col. Will Ransom, her CO, and he told her that his family had been investing with the Dalhousie Merchant Bank in Mobile for over 150 years and were extremely pleased. Will introduced Mary Jo to Emile, and she became a Dalhousie client. They had managed her money well, and today her account was valued at a little over $71,000,000.

The Dalhousie firm had sent several clients to Mary Jo for civil-engineering work, and, recently, Emile had arranged a client more suitable to her military skills. Mary Jo had solved the mystery of the disappearance of Jake Broussard, who was, at the time of his death in 1964, the U.S. Attorney for south Alabama. Mary Jo led the team that found out what happened, and, in the process, Jake's killer was brought to justice.

The speaker clicked, and Emile Dalhousie said, "Hello, Mary Jo. What can I do for you?"

Mary Jo picked up the receiver and replied, "Hi, Emile. Just wanted to give you a heads-up that I plan to buy a used Cessna Citation CJ4 while Maurice and I are in France."

"Do you know how much it will cost?"

"Yeah. I've made a deal for my Mustang and $2,800,000. I'll pick it up as soon as we get to Paris, and we'll use it during our trip."

"How do you plan to get your plane to Europe?"

"Maurice and I are going to fly it there."

"I didn't realize your little jet could handle that distance."

"It can't do the trans-Atlantic flight, but I plan to hop across the better part of the Northern Hemisphere."

"Wouldn't it make more sense to ship it by boat? I'll let you and Maurice fly to Paris on our Gulfstream."

"Yeah, it makes more sense, but it won't be half the fun. Thanks for the offer of the Gulfstream, but we'll be just fine."

"I know better than to argue once you've made up your mind. The funds will be available from our branch in Paris, and I'll email you the manager's contact info. When do y'all plan to leave?"

"We'll leave next Monday and return before New Year's Eve. Maurice is planning to fill you in today."

"Yes, he and I have a meeting scheduled for 3:00 this afternoon. I know he's concerned about leaving for a month since Dan Cannon left us for Brooks Capital, but I'm sure we'll be fine. He does realize the risk of flying your plane to Europe, doesn't he?"

"Of course, and don't try to talk him out of it! We'll have a wonderful trip. Are you concerned about security with Maurice gone for a month?"

"Not at all. He's arranged for Bill Prisock, who's been with us for over five years, to be in charge while he's gone. By the way, what do you hear from Brooks?"

"Quite a lot. Thibodaux Engineering is working on two projects for him. We're designing and constructing the test tower for the Tesla project at Will Ransom's plantation in Mississippi, and we're designing the pitchblende processing plant that will be built on the Jicarilla Apache reservation in West Texas. How's the decimal-skimming system working?"

"Just like we planned. Alan is only running it a couple of hours a day, but we are still booking close to a $1,000,000 each trading day."

"That ought to keep the ranch working. I know he's anxious to see the results of the Tesla project. If it works as we hope, it can provide the power needed to run the pitchblende plant, as well as supply the Jicarillas with all the power they'll ever need."

"Well, money will never be the problem for him. Incidentally, did you get an invitation to Maria Broussard's New Year's ball?"

"I did, and Maurice and I plan to return in time to be there. I haven't seen enough of Maria since we took care of John Henry. I'm sure the Littons will be invited, but I don't know if General Litton will be up to it."

"Since the John Henry business, Jack and I have become much closer. In fact, he's joined our weekly poker game, and he's killing us."

"After spending a career as a spymaster, I suspect he's a formidable poker player."

"Oh, he's one of the best I've ever seen. I hope the rest of us can afford to fund his winnings."

"I'll give him a call before I leave for Europe and wish Karen and him happy holidays. He and Amy Wilson keep in touch, so I know he'll be up on what's going on at Brooks Capital."

"Good. Is there anything else I can do for you?"

"Just remind Constance that I'm sorry we can't attend your Christmas party, but I hope we'll see y'all at Maria's ball."

"You and Maurice have a wonderful time in Paris, and, if you need anything, our manager in the Paris office is at your disposal."

"Thanks, Emile; I'll meet him when I pick up the check for the plane, so I'll know where to find him. I hope you and Constance have a wonderful Christmas, and I look forward to seeing you when we get back."

Mary Jo replaced the receiver and turned to her computer. She logged on to the flight-planning software and entered the tail number of her Cessna Mustang. The screen filled with all of the data about her plane. Then, she entered Mobile, Alabama, as the starting point and Paris, France, as the destination. The screen filled with the details of her proposed flight, including the weather forecast for the entire trip.

Mary Jo looked the proposed flight plan over and decided that it would work. The software had built in a 20% margin of error and did not have any single leg of the trip over 900 air miles. The Mustang had a fully fueled range of nearly 1,200 miles. The long-range weather forecast didn't show any problems for flying the North Atlantic the next week, but that could always change, and the go/no-go decision would be made next Monday.

Mary Jo also liked the fact that the system converted all time to local, so they would have time to eat dinner and relax in Halifax and Reykjavik without rushing to get back in the air. She decided to book the flight plan, which would automatically send her notice if weather conditions turned bad. Then, she called Carson Aviation and requested that they do a full check-over of the little jet before the trip. If something was about to break, then she didn't want to be at 30,000 feet over the Atlantic when it happened.

By the time Mary Jo had completed her flight plan, Laurie, her housekeeper and cook, had buzzed her to tell her that lunch was ready. Mary Jo made a few last-minute adjustments and then took the elevator down to the first floor. Her home at 737 St. Louis Street was a three-story brick town house, built as a family home in the 1840s after a fire had destroyed the original 18th-century structure. The old house had seen many renovations and commercial uses since being put on the market in 1953. Mary Jo bought the building from the estate of an attorney, and she had completely restored it, along with adding many modern conveniences, such as an elevator and a state-of-the-art security system.

When Mary Jo walked into the kitchen, she saw Laurie placing a steaming bowl of red beans and rice on the breakfast-nook table. All along the Gulf Coast, Monday was traditionally wash day. In the old days, washing the family's clothes took all day, with multiple washtubs of soap, bleach, whitener, and starch. It made a lot of sense to put on a pot of red beans early in the morning and let it simmer all day until the washing was done. With a little white rice and butter, and some French bread, supper was on the table with relative ease. The advent of modern washers and dryers made short work of the dirty clothes, but bowls of red beans and rice were still often Monday's main offering.

After lunch, Mary Jo returned to her private suite on the third floor and stripped out of her clothes. As she stood naked in front of a full-length mirror, she thought to herself, "I guess I still look pretty good, for 37." All in all, she was holding together well. She smiled when she saw the Airborne insignia tattooed on her left thigh, courtesy of a night on the town after graduation from the Parachute School at Ft. Bragg. The gold sphinx insignia of Army Intelligence on her other thigh had been added later — to provide balance.

Mary Jo worked out regularly, could still run 20 miles with a full pack, and could swim to Panama and back if she had to. It had been three years since she left the army, but one never knew. She intended to be ready in the event she needed any of her hard-earned skills.

After a shower, Mary Jo wrapped herself in a full-length robe and sat on the edge of her bed, looking at her closet and realizing that she didn't have nearly enough appropriate outfits to spend several weeks in Europe — or anywhere else for that matter. Mary Jo owned two little black dresses and one formal gown, and the rest of her wardrobe leaned toward jeans and t-shirts. She thought, "Oh hell, I'd rather have a root canal or a pelvic exam, but I'm just gonna have to bite the bullet and go shopping. I've got to have some help though. This seems like the perfect time to give Constance a call."

THREE

MARY JO TOOK ANOTHER LOOK in her closet, sighed, and placed a call to Constance Dalhousie. Constance was Parisian to her core, and she exuded the chic elegance of French femininity. She and Emile had met during the two years he had spent working in the firm's Paris branch. He had been in his late twenties, had graduated from Texas A&M, had served two tours in Vietnam, and had completed the banking course at the London School of Economics. Constance Leclerc was a student at the Sorbonne, and they met during a weekend at her family's chateau in the Loire Valley. They were married within the year and returned to Mobile when Emile came back to train as the firm's managing partner in North America. The offices in New Orleans, Charleston, Boston, and Montreal were to be his responsibility.

Constance answered the phone with her slight French accent: "Hello, Mary Jo. Glad you called. Emile tells me that you and Maurice are spending the holidays in Paris."

"Well, we'll leave Paris just before Christmas to go to Maurice's home in Corsica, but we'll have over a week in Paris before we leave, and that's why I'm calling. I need some help putting together a wardrobe for the trip, and, Constance, you know how much your approval means to me. I think you're the final word on fashion and style."

Constance, who did her shopping in New York and Paris, and probably had never been in a local store, replied, "You are far too kind. I suspect you have elegant taste, but I question your love of shopping."

"You've hit the nail on the head. I truly hate to shop."

"I would love to do whatever I can to help," replied Constance. "What do you have in mind?"

"First of all, I have no idea what I'll need. I know we'll be eating lunch and dinner out and visiting all of the Parisian tourist sites. Maybe you can help me put something together?"

"When do you plan to leave?"

"Weather permitting, we'll take off next Monday and arrive in Paris on Wednesday afternoon."

"You said, 'weather permitting.' Is there a storm coming?"

"No, but we're going to take my little jet across the top of the world, and weather in Greenland and Iceland can be tricky this time of year."

"You're so adventurous, my dear. Well, that doesn't leave us much time to work on your wardrobe, but I think I know the solution."

"I'm glad to hear you say that. I'm near panic mode."

Constance paused for a moment and then said, "I don't believe we have enough time to do justice to a shopping trip in New York. I usually spend several days, at the very least, when I go, but don't despair. My younger sister, Collette, lives in Paris and is a shopping maven. I'll call her and arrange for her to meet you when you first get there."

"Oh, Constance, I hate to be such a bother. Please don't drag your poor sister into my wardrobe dilemma."

"Don't be silly. Collette will be thrilled to help you, but I must warn you — have your checkbook ready. Collette's husband, Augustin Beaumarchais, is chairman of one of France's largest industrial companies, and he indulges her every whim. Frugal she's not."

"She sounds like just what I need. When you talk to her, tell her that money will not be an object."

"Maybe that's not such a good plan. Collette will have you decked out in Coco's most elegant creations, wrapped in sable. Let's give her some budget guidelines."

Mary Jo asked, "What do you think?"

"If it were for me, I would insist that she not exceed $50,000. She'll argue that it will be insufficient and finally agree to something near $100,000. The good news is that she will leave you with the foundation of a world-class wardrobe. Of course, you and I will be responsible for keeping it up to that standard, so you'll have to accompany me to New York twice a year."

Mary Jo's head was reeling. Never in her whole life would she expect to spend anywhere near that much on clothes — guns maybe, but never clothes. Mary Jo managed to choke down her shock and replied, "Constance, I can't wait to meet Collette. I'll bet she's a real piece of work."

"That she is. As Emile is quick to say, 'Collette is hard to guard.' If you'll give me your contact information in Paris, I'll give her a call and set it all up."

"We're staying in Maurice's family flat somewhere on the Left Bank. I'll ask him to let Emile know the address and phone number."

"I'm envious of the two of you turned loose in Paris with the whole city to shop. I'll expect a full play-by-play account when you return."

"I just hope I'll have gas money to fly back, but, now that I think about it, I realize that I'm spending nearly $3,000,000 on a new jet. What's a hundred thousand on a few dresses? I may have to retain you as my lifestyle coach."

"We'll talk about that when you return. I might just have some ideas along those lines too."

"I can't wait to hear them. Thanks, Constance. You're a lifesaver. We'll talk when I get back."

"Adieu, my dear. You and Maurice enjoy your trip and hug Collette for me."

After finishing her conversation with Constance, Mary Jo decided to make the other two calls she had on her "before leaving for Paris" list. She wanted to be certain that she had time to catch up with three special people. Mary Jo dialed a number and waited until a deep, resonant male voice answered: "You have reached Terrebonne Plantation. This is Justin. How may I help you?"

"Good afternoon, Justin. This is Mary Jo Thibodaux. Is Maria available?"

"Madam is having tea in the study. I'm sure she will be pleased to hear from you. And, Miss Thibodaux, I've never had the opportunity to tell you how much I appreciate what you did to solve Mr. Jake's murder. It has made a difference in Madam's frame of mind. She seems to be at peace finally."

"I'm pleased to hear this, Justin. You are kind to mention my involvement."

"Of course, and now I'll take the phone to Madam."

In a moment Maria Broussard answered: "Why, Mary Jo, it's good to hear from you. It seems ages since we last spoke."

"It has been too long, and I apologize. I spent the last month or so helping a friend set up a business in the wilds of West Texas."

"Did it involve the kind of work you did for Jake and me?"

"Just a bit, but it all worked out, and now I'm preparing to leave for Paris next Monday."

"How exciting! I love Paris, and it's been eons since I've been there. I hope Maurice is going with you."

"He is, but how could you possibly know that?"

"Good news travels fast in my circle, and I've visited with Constance Dalhousie."

"I should've guessed. Well, Constance is helping me put a wardrobe together, or at least her sister in Paris will be helping."

"Oh, my heavens! Don't tell me you're going shopping with Collette?"

"That's the plan. Should I be worried?"

"Not if you can afford it. I met Collette when Constance was Queen of Mardi Gras. She and Augustin spent nearly a month in Mobile and New Orleans. I accompanied Constance and Collette on a shopping trip to New York. I always thought I was a world-class shopper, but I paled in comparison to Collette."

"Well, she's going to help me when I get to Paris, so I guess I better increase the limits on my credit cards."

"You needn't worry about credit cards. Where Collette shops, they just bill her husband. I'd set something up with

Emile before I left if I were you. I hope y'all will be back in time for my New Year's Ball."

"Absolutely! We wouldn't miss it, and I should have something fabulous to wear."

"If Collette is responsible, you'll be the belle of the ball for sure."

"I'll settle for something on the upper side of dowdy."

"Mary Jo, my dear, you couldn't do 'dowdy' if you tried. I envy your natural beauty, and, speaking of envy, I'm quite jealous that you're getting to shop in Paris with Collette. I can't wait to see the results."

"You'll get those results on New Year's. I hope you have a happy holiday season, and I'll see you December 31st."

"I can't wait. You and Maurice have a great time."

Mary Jo disconnected, leaned back in her chair, and thought about the day Emile introduced her to Maria. Mary Jo had gone to the Dalhousie offices to discuss a different type of consulting assignment, and Emile wanted to present her to the client. When they entered the conference room, Maria Broussard stood to greet them. She was dressed all in white, including a large, white garden hat. Nature had blessed Maria with a pale, clear complexion (usually described as ethereal), bright green eyes, short gray hair, and the figure of a Dallas Cowboys cheerleader. If Mary Jo had done the math right, Maria should've been somewhere in her eighties, and, yet, there was not a wrinkle or worry line to be seen. Either she was a genetic miracle, or she had a fabulous plastic surgeon. Either way, Maria looked like an angel descended to earth. Mary Jo thought, "My gracious! She's the most beautiful woman I've ever seen. She could be a movie star!"

In the aftermath of the assignment, Mary Jo and Maria had remained close friends and tried to see each other as much as possible. Today's visit was the first conversation they'd managed since Mary Jo had accepted the assignment in Texas. It was good to catch up.

Mary Jo wanted to make one more call before Maurice came over for dinner, so she dialed it now, and Karen Litton answered. "Mary Jo, you must be back from Texas."

"I am, and I've meant to call to check on you and the General. How are y'all doing?"

"I'm fine. Beginning to feel my age a bit, but I guess that's to be expected. Jack is still doing too much; he's fallen in with Emile Dalhousie and his buddies. They're playing poker once a week, and, so far, they haven't figured out Jack's fatal poker flaw — he's cleaning them out."

"Yes, I was talking to Emile earlier, and he mentioned something to that effect. I'm surprised to hear that the General has a flaw in his game."

"Oh, he does, and they'll catch on quick enough. Jack plays poker like he plays gin. He plays every hand."

"You're right; that'll catch up with him sooner or later. In the meantime, he has it all his way. Is he available?"

"Yes, he's sitting right here itching to talk to you. Let me hand him the phone."

Jack Litton came on the line and said, "Mary Jo, Amy Wilson has filled me in on your adventures in West Texas, but I want to hear all about it from you. Can you join Karen and me for lunch tomorrow?"

Mary Jo thought for a moment and then said, "I'd love to. I've got a lot to tell you."

"Shall we say about noon then?"

"Noon will be fine; I'll see y'all tomorrow."

Mary Jo looked at her watch and decided she still had time before the day ended to check in with Allie, her engineering firm's office manager. Mary Jo walked across the hall, tapped on Allie's office doorframe, and said, "Hey. You got a minute before you leave?"

"Sure, come on in."

Mary Jo took a seat in one of the chairs facing Allie's desk and said, "Just wanted to touch base. We're still planning to leave for Europe next Monday, and I thought we'd better go over all of the projects before I leave."

"Yeah, good idea. We're in pretty good shape. We just received the final check for the Ono Island project. I talked to Bill Thornton yesterday, and he's completely pleased. The catfish project up in Greensboro is close to finalized. Auburn's School of Fisheries is sending their final changes to me this week, and we'll be ready to put the construction job out for bids when I get them. I'm working with Mississippi State on the chitosan project for Frank Carcello. Their engineering department is still working on a test plant, but it'll be several more months before we can get involved, so that's pretty much on hold."

"How about the stuff for Brooks Capital?"

"Well, that's moving along a little faster. Dr. Volanov has constructed a small test tower at Mississippi State, and it worked. He's sending me the plans, and I'm going to scale it up to full production size. We'll be ready to start construction sometime after the first of the year. The pitchblende project on the Apache reservation is waiting on the power project. I've pulled info from the web about a pitchblende processing plant though, and it's going to be complex. You've got a hundred permits and studies to do, and the NRA gets involved."

"Yeah, but I don't think anything will break on it before I get back from Europe," Mary Jo said.

"No, and I can handle anything else that comes up, so go and have a great Christmas in Corsica," Allie replied.

"Will do. Maurice is coming over for dinner, so I'll see you in the morning."

"Great. I'll be leaving in a few. Want to finish up on something, and then I'm outta here."

Mary Jo took the elevator back to her suite and decided to fix her hair and what little makeup she used before Maurice arrived. When she'd freshened up, Mary Jo took the elevator to the first floor, and, just as she entered the hallway, she heard the buzzer indicating someone wanted into the parking area. She walked to the control panel and pushed the "Enter" button.

Maurice came bursting through the garage door and said, "What smells so good? Laurie, what wonder have you come up with?"

"Go on, Mr. Maurice. I ain't got no wonder, just shrimp and grits."

"Your shrimp and grits dish is indeed a wonder to behold, and will there be andouille in it?"

"You know my shrimp and grits recipe has andouille in it, and you know there'll be French bread and butter too."

"Laurie, you are the chef of my dreams. If you were single, I'd propose."

"I 'spect you better save your proposals. You may be needing 'em," Laurie retorted with a grin.

After dinner, Mary Jo and Maurice sat in the courtyard, listening to music and sipping brandy until bedtime. Later, when they were lying in bed, Mary Jo thought how comfortable they had grown with each other, and how their lovemaking flowed naturally. She realized that Maurice was everything she'd dreamed about and fell asleep in his arms.

***

The next week flew by in a blur. Mary Jo spent her time checking on the Mustang, running last-minute errands, and visiting with the Littons, while Maurice made sure that all would run smoothly at the Dalhousie firm while he was away. On Monday morning, Bill Prisock dropped them off at Carson Aviation and helped Maurice load their luggage on the Cessna, while Mary Jo did another check on the weather and filed a final flight plan.

Doug Hastings, Carson's manager, joined the couple as Mary Jo filed the plan. Doug said, "I just went over all of the paperwork on your plane. Everything is in order for the trade-in for your CJ4."

"Thanks, Doug," Mary Jo replied. "I appreciate the work y'all did on such short notice."

"No problem. Y'all have a safe flight, and I'll see you and your new plane at the end of the month."

Mary Jo took Maurice over to the flight-plan monitor and called up their plan. She turned the monitor so that Maurice could view it and said, "As you can see, today, we'll refuel in Richmond, Virginia, and spend the night in Halifax, Nova Scotia. Tomorrow, we'll refuel at Goose Bay, Newfoundland, and Nuuk, Greenland, before spending the night in Reykjavik, Iceland. On Wednesday, we'll refuel on the Isle of Skye in Scotland and land in Paris shortly after noon.

Maurice studied the plan and said, "Your little jet can handle all of this?"

"With ease. No flight is more than 900 miles, and the Mustang has a fully loaded range of 1,200 miles. We'll have a 25% margin for error if we encounter headwinds or weather."

"Where will we spend the nights, at the airport?"

"No, we have rooms at first-class hotels and dinner reservations in top-rated restaurants in Halifax and Reykjavik, and plenty of time to enjoy them, thank you very much."

"Well, you seem to have covered everything. Let's get this show on the road."

Mary Jo lifted off from Mobile at 6:55 CDT and landed for fuel in Richmond at 10:30 EDT. The flight to Halifax took a little over three hours, and they landed at 5:00 local time. After Mary Jo attended to the plane, they caught a taxi to the Lord Nelson Hotel.

The hotel was elegant and comfortable, and the couple made love before showering together and dressing for dinner. Mary Jo had learned that the Victory Arms restaurant in the hotel was considered to be one of the best in Halifax, and they had a great meal and impeccable service. They slept soundly that night and were up and back at the airport by 6:00 the next morning.

The first leg of the day's flights from Halifax to Goose Bay, Newfoundland, only took two hours, but Mary Jo wanted a full load of fuel before they flew across the ocean to Greenland. They refueled in Nuuk and landed at Reykjavik at 6:30 local time. It was close to dinnertime when their taxi dropped them at the main entrance to the Hotel Borg.

After a quick change of clothes, the two hailed a cab, and Mary Jo told the driver to take them to Restaurant Sjavargrillid. On the short ride to the restaurant, she said, "It didn't take long to figure out that eating in Iceland pretty much means fish. I know you love steak, but tonight it's going to be seafood."

Maurice grinned and said, "I'm fine with seafood. Remember, I grew up on an island."

"We'll put that to the test tonight."

The meal was fabulous; the fresh Atlantic cod was cooked to perfection, and the service was outstanding. The couple made it back to the room in time to shower together, and they fell asleep shortly afterward. They caught an early breakfast in the hotel dining room and were airborne by 7:00 a.m.

The travelers refueled on the Isle of Skye and crossed the English Channel before noon. Mary Jo had decided to use Orly Airport, just to the south of Paris, partly because it was friendlier to private aviation but also because it was the home field of her new CJ4. She set down just before 2:00 local time and followed the guides to the private aviation terminal.

Maurice took over managing their luggage while Mary Jo made arrangements to have her plane cared for. They met at customs and were soon waiting in line for a cab. When the bags had been loaded into the taxi, Maurice told the driver to take them to 8 Rue de Saint-Simon.

FOUR

THE TAXI FOLLOWED THE SIGNS to Paris, and, soon, the travelers were on the péage, moving north with the traffic. They were speeding above the southern suburbs of Paris, and Maurice carried on a monologue about points of interest. Mary Jo smiled to herself and relaxed. The flight was over, and they were on Maurice's turf. She was glad to relinquish control.

When the taxi turned onto the Boulevard St. Germain, Maurice began to reach for his wallet. The driver turned left onto Rue de Saint-Simon and pulled to the curb at number 8. Mary Jo stood on the narrow sidewalk and watched as Maurice and the driver unloaded their luggage in front of a three-story town house.

Maurice opened the front entrance, and the couple walked into an elegantly decorated foyer with a winding staircase. There was a study to the right — with a fire crackling in the fireplace — and a dining room to the left. Mary Jo looked at the fire and said, "Seems that we were expected."

Maurice smiled and said, "Yes, I called ahead. Louie, our caretaker, has been at work."

Just then, a senior man, dressed in dark pants and a white shirt buttoned to the top, came through the hallway. A huge grin crossed his weathered face, and he embraced Maurice, chattering in a language that Mary Jo had never heard. Maurice hugged the man tightly and said something in the same language.

Louie Pastise nodded in agreement and said in English, "Of course, Mon Patron, English it will be."

Pastise turned to Mary Jo and added, "Welcome to Paris, Miss Thibodaux. We have been looking forward to your visit."

"Mary Jo, this is Louie Pastise. He and his wife, Portia, are our caretakers."

Mary Jo took Louie's outstretched hand, shook it, and said, "I'm pleased to meet you, Louie, and your English is perfect."

"Oui, I'm afraid that it is much better than my French. Now, you must excuse me. Portia needs my help upstairs."

When Louie had disappeared, Mary Jo asked, "What language were you and Louie speaking at first?"

"It's Corsu, the patois spoken by the natives of Corsica. It has its origins in ancient Etruscan."

"Well, I hope to *never* have to learn it. It sounds impossible to the ear."

"Most of my family speaks it, but we only use it when we don't want to be overheard. They all speak English and will probably use it exclusively if you're present."

"I'll appreciate that. What are we planning for the rest of the day?"

Maurice grinned and said, "Unless you have something pressing, I thought we'd spend the afternoon relaxing and then go around the corner to a small neighborhood café for dinner."

"Sounds good to me. I need to get in touch with the Dalhousie office here, and I'll want to contact Collette tomorrow."

"Well, then, let me take you upstairs and show you the bedroom.

***

The next morning, when the couple came down, Portia had a tray of brioches and croissants, along with a fresh urn of coffee, waiting on the breakfast table. Mary Jo and Maurice were finishing a second cup of coffee when the doorbell rang, and Louie came and handed Mary Jo an envelope.

Mary Jo slit the sealed envelope and read the card. When she finished, she looked at Maurice and said, "We seem to have our first Parisian invitation. Collette and her husband have invited us to dinner at their home on Saturday evening."

"Oh shit," Maurice said. "I guess it's formal."

"I have no idea; it says 'vetement decontracte,' whatever that means."

"It means business casual, so I can probably handle that. How about you?"

"I have my little black dress, so I guess it'll have to do. I'm sure Collette will be planning to take me shopping and repair my woefully inadequate wardrobe. You might consider doing some shopping, as well. Business casual probably won't cut it for dinner at a three-star joint."

"You're joking, but I do need some clothes. Will we have a problem going home with more baggage?"

"Shouldn't be a problem. The new plane will have additional baggage capacity, and we didn't even half fill the Mustang."

Maurice asked, "Is the invitation RSVP?"

"Yes, there's a telephone number provided. I'll call and accept later this morning. I need to get in touch with the Dalhousies and the broker who's handling my purchase of the CJ4."

"While you're doing all of that, I'll call Corsica and let the family know we're safely in Paris. My father seemed a little concerned when I told him how we were getting here."

"While you're talking to him, ask which airport we'll need to use."

"There's a commercial field near our home in Ajaccio. I've flown into it before, and it can handle big jets."

"I'll get our flight plan put together when I boot up my computer. We do have a high-speed connection, don't we?"

"Of course. My father is in the shipping business, so he is never far from a computer."

Maurice wrote something on a pad, handed it to Mary Jo, and said, "Here's the connection. You won't even know you're in a third-world country."

"Don't be a smart ass. I knew Paris would be equipped, but Corsica may be another story."

"You'll just have to wait and see," Maurice replied. "But, for now, I'll let you use the office on the third floor, and I'll use my cell."

After another cup of coffee, Mary Jo climbed the stairs to the office and booted her computer. She found the email from Melissa, giving her the contact information for the Dalhousie Paris office. Mary Jo dialed the number and was connected immediately. A young man answered in French: "Bonjour, c'est la firme Bancaire Dalhousie."

"Bonjour. Do you speak English?"

"Oui, Madam. How may I assist you?"

"My name is Mary Jo Thibodaux, and I'd like to speak to Monsieur Benoit."

"I will see if Monsieur Benoit is available."

After a slight pause, Benoit picked up and said, "Ah, Mademoiselle Thibodaux, I've been expecting your call. Did you have a pleasant flight?"

"Yes, pleasant and uneventful, thank you."

"Wonderful. Now, I believe you will be buying a new airplane while you are here?"

"Yes, and I'll need to draw against my account to pay for it."

"That will be no problem. Simply give the representative my telephone number, and either I or my assistant will take care of everything. Do you know when you'll complete the purchase?"

"No, but I'm sure it will be this week. I wanted to talk to you before I called the seller."

"Very well. We'll take care of it when you are ready. Now, is there any other way I can be of assistance?"

"As a matter of fact, there is. I'll be doing some shopping while I'm here, and I'd like for the bills to be paid from my account. Can you make such arrangements?"

"Of course. Do you know where you'll be shopping?"

"I have no idea, but I'll be shopping with a local lady who knows her way around Paris."

"Do you mind if I ask her name?"

"Not at all. The lady's name is Collette Beaumarchais."

"Ah, the lovely Madam Beaumarchais. She and Augustin are clients, and we handle all of Madam's purchases. We have a complete list of her shops and will set up direct billing for you. Do you want a limit at any one store or an aggregated limit for your visit?"

"No, just let me know if I'm close to running out of money."

Benoit laughed and replied, "Even shopping with Madam Beaumarchais would not exhaust your funds."

"After what I've been told about Collette, I'm not so sure about that."

"I'll be certain you're covered. Is there anything else I can do for you and the sergeant major during your visit?"

Mary Jo hesitated and then thought, "Of course, the firm would know Maurice was with me."

Mary Jo regained her composure and said, "Not at the moment, but we won't hesitate to call if something comes up, and thank you for handling my shopping expenditures."

"It is our pleasure; both you and Maurice are valued clients of our firm. Please call if we can be of further service."

"Yes, thank you," Mary Jo replied and broke the connection.

Mary Jo pondered Benoit's remark about Maurice's being a client and realized they'd never talked about his finances, other than his father's Mafia connections. It would seem that Maurice was a client as well as an employee. "Well, that's interesting," Mary Jo thought.

Mary Jo decided to call Collette and accept the dinner invitation before dealing with the aircraft broker, so she dialed the RSVP number.

A male voice answered in French: "Bonjour, ceci est la résidence de Beaumarchais."

Again, Mary Jo asked if he spoke English, and the man answered with a pronounced French accent: "Oui, Madam. May I help you?"

"Yes, I would like to respond to an invitation from Madam Beaumarchais."

"This must be Mademoiselle Thibodaux. Madam asked that I call her to the phone immediately if you rang. One moment please."

Collette Beaumarchais picked up and said in slightly accented English, "Mary Jo, I'm so glad to hear from you. I feared you'd disappeared into the Atlantic."

"No, Collette, to everyone's amazement we made it here without a problem. I'm calling to accept your kind invitation to dinner Saturday evening."

"Oh, wonderful. Augustin and I are excited to meet you and Maurice. We've heard so much about you both. I understand that you are staying in a flat on Rue de Saint-Simon?"

"Yes, it belongs to Maurice's family, so we're using it during our visit."

"That is in the 6th, our arrondissement. Our home in the city is in Saint-Germain des Pres, only blocks away. Our chauffeur will pick you up at 8:00, if that is satisfactory."

"That's very gracious; we can certainly take a taxi if you are so close."

"No, it will be our pleasure. After dinner, you and I will have time to plan our shopping spree, while the men have their cognac and smoke their smelly cigars. I can't wait to show you the best shops in all of France."

"We'll be looking forward to the evening; I've heard so much about you from Constance and Maria that I can't wait to meet you finally."

Collette laughed and said, "I'm looking forward to our meeting, as well. Au revoir until Saturday."

Mary Jo said goodbye and disconnected the call. She looked at her watch and realized that it was getting close to noon — her brioches and croissants were letting her down. She found Maurice sitting at the kitchen table talking on the phone, and, when she came in, he motioned for her to take a seat.

Maurice was speaking that strange Corsican patois, and Mary Jo assumed he was talking to his father. When Maurice hung up, he turned to her and said, "That was my brother, Giovanni. He's stationed at NATO headquarters in Brussels, and he and his family are vacationing in Marrakesh. He plans to fly back and arrive in Ajaccio two days before Christmas. He and I were very close as boys, so I'm looking forward to seeing him."

"I know you're going to enjoy visiting with your brothers, but what about your sisters?"

"They'll all be there. Their husbands work in the family business, and they all live in Ajaccio."

"Well, that will be great. I can't wait to meet them. Now, what are we planning to do for lunch?"

"I thought we'd go around the corner to a local patisserie and grab something light. Tonight, we're going to Chez l'Ami Louis for dinner, so we don't need a big lunch."

"That sounds fine. Tell me more about our evening plans."

"Chez l'Ami Louis is my favorite Paris restaurant. I try to make it at least once on every visit. It's not particularly fancy, but the food is solid country French, and I think you'll love it."

"I'm sure I will, but let's hit the patisserie. I'm getting pretty peckish."

The couple barely beat the lunch crowd, and they both had Croque Monsieur, with a glass of house white wine. The sandwiches were rich and toasty — and surprisingly filling. Maurice and Mary Jo were strolling back to the flat, enjoying the bright, clear December weather and doing a little window shopping, when Maurice asked, "Well, did you get all of your calls made?"

"Not all. I've still got to get in touch with the broker who's handling my airplane. I'd like to get that done and out of the way so that I can concentrate on shopping with Collette next week. We're on for Saturday night; their chauffeur will pick us up at 8:00."

"It's nice to be back in France where no one dines until 9:00. I've never adjusted to having my evening meal at 5:30."

"I suppose the Legion always dined at the proper hour," Mary Jo said with a glint in her eye.

"We did, even if we were deployed. We made every attempt to have a hot meal and a couple of glasses of wine."

"*We* considered ourselves lucky to get an MRE warmed on a can of Sterno if we were in the field," Mary Jo countered.

"That's one of the basic flaws of U.S. military strategy. No class."

"At least the French always welcomed us when we came and saved their asses."

"We have always assumed that you were paying us back for Yorktown where we pinned the British down and held them for your General Washington."

"Yeah, there's that. I guess both countries have a mutual assistance program."

"When are you going to deal with your plane?"

"I'll go up and do it now. I'd like to have a little quiet time with you before dinner."

"Another advantage to eating late," Maurice said with a wide grin.

After lunch, Mary Jo placed a call to the broker and gave him the Dalhousie contact information, and they made an appointment to meet at 10:00 on Friday morning. The broker gave her directions to his office in the Private Aviation Terminal and assured her that he would be prepared to complete the transaction.

After talking with the broker, Mary Jo pulled the file on her Mustang and checked it to be sure she had all of the documentation on maintenance, insurance, and licensing that she'd need. Once satisfied that all was in order, she went back downstairs and found Maurice reading in the library.

Later that evening, the couple caught a cab to Chez l'Ami Louis, which was tucked into a small side street in the neighborhood of the Picasso museum. The small café had only 12 tables, and there was a crowd spilling onto the sidewalk and waiting to be seated. Maurice and Mary Jo went to a side door, were admitted at once, and were seated at a table for two.

Mary Jo smiled across the table and said, "Do I detect the long arm of the Mafia at work on our reservation?"

"Not really. I'm truly a loyal customer, and I always call ahead."

A waiter came to the table, spoke to Maurice in French, and asked if the couple would like a bottle of wine. Maurice ordered a carafe of the house Bordeaux, and they had a glass as Maurice explained the menu: "As you know, I love foie gras, and this is the best I've ever had, so I'm taking the liberty of requesting an order for both of us."

"You can't go wrong with foie gras," Mary Jo agreed.

"The specialty of the house is poulet roti, a perfectly roasted chicken, served with the best pommes frites in Paris. The chicken is huge, and we can easily split one. If you don't want chicken, then they also do a great duck confit."

"The chicken sounds good, and I'll be glad to split it, but I'm interested in the desserts."

"Well, I don't think you'll be disappointed."

The meal was served, and the chicken lived up to Maurice's billing. It was perfectly roasted and proved to be more than enough for two. After dessert, Maurice suggested that they walk back to the flat, so they bundled up against the frosty night and walked arm in arm across Paris. As they crossed the Seine, they paused on the bridge and looked at the brightly lit Eiffel Tower downriver and Notre Dame upriver.

Mary Jo had been to Paris several times during her days as a counterintelligence agent, but this was her first visit with a lover, and she was really seeing Paris for the first time. It was indeed the City of Lights. They stopped in a small café across from the flat, had a brandy, and talked about the places they had visited in their past. It was well after midnight when they climbed into bed and gently made love before falling into a deep, peaceful sleep.

Maurice had asked Portia to wake them for an early breakfast on Friday morning, and, as the couple finished their second cups of coffee, Mary Jo said, "Do we have dinner plans for this evening?"

Maurice looked up from his newspaper and said, "No plans, but, after stuffing ourselves last night, I thought we might try a small local café for a light lunch, just a few blocks away."

"We might need to visit that café another day because today's lunch is covered. Breton Aviation indicated that a celebratory meal would be provided after we sign the paperwork for the new plane — and be sure to bring your passport. I want to take my new toy for a test flight after lunch, and I know a great little dinner spot in Rome."

"It's going to take some time to get accustomed to petit déjeuner in Paris and dinner in Rome, but I'm game to try. How long will the flight be?"

"I checked, and it's about 700 air miles. We can be there easily in two hours. We can have dinner and be back here just after midnight."

"Okay, why not? We can do whatever we want, and dinner in Rome sounds magnificent."

"Well, now that we have dinner plans, call a taxi and let's go buy a plane."

FIVE

AFTER THE TAXI DROPPED THEM off at the private aviation terminal at Orly, Mary Jo and Maurice quickly found their way to the offices of Breton Aviation, Ltd. Mary Jo walked up to the young woman, who was behind the reception desk, and said, "Good morning. I'm Mary Jo Thibodaux. I have an appointment with Clive Breton."

In a heavy British accent, the woman replied, "Yes, Miss Thibodaux, Mr. Breton is expecting you. Please follow me." The woman led them to a conference room where she opened the door and said, "Mr. Breton, Miss Thibodaux is here."

A tall man in a Savile Row suit and regimental tie took Mary Jo's hand and said, "Welcome, Miss Thibodaux. I'm Clive Breton. I believe we have everything ready to complete our transaction."

"Nice to meet you, Mr. Breton," Mary Jo replied. "This is my friend Maurice Lebeaux."

Breton and Maurice shook hands, and everyone took a seat. Breton handed Mary Jo a manila file folder and said, "If you'll open your folder, we'll get through all of the paperwork, and then I'll take you out to see your new plane. First, let me say that we have thoroughly inspected your Mustang and found everything to be in order, so now let's make it all final."

Breton went over each form in the folder, explaining its purpose, and he and Mary Jo signed and countersigned each of them. Finally, the last form had been completed, and Breton turned to Mary Jo and said, "Miss Thibodaux, I noted that you are thoroughly checked out in twin-engine jets and have over 10 hours in the CJ4, so you are good to go. Do you plan to leave Paris today?"

"No, we plan to take a test flight to Rome this afternoon, but we will return this evening. I would like to have my plane hangared here at Orly until December 22nd."

"Fine, that will be no problem. I'll set everything up, and you can check with operations when you file your flight plan to Rome. I believe we've completed the purchase, so let's take a look at your CJ4. Then, I'd like for you and Mr. Lebeaux to be my guests for lunch."

Breton led them through a side door in the terminal and ushered them into a waiting golf cart. They drove across the tarmac, halting inside an open hangar. When they'd reached the back of the hangar, they stopped in front of a gleaming-white twin-engine jet with its cabin stairs down. Breton stood at the foot of the stairs and said, "Well, here she is, sporting a brand-new paint job and a completely redone interior."

Breton continued, "As per your specifications, we limited the seating to six first-class seats, two of which can recline for sleeping. Since you pilot yourself, the flight deck is designed for easy access to the instruments from the left-hand seat. The copilot's seat can be used for an extra passenger, giving you a total of seven seats."

Mary Jo walked around the plane and noted the increased size over her Mustang. She did what amounted to a preflight check and returned to the stairs. "She's beautiful. But the main reason I wanted to trade up from my Mustang was the increased range, and she can go almost twice as far. The added seating and speed are what we in Louisiana call a lagniappe." She looked at Maurice and asked, "Well, Mon Cheri, what do you think?"

"You're right," Maurice replied. "She's definitely beautiful. Let's check out the interior."

The two climbed aboard, and Maurice admired the polished inlaid wood, the high-quality leather upholstery, and the plush carpeting. He took a seat and sighed, "No doubt about it…these are first-class seats. Now, show me the bar and the head."

Breton opened the hatch to the small lavatory and toilet and then pointed out what he referred to as "the refreshment center." Maurice smiled and said, "That about covers my questions. What do you think?"

Mary Jo said, "She's exactly what I'd hoped for. She can go much faster for much longer distances and still get in and out of the small fields I sometimes have to use. Also, I like the increase in operating cciling. Sometimes a few extra thousand feet can get you over some nasty weather."

Mary Jo glanced at her watch and said, "I believe everything's in order. Now, I think we'll accept your invitation to lunch before we leave for Rome."

"By all means. I have reservations at Le Meil-Melo in the main terminal. A Lebanese family owns the restaurant, and it's probably the best airport café in the world."

The little café lived up to Breton's review, and, after lunch, the couple bid goodbye to Breton, and Mary Jo led the way to flight operations. She filed a flight plan to Rome and found that her new plane had been moved into position for boarding. She did her preflight and took the left-hand seat, while Maurice settled into the copilot's seat. Soon, they were cleared for takeoff, and, once airborne, Mary Jo eventually leveled out at a cruising altitude of 27,000 feet.

After the plane was released from Orly control, Maurice adjusted his headset and said, "How long will it take to get to Rome?"

"We're flying into Urbe rather than da Vinci, which is almost 700 miles. We'll cruise at 400 miles per hour, and, because Urbe is in the northern part of the city, we won't get caught up in the traffic we would have faced using da Vinci. It's 2:30 now, and there's no time difference, so we should be touching down about 4:00 Rome time."

"Sounds like we'll be hitting the evening rush hour. Is the restaurant far from the airport?"

"Yeah, it's pretty much across town, but it's near the area I lived in when I was stationed in Rome back in 2006. Rome was my last posting before I was promoted and recalled to D.C. We'll have an hour's ride."

"I suppose there'll be plenty of taxis at the airport."

"Actually, someone is picking us up. In addition to wanting to take a test flight, I also wanted to introduce you to some friends in Rome. While I was working out of the embassy in Rome, I worked closely with the CIA station chief and the Italian version of our FBI. We were all involved with an undercover operation that went bad."

"Who's picking us up?"

"Carlo Baggetti. Carlo was station chief, but he was forced into retirement after an op went south."

"Baggetti sounds Italian. How'd he get to be with the CIA?"

"Carlo is an American of Italian descent. He grew up in Boston and attended the Naval Academy. Since his retirement, he lives in Rome and sorta freelances."

"I know you had an interesting life before we met, and I suspect you'll tell me what you can. In the meantime, I'm going to sit back and watch the movie."

Mary Jo landed at Rome's Urbe airport just before 5:00 Rome time, and, after arranging for the plane to be refueled, she and Maurice entered the main lobby of the small terminal. Mary Jo looked around the room until she spotted a well-dressed man holding a sign that read "Shiva." When the two made eye contact, his face lit up, and a huge grin spread across his handsome visage. Mary Jo ran across the room and leaped into his outstretched arms. He held her tight and made a full circle with her feet off the floor. When he set Mary Jo back on her feet, he reached out, grabbed Maurice's hand, and said, "You have to be the Foreign Legionnaire that has destroyed any hope I had of winning the heart of Mary Jo. I originally planned to kill you on sight, but you seem to be a nice guy, and she is clearly nuts about you."

Maurice shook the guy's hand and said, "I'm glad to have dodged your earlier plan, but you have me at a disadvantage. I haven't had the opportunity to read your file."

Mary Jo could see the irritation in Maurice's face, so she jumped in at once. "Oh, Maurice, I apologize. I should have given you more of a heads-up that we'd be meeting some of my old friends. This charmer is Carlo Baggetti, an ex-employee of the puzzle farm in Langley, Virginia. I was, at one time, the liaison between U.S. Military Intelligence and Carlo's office. I asked, and he kindly agreed to be our chauffeur for the evening."

The three continued to talk on their way to the parking garage. Maurice took note of the fact that they bypassed immigration and customs, and Carlo led them to a black Jag convertible. After clearing the airport, Carlo drove through the magic-filled city streets of Rome at night. There was a full moon and light traffic as he maneuvered through the quiet neighborhoods, purposefully avoiding the freeways. Mary Jo tried to make small talk during the ride until they pulled up to the valet parking stand of Cacio e Pepe. With a cheerful greeting, the young attendant took Carlo's keys, and they entered the small trattoria.

The smiling maître d' recognized Carlo and said, "Ah, Signor Baggetti, your host for the evening is awaiting your arrival. Please follow me."

"Thank you, Cosimo. It's good to see you."

Cosimo led Carlo, Maurice, and Mary Jo to a small private room, screened from the main dining area by a curtain. A senior man was seated in the alcove, and he stood, extended his hand to Carlo, and said, "Carlo, it's been too long since we've shared a meal. I've been looking forward to seeing you since your call yesterday." Grasping Mary Jo's extended hand, the man pulled her into an embrace and kissed both cheeks. "Mary Jo, my angel of mercy, your visit to Rome is long overdue. I'm delighted to see you."

Mary Jo blushed and said, "Roberto, I had no idea that you would be here, but it's great to see you. Meet my good friend, Maurice Lebeaux."

General Roberto Morelli shook Maurice's hand and said, "Sergeant Lebeaux, I have been anxious to meet you. I served with the Legion on several occasions, and we may well have mutual friends."

Maurice shook his hand and said, "We may indeed."

When they all had taken their seats, Roberto turned to Mary Jo and asked, "Do you see much of Alan Brooks these days?"

"I do. In fact, Maurice and I just finished setting up a security system for Alan's new company. He still lives in West Texas and resigned his teaching profession to start his new enterprise."

Roberto smiled and said, "I always wondered about his love of that god-forsaken place, especially after he said that Afghanistan reminded him of home."

"No kidding. I suppose he would feel nostalgic about the back side of the moon. Aside from his insane choice of a place to live, he seems to enjoy his new business and running his family ranch."

Carlo spoke up and commented, "Yeah, a little over 16,000 acres is enough to keep a guy down on the farm, even after he's seen Kabul."

Roberto and Mary Jo looked at Carlo, and Mary Jo said, "Well, well...I see that old habits die hard. You did your homework on the lot of us, didn't you?"

Carlo said, "Simply being thorough; knowledge is the currency of our mutual businesses, isn't it?"

"I'll have to second that," said Morelli. "We're all in the knowledge business, even the famous and lovely Mary Jo, late of special ops."

Mary Jo lifted her glass and said, "To knowledge!"

Roberto and Carlo clicked their glasses to hers and Maurice's and said, "Hear, hear!"

Cosimo pulled back the curtain and entered the small room. He smiled and said, "Tonight is a special occasion for Cacio e Pepe; it is a rare evening when we have the pleasure of serving one of the holders of Italy's Military Medal of Valor. The staff and I would like to extend the hospitality of our little trattoria to Lieutenant Colonel Mary Jo Thibodaux, a Knight of the Military Medal of Valor presented by a grateful Republic of Italy." He stood aside, and the entire staff of the restaurant broke into song, as only Italians can do, with a raucous rendition of "The Star-Spangled Banner."

They all stood during the anthem, and Mary Jo graciously acknowledged the tribute as the curtain was restored. She sat down, looked sternly at Carlo, and said, "Did you know that was coming?"

Assuming the look of total innocence, Carlo replied, "Moi? No way. That was all the work of your pal Morelli. Isn't that so, Roberto?"

"Si, I am the guilty party. It is our equivalent to your Medal of Honor, and it means a great deal to all Italians. I hope you're not offended."

"Of course not — embarrassed maybe, but not offended. I'm honored."

Carlo raised his glass and beamed, "To fallen friends!"

Everyone clinked their glasses and replied, "Hear, hear…to fallen friends."

Roberto Morelli turned to Maurice and said, "May I call you Maurice?"

"Please do, General," Maurice replied.

"I believe we owe you a little background information. Before I became a spook, I served in the Italian Army's equivalent of your special forces and worked closely with your SEALs in Afghanistan. I first met Mary Jo when she pulled me from the wreckage of a helicopter and carried me to safety. In the process, she fought her way through the surrounding Taliban and united many of them with their waiting virgins. The U.S. Army could not acknowledge her bravery because we weren't supposed to be where we were. The Italian government felt no such restraint and awarded her our highest honor for gallantry, and she earned my love and respect forever."

Maurice listened with interest and said, "General, I'm not surprised. I've had the opportunity to see 'Shiva' in action. It always seems to be my lot to clean up after her."

Roberto grinned and said, "I've taken the liberty of ordering for the table. I hope you don't mind. Cacio e Pepe is considered by many to be the quintessential trattoria and usually is listed as one of the top restaurants in Italy. I've ordered a sample of all of the house favorites. I hope they prove interesting."

"That sounds wonderful," Mary Jo said. "Now, tell me, Roberto…how have you been since your apparent full recovery?"

"Aside from the sad reality of no longer being a competitive alpine skier, I, indeed, am completely recovered from my brief visit to Afghanistan. I retired from the Alpini Regiment after our little adventure and joined the faceless ranks of the Italian bureaucracy. Today, I push paper from one side of my desk to the other."

"Yeah," Carlo interjected, "and I was the commercial attaché at the embassy. Roberto continues to have an incredibly active operational role."

Morelli smiled and said, "Why, Carlo, I have no idea where you get such ideas. I'm a simple policeman, serving and protecting the citizens of our Republic. Not nearly as exciting as the professional lives we all once knew."

Mary Jo nodded in Carlo's direction and said, "Maurice and I are enjoying a visit to Paris before we go to Corsica to spend Christmas with his family."

Carlo smiled and replied, "I've been to Corsica on several occasions, both for business and pleasure, and still have friends on the island. Maurice, there was no mention of your ties to Corsica in your file."

"No, like many Legionnaires, my life began with my enlistment. Lebeaux is my Legion name; my family name is Capriati."

Roberto looked interested and asked, "Are you related to General Giovanni Capriati by chance?"

"Yes, Giovanni is my brother. Mary Jo and I will be visiting with him and the rest of the family just before Christmas."

A cloud passed across Morelli's face but quickly disappeared, and he continued: "Please give Giovanni my warmest regards. He and I have a long-standing personal relationship."

"I'll be sure and tell him about our meeting. We, indeed, live in a small world."

Carlo touched Maurice's arm and said, "Earlier this evening, I mentioned your relationship with our girl, Shiva."

"Yes, it is true; my heart has been taken hostage by Shiva the Destroyer, a label that can be a little troublesome."

"Any more of that Shiva crap and I can assure you that 'troublesome' will not do justice to the fate awaiting you," Mary Jo snapped.

"Now, now, children, try to play nice in front of Zio Roberto," Morelli said with a grin.

The meal was served in a series of courses, each accompanied by a fresh bottle of wine. Maurice noticed that Mary Jo was holding her hand over her wine glass and figured she didn't drink when she was flying. They talked of old times and mutual friends until the restaurant began to close for the evening.

Everyone hugged and said good night, and Carlo began the drive back to Urbe. This time, he used the freeways since the traffic had subsided. They reached the terminal just before midnight Rome time. Mary Jo hugged Carlo and said, "Thanks so much for including Roberto tonight. I have missed all of you since my days in Rome, and it was great to catch up. I never got the chance to ask, but how is your 'freelance' practice coming?"

"It keeps me in Jags and vino, so it's doing all I can ask for. How about your engineering practice?"

"It too pays the bills, but more and more I'm interested in doing 'freelance,' as well."

Carlo turned to Maurice and asked, "How about you, Sergeant Major? Does security work bore you?"

"I have to admit to yearning for my old life in the Legion, but, since I met Mary Jo, things have picked up considerably. Just cleaning up behind Shiva has raised the level of my professional life."

"I bet it has. We must all keep in touch. If there is ever anything I can do to assist you, all you have to do is ask."

"You too, Carlo, and thanks for a wonderful evening," Mary Jo said. "Now, we need to be airborne so that we can get back to Paris before dawn."

After another round of goodbyes, Carlo drove off, and the couple went into the terminal. Maurice and Mary Jo were taken out to the plane and soon were headed north. They landed at Orly just after 2:00 Paris time and were back at the flat asleep by 3:00.

SIX

THE COUPLE SLEPT WITH THE bedroom door open, and the pealing of church bells woke them at 9:00 on Saturday morning. The sun was streaming through the fluttering curtains, and the faint sound of neighborhood traffic played in the background. They slowly made love and settled back into the bed. Finally, Maurice rolled over on his elbow, kissed Mary Jo's bare breasts, and murmured, "I'm willing to begin every day like this."

Mary Jo smiled and said, "Me too. Maybe we ought to quit our jobs and move to Paris."

Maurice sat up, propped himself against his pillow, and then replied, "We've never talked about the future, and I don't want to break the spell of this wonderful morning, so I'm going to assume that was a rhetorical comment."

"I guess it was, but, now that it's been said, maybe we can begin to think about where we're headed."

"Well, before we start, let me say that I'll be content to be part of your life in any capacity you desire."

"Any? What if I told you I might want to be your wife?"

"It would make me the happiest man alive, and, while we're on that subject, would you marry me?"

"I never expected to hear those words, and please know that it's not something I expect."

"So…why don't you answer my question?"

"Well, okay, yes! I'll marry you!"

"Good! Now that's settled…let's talk about some coffee."

Mary Jo laughed, tackled Maurice, pinned him down, and planted a long, passionate kiss on his lips.

Maurice said, "Forget the coffee…let's go for round two…"

Later, the engaged couple sat on the small balcony overlooking Rue de Saint-Simon and watched the neighborhood families as they went about their daily lives. After their third cups of coffee, Mary Jo said, "You know, earlier we mentioned quitting our jobs and moving to Paris, but I suppose we ought to decide exactly what we're planning to do."

Maurice replied, "Yes, but first let's decide when and where we're going to be married. Do you have anything in mind?"

"Not really. I've never been the typical dreamy-eyed girl who has had every detail of her wedding planned since she was seven years old."

"Well, I've been thinking that when we see my family over Christmas, we can tell them about the engagement. I'm comfortable with having the actual wedding wherever or whenever you want."

"I'd like to give it some thought. I do know that I want a small, family thing, nothing grand…maybe in New Iberia or New Orleans. We don't have to decide now."

"No, but I will want to tell my family."

"No problem from me — I'll go along with whatever you decide on that score."

Mary Jo stood, began gathering the dishes from breakfast, and said, "What I do have to decide now is what to wear tonight."

Maurice looked at her quizzically and asked, "What's so important about tonight?"

"Did you forget? We're having dinner with Collette and her husband."

"Yeah, I guess it slipped my mind. What time do we need to be ready?"

"Their car is picking us up at 8:00. I'll need at least two hours to dress."

"Great. That leaves us all afternoon to walk around Paris. It'll give me a chance to show you some of the sights. Let's get up and hit the streets."

The betrothed couple dressed in jeans, sweaters, and warm jackets. It was just before noon when they left the flat and turned right on Rue de Saint-Simon. The sky was a deep blue, and there was a brisk breeze coming off the Seine. Maurice took Mary Jo's arm and said, "One of the great pleasures of Paris is to simply stroll through her neighborhoods and soak in the scenes. We're going to make a loop that will bring us back to the flat in about four hours, and, along the way, we'll see some of the city's most famous sights."

"Sounds good to me...you're my tour guide," Mary Jo replied.

After a couple of blocks, the two turned right on Rue de Grenelle, a narrow street with cars parked in any space available. Most of the buildings were two or three stories, with commercial space on the street and residential flats above. The sun couldn't get down to street level, and the jackets felt good. Soon, there was a splash of sunshine and an open park.

Maurice pointed to a large domed building made of white stone and said, "We're looking at the Dome des Invalides, which contains two of my favorite places in Paris, the tomb of Napoleon and the French Army Museum. We don't have time to do justice to the museum, but we can see the tomb."

"Maybe we can come back to the museum before we leave for Corsica."

"I'd like that, but what I'd really like to show you is the Legion's museum in Aubagne."

"Is that close to Paris?"

"Not really…it's the Legion's headquarters just outside Marseilles. Maybe we can catch it on another trip."

The couple entered the building and joined a tour group led by an English-speaking guide. The female guide led them to the vast open area containing a red quartzite sarcophagus resting on a green granite base. She explained that Napoleon's remains were removed from the Island of St. Helena in 1840 and reinterred here in 1842. When Mary Jo and Maurice were back in the park, Mary Jo said, "That was very interesting; I was surprised at the respect still paid to such a controversial man."

"Napoleon was never controversial in France. He represents the very apex of French national glory."

"I guess he's even more revered in Corsica."

"Not as much as you'd think, considering his lifelong love of his homeland. He grew up in Ajaccio and remained a Corsican until his death. The real hero of Corsican independence is Pascal Paoli, and he and the young Bonaparte disagreed on basic strategy. Corsica still claims the Emperor, but always with a footnote about Paoli."

"I can imagine that Corsica's history is a study unto itself."

"Yes, those of us of Etruscan descent look at everyone else as an invader."

The two strolled through the Esplanade des Invalides until they came to the Quai d'Orsay. They walked to an observation post on the Seine, and Maurice swept his hand along the river and said, "To me, this is the best river view in Paris. We can see the Eiffel Tower to our left and all the way to Notre Dame on our right. We'll stroll down the river walk to the tower, and, if it's not too crowded, we'll ride to the observation deck so that you can really get a bird's-eye view of the city."

The couple made their way along the riverfront until they reached the bridge known as Pont d'Iena. They turned left and continued their walk to the Eiffel Tower, but, when they checked the long line waiting to ride to the top, Maurice said, "We'll come back on a weekday when the crowd thins a bit. Let's cross the river here and walk back down the Right Bank to Avenue George V."

"Hey, I'm with you. You can't really see the tower from this point. It was meant to be viewed from a distance."

"Yeah, it's like seeing the Pyramids from Cairo. Perspective makes large monuments majestic."

The couple crossed the Seine on the Pont d'Iena and took the river-view path along the Right Bank paralleling Avenue New York. When they reached Avenue George V, Maurice stopped and pointed away from the Seine. "The next half-mile is probably one of the most expensive pieces of real estate in Paris. There are shops I suspect you and Collette will be visiting, and the centerpiece of it all is the Hotel George V. The hotel was built in 1928, and, until its purchase by the Four Seasons, was to Paris as the Ritz is to London or the Plaza to New York, the quintessential French hotel."

The two walked up to the large, stone hotel, and Maurice led Mary Jo into the opulent lobby. He said, "I would ordinarily suggest that we have lunch in Le Cinq, which is one of the two best hotel restaurants in Europe, the other being the Connaught in London, but I don't want to spoil our appetites for tonight."

"We can always come back before we leave, and, by the way, I've dined at the Connaught. It's in Mayfair, close to the U.S. Embassy. The ambassador took our whole office to dinner there. You're right. It is a great restaurant. That night was my first experience with foie gras."

"Our first experience with foie gras tends to stick with us…much like our first orgasm," Maurice said with a twinkle in his eye.

Mary Jo laughed and said, "Well, I love foie gras, but maybe not that much."

Maurice chuckled, "Now that I think of it, I may have overstated the effect of foie gras, but, speaking of food, I think we'll go on to the Champs Elysees and indulge in one of the city's major tourist ripoffs, a cup of coffee and a tart at the George V's small café around the corner."

The two walked the block or so to the wide, tree-lined boulevard, and Maurice pointed to the left and said, "You can see the Arc de Triomphe, which is the beginning of the street, and, down to my right, it ends at the Place de la Concorde."

Maurice turned to his right and pointed at the awning and tables facing the street. The awning and umbrellas carried the name George V. The two were seated at one of the outside tables along the wide sidewalk. They ordered coffee and a fruit pastry, along with a bottle of Perrier. The coffee was a rich, dark roast, and the pastries were amazing.

The lovers sat and watched the pedestrian traffic stroll by, and, finally, Mary Jo said, "I don't think you've been to Paris until you do this, and I don't really care what it costs."

"I'm glad to hear you say that because we could have a great dinner at NoJa for less."

"Oh, c'mon, Maurice, you're paying for location, even though the coffee and goodies are pretty darn good."

Maurice shook his head and said, "I suspected that beneath that hard Shiva surface lay the heart of a true romantic."

"Shiva is really a nice girl, when you get to know her."

"So far, I like what I've seen. Finish your water. We need to head back toward the flat."

Maurice paid the bill and left a generous tip. The two began walking toward the Place de la Concorde, enjoying some of the world's best window shopping. Soon, they passed the colossal glass-domed Grand Palais and the smaller Petit Palais, both home to art exhibits and special performances. Mary Jo made a mental note to go online to see what would be happening over the next week or so.

The couple's walk continued through the Place de la Concorde and into the Jardin des Tuileries, with all of its museums and statues. When they reached the Place du Carrousel, they turned back toward the Seine. They strolled down the riverfront Quai des Tuileries until they were opposite the Ile de la Cite and Notre Dame. They crossed the river on the Pont d'Arcole, made their way to the huge cathedral with the famous flying buttress, joined an English-speaking tour guide, and spent the next 45 minutes inside the beautiful church. When they emerged back into the fading sunlight, Mary Jo took Maurice's arm and said, "I know you aren't a practicing Catholic, but would you consider going to Mass with me tomorrow?"

"Of course I will. Do you want to come back here? There are many churches in Paris, and some other famous ones, such as the Sacre-Coeur, are just as close."

"Yes. I'd like to experience Notre Dame, and I'm delighted you're willing to go with me."

"No problem — as long as I don't have to go to confession. It's been awhile, and I'd have no idea where to begin."

"I think you can skip it tomorrow, but you might have to face it before we can be married in a church."

Maurice looked at his watch and said, "I suspect you're right, but I'll deal with that later. It's almost 4:30, and we wanted to be back no later than 6:00. We can walk back, which will take less than an hour, or we can get a cab. It's up to you."

"Let's walk. I don't want this to end. I'll have plenty of time."

The lovers crossed the other branch of the Seine on the Pont Saint-Michel and turned left when they reached Saint-Germain. Their walk took them through some of the most desirable addresses in Paris. Maurice's estimate of less than an hour proved correct. They showered, and, as Maurice lay on the bed watching Mary Jo begin to dress, he smiled contentedly and drifted off into sleep. "I'll meet you in the library," Mary Jo said when she woke him with a kiss at 7:00.

30 minutes later, Maurice found Mary Jo sitting in a wingback chair and holding a bourbon on the rocks. He walked to the bar, poured a scotch, and joined her. They sipped their whiskey and talked about the afternoon walk until they heard a knock on the front door.

Maurice opened the door to find a handsome, young man in full livery standing beside a gleaming, black Rolls-Royce Phantom. The chauffeur smiled and said with a heavy French accent, "Good evening, Monsieur Lebeaux. I am Felix, and I am here for you and Mademoiselle Thibodaux."

Maurice led Mary Jo to the waiting car, while Felix held the door open. They settled into the luxurious leather seats, and Mary Jo whispered, "There's a lot to be said for sheer luxury, no matter how ostentatious it is."

Maurice smiled. "In this case, ostentatious comes at a steep price; this is the extended wheelbase Rolls, and it can be yours for less than half a million, if you don't get too cute with the accessories."

"I just hope I can get through the shopping trip with Collette for that or less."

The big car moved comfortably and quietly through the streets of Paris, and Mary Jo realized that they were indeed retracing their walk route. Felix turned onto a quiet side street and stopped before a large wrought-iron gate. The gate began to swing open, and they could see a large, stone, three-story house with a circular drive leading to a gaily lit entrance.

As Felix parked the car, the door to the home opened, and a gentleman dressed in evening clothes came out to help Mary Jo out of the car. When Maurice was out, the car drove off, and the butler said in a very British accent, "Welcome, Miss Thibodaux and Mr. Lebeaux. If you will follow me, Le Comte and Madam are expecting you."

The gentleman led Maurice and Mary Jo through an elegant entrance hall to what appeared to be a library with a crackling fire. The butler ushered them in and said, "I have Miss Thibodaux and Mr. Lebeaux," and he quietly slipped away.

A tall man, dressed in flannel pants and a sports coat with an ascot, walked across the room, shook Maurice's hand, and bowed slightly. He kissed Mary Jo's hand while saying, "Welcome to our home. I am Augustin Beaumarchais." He turned to an elegantly dressed lady in her early forties and said, "This, of course, is Collette."

Mary Jo thought, "If central casting were looking for actors to play French aristocrats, they could never do better."

Mary Jo took Collette's hand and said, "Collette, I'm so glad to meet you. I can't begin to tell you how grateful I am for your help with my wardrobe and your kind invitation to your beautiful home."

"Ah, Mary Jo, it is I who should be thanking you. I can't believe that we will have days of shopping, and I won't have to spend a sou."

Augustin looked at his wife incredulously and said, "Unless aliens have kidnapped my Collette, I doubt you are capable of shopping and not buying."

"Oh, Augustin, if you insist, I'll try to find a little frock or two while assisting Mary Jo."

Augustin grinned at Maurice and said, "I suspect the merchants of Paris are in for a very profitable week. What are your plans while Mary Jo and Collette boost the local economy?"

The butler returned and said, "Comte. May I serve cocktails or wine?"

Augustin replied, "Yes, Judson, Madam and I will have our usual, and I'm sure our guests will want to join us."

Maurice looked at Mary Jo, and she gave him a slight nod. He said, "Miss Thibodaux will have bourbon on the rocks, and I'll have a scotch neat."

Everyone took a seat by the fire, and Judson returned with a tray full of glasses. When they were all served, the butler quietly left the room.

Maurice turned to Augustin and said, "To answer your question about what I plan to do while the ladies are shopping, I thought I might visit the French Army Museum — at least for one day."

"I too enjoy the museum and have visited it many times, even though my military days are far behind me."

"I take it that you once were on active duty?"

"Yes, I served with the 11th Parachute Brigade until 1990. Did you serve, Mr. Lebeaux?"

"I too served with the 11th Parachute Brigade as a member of the Legion's 2nd Parachute Regiment. It is possible that we may have seen action together."

"I had no idea you were an officer in the Legion."

"Not an officer, but I retired as Sergeant Major of the 2nd."

"I never had the pleasure of serving in the Legion, but the 2nd jumped into Chad with us in 1986. Were you there?"

"Yes, we were based in Corsica at that time. We fought alongside the Chadian army until the Libyans withdrew to Libya."

"Collette tells me that you are Corsican by birth."

"I am. My legal name is Lebeaux, but my family name is Capriati."

"Capriati? I went to Saint-Cyr with a Giovanni Capriati from Corsica."

"Yes, Giovanni is my older brother. We'll be spending Christmas with him at home in Ajaccio."

"You must tell Giovanni hello for me. The last time I saw him, he was at a reunion of our class. I believe he was a colonel at the time."

"Yes, he was recently promoted to major general and is serving on the NATO staff in Brussels."

"Well, I'm not surprised; he was always a serious student and ranked at the top of our class academically. Give him my congratulations."

Collette smiled and said, "I hope you and Maurice are not under the impression that you will spend the evening reliving the past. Mary Jo and I refuse to be ignored."

Augustin returned her smile and said, "Ah, Mon Cheri, it is highly improbable that you or Mary Jo will ever be ignored by any man. Perhaps we can use our combined military experience to help you plan your shopping expedition."

"I doubt it. Shopping is my area of expertise, and I'd leave both of you in my dust. Mary Jo and I will launch our attack at 10:00 on Monday morning, and, by Wednesday afternoon, the mission will be complete."

The door to the library opened, and Judson announced, "Dinner is served."

Judson led them down a vast hallway past a large dining room with a table, which could seat at least 20. They continued to a smaller dining room that had a table for four set with rich linen, gleaming silver, crystal, and antique china. The room was large enough for a fireplace and a small sitting area.

The ladies were seated, and Collette said, "Our meal has been prepared by our chef, Tony Lusco. Tony trained with Joel Rubuchon at his restaurant in Bordeaux. We were lucky to be able to woo him to Paris. I think you'll be pleased with his dishes."

"Pleased" didn't begin to cover the seven-course dinner. Everything was perfectly prepared and presented, from onion soup and freshly baked bread to the cheese and desserts. Judson served wine with each course, and even Mary Jo could tell that the quality of each bottle was superb.

After dinner, the couples returned to the library, and Judson served a snifter of excellent cognac and offered a box of Cuban cigars. To Mary Jo's surprise, Collette accepted a cigar, and Judson expertly clipped the tip and lit it. The four sipped brandy and smoked, and Mary Jo shared her story of growing up in South Louisiana.

It was close to midnight when they thanked Augustin and Collette for a pleasant evening and were driven back to the flat. The couple agreed that, after the long walk and the lengthy dinner, they were ready for bed, where they immediately fell asleep, cuddled in each other's arms.

SEVEN

ON SUNDAY MORNING, Mary Jo and Maurice attended Mass at Notre Dame and then came back to the flat. Maurice made an omelet, which they shared on the balcony, while seemingly all of the church bells in Paris, sounding like a massive wind chime, serenaded them. Maurice walked a couple of blocks to a newsstand and bought a copy of the London *Times*. The couple spent the rest of the morning reading the paper and sipping coffee. Finally, Maurice looked up and asked, "What time are you and Collette going out tomorrow?"

"She and Felix are picking me up at 10:00. What's on your agenda?"

"I think I'll go over to the Dalhousie office and check in with my counterpart, and then I might take in the Military Museum. What time do you think you'll be back here?"

"Collette said that all the shops would close by 5:00, so I guess sometime around that."

"I'll plan on meeting you back here around 5:00. I'd like for us to have dinner at a small neighborhood café, so we won't have to worry about dressing up," Maurice added. "In the meantime, let's see what we can find to do to kill the rest of today."

***

Mary Jo had set her phone alarm to ring at 7:00. When it beeped Monday morning, she got up and began to get ready for the day. Maurice stirred when the alarm rang but settled back into a deep sleep while Mary Jo bathed and dressed.

Mary Jo was sitting at the kitchen counter eating a brioche and drinking coffee when Maurice came to the door in his robe. She smiled and said, "Good morning, sleepyhead — thought I'd let you rest and regain some of your stamina."

"What's wrong with my stamina?" Maurice asked this with a smile. "You're looking very chic this morning. Collette will have to work hard to make any improvement. Do you have any idea where you and Collette are going this morning?"

"None whatsoever. She said she had it all mapped out."

The lovers sat and talked for a while. Then, Mary Jo grew serious and said, "I'm going to be talking to Emile when I get back, and I'd like to tell him about our plans. Do you have any problem with that?"

"None at all…in fact, I want to shout it from the rooftops of Paris."

"I'm glad, but I wanted to check before I said anything."

"Tell anybody and everybody. I plan to tell my whole family when we get there."

There was a knock on the front door, and Mary Jo looked through the drapes and saw the big Rolls parked in the street. She gave Maurice a peck on the cheek and said, "Gotta run. Wish me luck and hope I'm not broke by this afternoon."

Maurice smiled and said, "May the Force be with you."

Felix wished Mary Jo a good morning and held the door for her. She slipped into the leather seat across from a beaming Collette, who said, "Bonjour, Mary Jo. Are you ready to begin building a wardrobe?"

"Actually, I'm terrified. I'm sure Constance has told you that I'm a complete neophyte when it comes to fashion and shopping. I'd much rather face an armed mugger than talk to a clerk in a boutique."

"Then, you should just relax. I'll handle the clerks, and you take care of the muggers. We'll make a great team."

Collette touched the intercom button and said, "Felix, first we'll go to Carine Gilson's on Rue de Grenelle."

"Yes, Madam."

"The logical starting point of any wardrobe is lingerie, so we will visit the studio of Carine Gilson. Carine's designs are traditional, and yet unique. She uses only the finest silk and lace."

Felix drove to Rue de Grenelle, and, finally, the Rolls pulled to a stop in front of a shop called Celine. Felix helped them to the sidewalk and said, "Madam, I will be nearby. Call when you are ready."

"Merci, Felix. We will be here for some time, so you may return to the town house and await my call."

Mary Jo assumed that they would be entering Celine, but, instead, Collette walked to a massive wooden door with a brass "18" on it. Collette rang the doorbell, and a soft, female voice replied, "Bonjour, Madam Beaumarchais. Michelle will be with you in a moment."

The big door swung open, and a young woman held it for Mary Jo and Collette. They walked into a large entrance with a winding staircase leading to upper floors. The foyer opened to four rooms, two on each side. The young woman indicated that they should accompany her to one of the back rooms, where she held the door for them as she addressed another woman behind an Empire desk. "Madam Gilson, Madam Beaumarchais and Mademoiselle Thibodaux."

A petite woman in her mid-forties stood and walked around the desk to greet them. She took Collette by both arms and kissed her on each cheek. "Collette, Mon Amie…how good it is to see you, and I gather that this is the young lady in question?"

"Oui, Carine. Mary Jo is the canvas, and you are the artist. I can't thank you enough for coming from Brussels to meet us here today."

"I would have gladly come from Brussels, but we are preparing for an upcoming show, and I'm spending the entire month at my home here in Paris. It is timely that you called when you did. Miss Thibodaux will have access to our latest creations."

"How exciting! I may indulge myself, as well, but, first, let's work on Mary Jo."

"Miss Thibodaux, or may I call you Mary Jo?"

"Of course, please do," Mary Jo replied.

"Only if you will call me Carine. Now, Mary Jo, we must set the stage for our work together. Collette refers to you as the canvas and to me as the artist. This is the essence of a designer and a client relationship, and it requires the best of both of us. Have you ever experienced the sensation that fine lingerie can produce in a woman?"

"Carine, I'll have to admit that I've pretty much taken my underwear for granted."

"Oh, how sad…but you will soon understand that no outfit will feel right if you don't have elegant lingerie. Even the most talented designer in the world cannot create the perfect garment if the underlying surfaces are not perfect."

"Well, that makes sense to me. As an engineer, I can't build a perfect building if the foundation is flawed," Mary Jo replied.

"Excellent! Let us begin to build the foundation. Michelle, will you please escort Mademoiselle Thibodaux to our scanning chamber."

Michelle led the way to a small elevator and held the door for Mary Jo. They ascended to the top floor of the salon and entered a room that resembled a clinic. There was a screen blocking one corner, and, in the middle, there was a vertical steel tube with a sliding door. Michelle smiled and said, "Mademoiselle, if you will, step behind the screen, take off all of your clothes, and hang them on the hooks provided. There is a robe for you there, as well."

Mary Jo did as she was told. When she came back in, Michelle told her to enter the long tube, to place her feet in the indicated position, and then to stand very still with her arms at her side. Mary Jo assumed the position, and Michelle averted her eyes as she took the robe and closed the door. Michelle spoke through an intercom that Mary Jo could hear and said, "Now, we will begin the scan. You will hear a slight humming sound, and you will feel absolutely nothing. This will take several minutes, so stand as still as you can."

A low hum began, and the outer shell rotated around Mary Jo's naked body. She thought, "Well, I'll just be damned. I'm in some sort of MRI device, and here I thought garment design was an eyeball and guesstimate business."

Once the rotation and humming stopped, the door opened, and Michelle handed Mary Jo the robe. After Mary Jo had stepped behind the screen and re-dressed, Michelle led her back to Carine Gilson's office.

When Mary Jo walked in, Collette asked, "What does Mary Jo, the engineer, think about Carine's new toy?"

"Well, I have to say that I'm surprised. I assume I've just undergone a full body scan that will be beneficial in fitting me properly, probably by using some type of CAD/CAM system."

Carine stood at her desk, turned the monitor to face Mary Jo, and said, "Take a look."

When Mary Jo looked at the screen, she saw a three-dimensional rendering of a woman's body, slowly rotating on a vertical axis. There was a chart, just under the image, with blinking red numbers.

Carine explained, "You are right about the system. It was developed using CAD/CAM design software, but it has been programmed for use in the fashion industry. Now, I will show you the results of that programming."

Michelle walked to a draped figure and pulled the drape away to reveal a designer's padded mannequin standing upright on a swivel stand. Carine said, "Now, watch what happens next." She performed a few keystrokes, and the mannequin began to reshape itself. The waist grew smaller, and the hips and breasts grew bigger, until the mannequin had been transformed from the shape of a matron to that of a much younger woman.

Collette asked, "Well, Mary Jo, how does it feel to be looking at your own body?"

"Spooky and a little unnerving."

"I can assure you that the benefits far outweigh the slight intrusion of your privacy. Now, we can design garments uniquely for you, and the program will send the exact patterns to our cutting room…but you haven't seen the best part."

Mary Jo watched in amazement as a halo of light formed around the mannequin, and small dots of light spread across its surfaces. Carine performed a few more keystrokes, and a pair of panties began to take shape on the mannequin. The panties had open, lace-covered legs and shimmered in the light.

Carine smiled and said, "I can't speak for you, but I prefer the boxer-short panty to the tighty-whitey style. It just feels better, but we can model anything from a thong to bloomers, depending on your desires."

"Ladies, I'm afraid you're dealing with someone who bought her skivvies in the PX for years. I have no basis to form an opinion on fashion or styles. I must rely on Collette's taste and experience."

Collette mused for a moment and then said, "Constance and I have discussed your situation at length, and I believe I'm correct in saying that your wardrobe needs have expanded beyond the track shorts and t-shirt arena."

Mary Jo agreed: "Yes, I'll need more fashionable casual wear, business ensembles, and party dresses. My mind goes completely blank when it comes to particular outfits. Maybe the two of you can just make the decisions for me."

Carine looked at Collette and arched her eyebrows. Collette thought for a moment and said, "If you will help us with a few questions, I do believe Carine and I can cover it."

"Fire away. I'll do anything to get out of shopping."

Carine shook her head and replied, "I certainly hope that your dislike of shopping is not contagious. It could spell ruin to my business, but, I agree. Collette and I can do this for you, but, first, let me suggest that we retire to my dining room and have lunch."

Lunch was served in a private dining room, complete with white linen tablecloths and napkins. The table gleamed with Limoges china, Christofle sterling silver, and Lalique crystal. Carine's chef served a delicious celery soup and Chicken Divan, accompanied by a vintage white Chablis. No mention was made of the wardrobe, and Mary Jo enjoyed the fashion-world gossip.

After lunch, the balance of the afternoon was spent determining Mary Jo's needs and desires in order to accommodate her new wardrobe. It was decided that, considering Mobile's coastal location, there would be the need for a good deal of casual wear. Since the winters were mild by Paris standards, the bulk of the clothing would be determined by color choices rather than seasonal change.

Everything went well until Collette brought up the need for outfits suited to colder climes, such as New England and

Europe. This required what was essentially a completely different wardrobe, and Mary Jo agreed — until the subject of furs came up. Collette thought Mary Jo had the presence to wear a full-length coat, and Carine agreed, but they did, however, disagree on fur.

Carine was in favor of mink, but Collette was insistent on sable. They debated for several minutes until Mary Jo interrupted and said, "Sorry, ladies, but I will not wear animal skins. I would much prefer warm cloth coats. I hope that isn't a deal breaker."

"No, not at all," Collette replied. "We realize that your desires must be fulfilled, and there are many elegant and stylish coats to be had. Now, Carine, do we have everything that we'll need?"

"Oui, I believe we do, and we can always contact Mary Jo if we need to."

Collette looked at Mary Jo and said, "It seems you are free to spend the rest of your visit to Paris enjoying the city's many delights. Carine and I will give you a daily report on our progress."

A blank look took shape on Mary Jo's face; she hesitated and then replied, "Do you mean that I'm done with the shopping?"

"Yes. Carine will email your image to our other shops, and we will work with them to design your wardrobe. Each evening, we will forward the results of our efforts to you for your approval. We would like to have some guidance on your budget before we start."

"Collette, I'm sure you know that I'm a client of the Dalhousie firm, and I believe they have made arrangements at your favorite stores. As far as the total amount, what do you suggest?"

Collette and Carine whispered between themselves, and, finally, Collette said, "Carine and I believe we can do the entire wardrobe, including shoes and accessories, for less than €200,000, especially with no furs to consider."

Mary Jo thought, "Oh, my heavens! I can't believe I'm even considering spending that much on clothes, but, on the other hand, I don't have to spend the next week shopping, so that's almost worth the whole amount."

Mary Jo smiled at Collette and said, "I'm comfortable with that figure, and I think you can guess that I'm relieved to be set free."

"Oui, it shows on your face," Carine said. "There's one more item we must cover, which deals with upkeep. I believe you will be better satisfied to stick to the classic designs that never really go out of style. This will mean that you will be able to maintain a classic wardrobe and not be captive to next year's gimmicks."

"I agree with that," said Mary Jo. "I'll be more comfortable, and it will mean that Constance will have much less hassle keeping me up to date."

"Then, we all are in agreement. Carine and I will begin in the morning, and I believe we are done for the day."

Felix and Collette dropped Mary Jo at the doorstep to the flat, and, after hugs and kisses, drove away. Mary Jo opened the door, stepped into the foyer, and yelled, "Maurice, I'm back."

Maurice came in from the den (with a glass of red wine in hand) and said, "Well, I want to hear all about it."

"First, let me get into something a little more comfortable and make a few calls. If you'll pour me a glass of whatever that is, I'll meet you in the den."

Mary Jo quickly changed into slacks and a sweater, and then went to the office and dialed Emile's number. It was 4:30 p.m. in Paris and 10:30 a.m. in Mobile. Melissa picked up and said, "Good afternoon, Mary Jo. Emile is awaiting your call."

Emile Dalhousie immediately came on the line and said, "Mary Jo, are you having a wonderful visit to Paris?"

"We really are, and I just spent the day with Collette. She and a fashion designer friend of hers are putting together a wardrobe for me."

"Yes, Collette and Constance just talked. I understand you were able to escape the clutches of Collette for a mere €200,000."

"Indeed, and, surprisingly, I consider it a deal. What's on your mind?"

"Nothing much. Mainly I wanted to make sure you still planned to be back here in time for Maria's New Year's bash. I may have a new client for you by then."

"Not only are we planning on being there but we have some news of our own."

"Really, do I hear wedding bells in the distance?"

"Loud and clear. Maurice proposed, and I accepted. We'll tell his family over Christmas."

"Constance and I are delighted. Maurice is an outstanding young man, and we know the two of you will be perfectly matched."

"Thanks, Emile. I think you know that I consider you and Constance family. We can discuss the new client as soon as I return."

"We will, and the two of you enjoy the rest of your stay in Paris."

"Thank you. Talk to you soon."

Mary Jo walked into the den, and, when she had some wine, she sat close to the crackling fire and said to Maurice, "You are not going to believe just how high-tech the fashion industry has become."

Mary Jo walked Maurice through the entire experience, complete with her assessment of the technology. It was close to 7:00 when she finished. Maurice swirled the wine in his glass and said, "I shudder to think what all of this is going to cost."

Mary Jo thought for a moment and then replied, "Close to 200,000 euros, but, considering that I'm going to have a complete world-class wardrobe without the agonizing hours of shopping, it's beginning to sound more and more like a bargain."

Maurice didn't change expressions and said, "I suppose this means no more jeans and football jerseys."

"Not at all, but it does mean that I can dress appropriately if we go to the beach *or* to the opera."

"In that case, I'll see what I can arrange for myself before we leave Paris. Now, let's walk around the corner to Chez Moliere and enjoy a little slice of heaven."

Chez Moliere was only two blocks away, and, when Mary Jo and Maurice walked in, you'd have thought Maurice owned it. The two were immediately seated at a table near a roaring fireplace. Maurice ordered for both of them, and the resulting four-course meal was a perfect example of the cuisine of Normandy. The rich dishes were true comfort food. The desserts of apples simmered in Calvados were the ideal foil for the rich dark-roast coffee.

While they ate, Maurice told Mary Jo about his visit with the security people at Dalhousie's Paris office and his trip to the museum. It was nearly 11:00, and there was a chilling wind coming from the Seine when the couple returned to the flat. The fire was dying down, but they cuddled in front of the embers and had a glass of brandy before they turned in for the night.

EIGHT

WHILE THEY WERE EATING their breakfast on the balcony, Maurice told Mary Jo that he planned to get on the phone as soon as they finished eating and plot out the balance of their stay. She reminded him to check out what was going on at both the Grand Palais and the Petit Palais while he was at it.

Mary Jo cleared the breakfast dishes, stacked them for Portia, and then called Collette's cell phone.

Collette cheerfully answered, "Bonjour, Mary Jo. What can I do for you?"

"I thought I'd better call and check to see when some of my new wardrobe will be available. Maurice is planning a week of events and dinners."

"I'm on my way to meet Carine, and we'll get started this morning. You should have all of your lingerie delivered this afternoon, and we'll get right to work on the rest. If you can call back and give me an idea of where you will be going, I can be sure you have the proper ensemble to wear."

"Will you be able to turn it around that fast?"

"My dear, we have your body measurements and your funds at our disposal. Now, it's only a matter of persuading the various shops to meet our deadlines, and Carine and I can be very persuasive."

"I'll email our schedule as soon as Maurice completes it."

"If you will do that, then I'll see that an outfit is delivered each day for the following day's activity, as well as for dinner."

"Collette, you're a miracle worker. I'll never be able to thank you enough."

"Mary Jo, I'm having the time of my life doing this. I need to thank you for your trust and confidence. Now, get your schedule to me as soon as you can."

Mary Jo found Maurice sitting at the kitchen table talking in French on his cell phone. She could see the concern on his face and decided to wait until he finished to ask about it.

When Maurice put the phone down, he said, "That was my brother Giovanni, the army officer. He and his family are vacationing in Marrakesh, and it seems that they cannot get a flight out in time for Christmas. The only flight available is on December 28."

"How in the hell did he get stranded without a return flight?"

"As a general officer, he and his family are allowed to fly on Air France for half price, if they'll fly standby. It seems that he has been bumped by someone with a higher priority."

"When were they planning to leave?"

"Their hotel reservations are prepaid until December 18th. He was planning to return to Brussels and then fly on to Corsica."

"I don't see a problem, since we own a jet and can pick them up and take them to Corsica with us."

"That would mean that we'll have to leave Paris next Monday, almost a week sooner than we planned."

"So what! It'll give us more time to spend with your family."

"Are you sure you don't mind?"

"No, in fact, I like the idea. You might be sure that they have everything they need and won't have to return to Brussels to repack."

"Yes, I'll call right back and set it all up. In the meantime, take a look at this and tell me what you think."

Maurice passed a legal pad to Mary Jo, and she began to read an agenda of activities and dinner reservations, starting the next day through the coming weekend.

Mary Jo smiled and said, "You've been a busy boy. You call Giovanni back while I email this to Collette. She promised me a proper outfit for each occasion, and I want her to get started. Since it appears that we'll be on the go beginning tomorrow, maybe we need to check your fluid levels tonight."

"That's a good plan. I'll have Louie run out and get us some bread and cheese so that we can eat in bed."

The lovers were asleep in each other's arms when the doorbell woke them, and they heard Portia go to the front entrance. She had a brief conversation with someone, and Maurice raised himself on an elbow and muttered, "Who do you suppose that was? Were you expecting anyone?"

"No, but I bet I know what it was."

"Yeah, what?"

"My underwear delivery."

Mary Jo pulled on a robe and went downstairs. Maurice heard her talking to Portia, and soon they came in carrying a stack of boxes with Gilson printed on the side. Mary Jo opened the first one. It contained at least 20 pairs of panties and bras. Each subsequent box contained other pieces of lingerie, including nighties and robes.

Maurice watched as Mary Jo opened each package, and, finally, he said, "I think we need a fashion show of your new unmentionables."

Mary Jo smiled, stepped out of the robe, and said, "Think your fluid levels can stand the strain?"

"There's only one way to find out."

A short modeling session achieved the desired result, and the two were basking in afterglow when the doorbell rang again. Maurice groaned and said, "Just how much underwear did you buy?"

Mary Jo donned the robe and came back carrying a smaller stack of boxes marked "Chanel." She opened one box and read a card from Collette: "Here is your outfit for tomorrow's trip to the Louvre and dinner tomorrow evening. Have fun. Collette."

Mary Jo read it aloud and then hung the new items in the closet. There was a separate box containing shoes and accessories, which Mary Jo placed in the top of the closet. She walked back to the bed and jumped in. "Okay, let's get back to checking your fluids."

The next morning, Mary Jo pulled the clothes assigned for the day, and, to her surprise, everything fit perfectly, including her new underwear. She felt feminine and sexy. The couple caught a cab to the Louvre, where they met an English-speaking guide. The guide bypassed the long line of people who were waiting for entry and led Mary Jo and Maurice to a side door and straight into the museum.

The couple saw everything from the Winged Victory to the Mona Lisa, but Mary Jo was particularly fascinated with the extensive Ancient Rome section. After a tasty lunch in the Café Mollien, Mary Jo insisted that they return, but, by the end of the afternoon, one thing had become abundantly clear. You cannot see the Louvre in one day.

That evening, Maurice and Mary Jo attended a performance of *The Nutcracker* at the Palais Garnier and then had dinner at Joel Robuchon's restaurant on the Left Bank. Maurice was handsome in his dinner jacket, and Mary Jo turned heads in her Chanel. She began to sense the difference well-styled clothing could make in one's enjoyment of an evening.

On Thursday, the couple visited the Rodin museum just around the corner from the flat and then taxied to George V to lunch at Le Cinq. After lunch, they took in the Picasso museum before returning to the flat to dress for the evening. Mary Jo's outfit had been delivered, and she looked elegant in a Celine dress and shoes by Lobato.

Maurice and Mary Jo returned to Palais Garnier for a performance of *La Bohème*. The haunting music of Puccini and Belle Époque Paris was perfect to set the mood for dinner at the quintessential Paris café, Brasserie Haussmann. After dinner, they rode home in one of the horse-drawn taxis. With the music still ringing in their ears, the lovers had a snifter of brandy while sitting on the balcony wrapped in woolen blankets.

The next morning, a delivery van pulled up just after breakfast and delivered the balance of Mary Jo's wardrobe. Included in the delivery was a set of Louis Vuitton soft-sided luggage.

Mary Jo spread the collection of clothing, shoes, and accessories on the bed and said, "There is no way we can fit all of this, along with your brother and his family, into our plane. I'll have to pack only what I'll need on Corsica and leave the rest here. We can pick it up when we return, and we'll have plenty of room in the cabin area to haul it back to Mobile."

"That ought to work; we can spend the night here and leave early the next morning."

"I noticed that we don't have anything scheduled for today. That'll give me a chance to sort through all of this and figure out just what I'll take to visit your family."

"We do have a dinner planned for Arpege this evening, but it's not until 8:00."

"Let me get started, and you can find a way to amuse yourself."

"I'll run over to the Military Museum and have lunch there. I'll see you later in the afternoon."

Mary Jo spent the next couple of hours opening and inspecting her new wardrobe. She decided what to take and what to leave at the flat, and, when she finished, she called Collette's cell.

Collette picked up after two rings and gushed, "Oh, Mary Jo, I'm so glad you called. Was everything delivered?"

"Collette, I can't imagine that there could possibly be more. I've used every surface in the flat to lay it all out. I'm worried that I'll have to add closets to my home in Mobile to hold it all."

"You may want to consult Constance about that; she is an organizational genius."

"I'll do that. I just wanted to call you to thank you again and to share my good news."

"You and Maurice are to marry. Constance was on the phone as soon as Emile told her. We are both pleased, and we stand ready to help with the wedding."

"We haven't made any firm plans for the wedding, and we'll be leaving Paris on Monday to go to Corsica."

"Oh my! Augustin and I were going to suggest that you join us at our country home near Orleans for several days before you leave."

"We're going to fly to Marrakesh and pick up one of Maurice's brothers and his family. They're on vacation and got bumped off their return flight. We'll go on to Corsica after we pick them up. I hope we can have a rain check on that invitation."

"Of course. I'm sure you and Maurice will be returning to Paris often."

"Thanks, Collette. We'll keep in touch and look forward to your next visit to the States."

"Yes, and don't let Constance allow your wardrobe to slip. Trust her and she'll keep you up to date. Let me hear from you."

The engaged couple's dinner at Arpege was a culinary delight, and Mary Jo looked radiant in an outfit by Tom Greyhound. On Saturday, they took another long walk, ending up at the Moulin Rouge in Montmartre. Saturday evening, they boarded a riverboat near Notre Dame and enjoyed a five-course dinner and dancing until after midnight.

On Sunday, the travelers slept in, read the London *Times*, and made love in the afternoon. They decided to get packed for the trip to Corsica and snacked on bread and cheese for dinner. They fell asleep with the BBC in the background.

On Monday morning, the couple took a taxi to Orly, and Mary Jo immediately filed a flight plan from Orly to Marrakesh and on to Ajaccio, Corsica. The ground crew pulled her plane to the tarmac, and she and Maurice loaded their bags. Mary Jo received clearance to take off at 9:00 a.m. Paris time. When she cleared Paris air control, Mary Jo switched to the intercom and said, "Well, we're on our way. I think I'll want to come back to Paris soon. Thank you for such a lovely time."

Maurice said, "It *was* a lovely time, and I enjoyed every minute. Now, we're off to the next stage of our adventure. How long will it take to get to Marrakesh?"

"It's 1,300 air miles, and we'll be cruising at 375 MPH, so it'll be close to four hours. We'll be flying over Southern France and Spain, and we'll cross into Africa over the Strait of Gibraltar."

"I spent a good deal of time in Morocco and Algeria during my service in the Legion, and I've even been to Casablanca."

"Well, play it again, Sam."

The weather was clear with only scattered clouds, and the only turbulence lasted for a few moments as they crossed the Pyrenees. They flew almost directly over the Rock of Gibraltar and were soon receiving instructions from the Marrakesh airport. From the air, Marrakesh gleamed in the desert sun, and Mary Jo set the jet down with just a little bump at noon local time. She followed the Jeep sent to greet them to a parking spot within walking distance to the terminal.

Mary Jo shut the engines down while Maurice opened the cabin door and lowered the stairs. Mary Jo gave instructions to refuel the plane and have it ready for takeoff at 2:00 local time. They passed through Moroccan immigration, and, as they entered the terminal, Maurice saw a tall, erect man in a tan suit waving at them.

Maurice shook the man's hand, turned to Mary Jo, and said, "Mary Jo Thibodaux, I want you to meet my brother Giovanni. Giovanni, this is my fiancée, Mary Jo."

A momentary look of puzzlement crossed Giovanni's face but was quickly replaced with a wide grin. He took Mary Jo's hand and said in a heavy French accent, "My dearest girl, I will hold my younger brother down, and you'll have an opportunity to escape a fate I'd wish on no woman."

Mary Jo chuckled and replied, "I appreciate the thought, but I've tamed your baby brother, and I have him eating out of my hand."

Giovanni laughed. "That's what the Legion thought, but don't ever say you never had a chance to escape. If you are determined to go through with this, then you have my blessing. Come, Nicole and the boys are waiting in the restaurant."

Giovanni led the way to a table overlooking the flight operations, and, as he approached, two young men rose to their feet. Giovanni turned to a beautiful woman in her forties and said, "Nicole, I want to introduce our savior and Maurice's fiancée, Mademoiselle Mary Jo Thibodaux. Mary Jo, this is my wife, Nicole, and my two sons, Ernesto and Henri."

The two young men smiled and acknowledged the introduction. Maurice and Mary Jo took seats at the table, and Mary Jo turned to Giovanni and said, "We've been instructed to bring you greetings from an old classmate, Augustin Beaumarchais. We were dinner guests at his home a week or so ago."

"Augustin. Well, it is a small world. He is CEO of one of France's largest conglomerates. I haven't seen him since our last class reunion. How did you and Maurice happen to be his guests?"

"His wife, Collette, is the sister of one of my good friends from Mobile. Her sister, Constance, kindly asked Collette to assist me in some shopping while we were in Paris."

Giovanni turned to Maurice and asked, "Did you use the flat while you were in Paris?"

"We did, and Louie and Portia both send their love."

The rest of the lunch passed pleasantly, and, soon, it was time to re-board. As everyone settled into their seats and Mary Jo was doing the preflight walk-around, Maurice took Mary Jo aside and said, "Ernesto has just turned 17 and will be enrolling at Saint-Cyr next fall. He's planning on a career as a fighter pilot, and I know he would enjoy flying in the copilot's seat. I'll sit in the cabin, talk to Giovanni, and keep him in the loop about what I'm doing."

Ernesto squirmed to get his six-foot-plus frame in the seat, and then Mary Jo showed him how to plug into the communications system. She carefully explained what she was doing as she started the engines and began to taxi to the runway. He listened intently as the tower cleared them for takeoff and watched Mary Jo's every move as they started their climb-out.

Mary Jo flew the plane manually and did not set the autopilot. She leveled off at 26,000 feet and kept the airspeed at 375. She turned on the cabin intercom and said, "Welcome, ladies and gentlemen, to Air Thibodaux's jet service to Ajaccio. This is your captain, M.J. Thibodaux, and your First Officer, Ernesto Capriati. Our flight today will take us just north of the Atlas Mountains, and we'll cross over Algiers before we hit the Mediterranean. Our flight time will be three and a half hours, and our ETA is 6:30 local time. Enjoy your flight, and, if you need anything, just ask our flight attendant, Maurice."

Mary Jo allowed Ernesto to take the controls, and he got the feel right away. She let him fly the plane until they picked up Ajaccio air control. She took over and made the landing into the small airport just as the sun sank behind Italy. She followed the ground instructions to a private hangar on the edge of the airport. She was about to ask where they were going when Ernesto said, "This is my Grand-Pere's hangar and flight operations building." Ernesto pointed to a figure leaning against one of two black SUVs parked in front of the hangar and said, "That's Charles, my Grand-Pere's head of security. He must be meeting us." As Mary Jo and Ernesto unhooked the earphones and started to leave the flight deck, Ernesto said, "Miss Thibodaux, I'll never forget this flight. I have now actually flown a jet, and I can't wait to tell my instructor about it."

"Maybe we can do a little more flying while we're here," Mary Jo replied.

Everyone deplaned, and they were met by Charles Carbanno, the man Ernesto had described as the head of Capriati's security. He was dressed in hunting clothing and had a double-barreled shotgun on a sling. Maurice and

Giovanni embraced the man and then introduced him to Mary Jo. He smiled and said, "Mademoiselle Thibodaux, we are honored to have you as our guest. If everyone will follow me, we will depart for the villa."

Mary Jo, still dressed in her flight clothes and slip-on boots, said, "Maurice, I'd like to change, if I may."

Maurice looked at Carbanno and asked, "Will we have time for Mary Jo to change?"

"I would prefer to start for the villa; there will be plenty of time to change before dinner. I have taken the liberty of loading all of your bags into our vehicles, and I have made arrangements for our ground-service people to move your plane into our hangar."

"Of course, that'll be fine," Mary Jo replied.

Carbanno said, "I have one more request; I'd like Giovanni and Maurice to ride with me in the lead vehicle and the ladies and boys in the trailing one. I'd like a chance to brief both of them on a situation."

Maurice gave Giovanni a quizzical look. Giovanni just shrugged his shoulders as if to say, "Don't ask me." Maurice held the door to the black SUV, which Mary Jo recognized as a Mercedes. The driver stood by with an Uzi slung over his shoulder until everyone was seated. Then, he got into the driver's seat and waited. When the lead van pulled away, he slipped in behind them and followed them out of the airport.

As the group rode through the streets of Ajaccio, Mary Jo said, "Nicole, do you have any idea what's going on?"

"None whatsoever and I doubt that Giovanni does either. One of the things I've learned about Corsica is that women will be treated with great deference and respect but will not be included in business discussions. Giovanni, however, has always shared these things with me, and I'm sure Maurice will, as well."

Within minutes, the little caravan left the well-lit streets of the city and began ascending into the hills on a narrow, winding road. It was now full dark, and, other than an occasional light from a farmhouse, Mary Jo could see nothing. She turned her head and looked up the mountain just as a flash of light, followed by a trail of fire, came hurtling out of the night.

The animal part of her brain screamed RPG just as the van in front burst with an explosion and a ball of fire.

NINE

THE DRIVER SKIDDED to a stop, and Mary Jo threw open her door and immediately began pulling Nicole and the boys into a roadside ditch. The van was being riddled by automatic rifle fire, and Mary Jo could see that their driver was slumped over the steering wheel. She instructed Nicole and the boys to stay in the ditch and to keep their heads down; they were shielded from the gunfire by the bullet-pierced van. As Mary Jo looked up, she could see Giovanni pulling a man from the burning lead vehicle and dragging him down into the ditch.

Mary Jo crawled to the passenger door of the van she had been in and pulled the door open. After she confirmed that the driver was dead, she managed to pull two Uzis and six extra magazines of ammunition out. Mary Jo jumped into the ditch and crawled to Giovanni. Filled with horror, Mary Jo saw the prone body of Maurice lying in the ditch, half of his head blown away. With tears streaming down her face, she looked at Giovanni, who had a fierce light shining from his eyes. Mary Jo grabbed his arm and said, "You have to go form a defensive position around Nicole and the boys!" He nodded in agreement and began to drag Maurice's body down the ditch. Mary Jo stopped him and shouted, "He's gone, Giovanni; go take care of your family."

There was a long burst of automatic weapons, followed by a second RPG that hit the trailing vehicle and set it ablaze. Mary Jo all but pulled Giovanni to his family and handed him the Uzi and the extra clips.

"Take this and let's move everyone away from these cars. We need to find a better defensive position further down in this ditch." They steered Nicole and the boys further away, while the two burning cars were literally being shot to pieces.

Mary Jo found a deeper part of the ditch and said, "Stay here and keep as quiet as possible; only fire if you have no choice. I'll be back as soon as I can."

Giovanni looked at her with shock on his face. "Where are you going?"

"I'm going to kill those motherfuckers."

Mary Jo slipped out of the ditch and ran across the road to the opposite gully. Her mental clock was fully alert now, telling her that 37 seconds had elapsed since the first RPG had hit. She estimated that she had less than a minute or two before the assailants began to withdraw. She glanced over the rim of the ditch and saw two flashes of machine-gun fire, followed by a stream of tracer rounds projecting into the wreckage. "They assume they've neutralized their target, so they're not afraid of revealing their position with tracers," she thought.

The horrifying image of Maurice's destroyed head flashed through Mary Jo's mind, but she quickly placed it in a separate compartment to be dealt with later. She eased out of the ditch in a low run, keeping the firing points in her peripheral vision, running parallel to the assailants' position. She reached down into the physical reserve that had made her a track star and shifted into another gear. She ran for close to 30 seconds and calculated that she should be able to flank the gunners. Mary Jo turned to her right and slowed to a low prowl as she reached into her back pocket and removed her ivory-handled straight razor, palming it in her right hand.

Mary Jo had extraordinary night vision, and she could see every burst from what sounded like a couple of AK-47s. She sensed that she was now behind their firing positions, so she dropped into a low crouch and eased forward. The burning cars provided sufficient contrast, and soon she could see the outline of a man advancing slowly toward the vehicles while firing from the hip.

Mary Jo knew the man was headed to finish off any survivors and wouldn't keep a watch on his rear. Shiva the Destroyer took off at a dead run, leaped on his back, and cut his throat from ear to ear. Before he hit the ground, Mary Jo had his rifle and was headed toward the other shooter. Another man spotted the movement from the corner of his eye and spun toward her. He was a nanosecond too late. Mary Jo hit him at full speed and struck him in the gut with the butt of her rifle. He crumpled to the ground and threw up.

Several minutes had passed since the attack began, and Mary Jo could hear the wail of sirens in the distance. Her battle instincts alerted her to movement to her rear, and she saw two figures running to the crest of the hill. She fired a burst and saw one of the fleeing bodies go flying into the air. His partner grabbed him and pulled him over the crest.

Mary Jo decided not to give chase. Just then, she heard a high-powered engine come to life and disappear into the night. She walked back to the figure on the ground and kicked him with her boot. He groaned and tried to defend himself with his arms. She rolled him onto his stomach and, using the strap of his rifle, tied his hands securely behind him and then yanked him to his feet. She jabbed him in the ribs and started marching him down the hill, just as the first of the police cars pulled up next to the burning vans. Before they came into the circle of light that was thrown off by the fires, Mary Jo pushed her prisoner to his knees and whispered, "I hope you speak enough English to understand this. I'm going to tie your feet and leave you here for a few minutes. If you make a sound or try to get away, I'll be back and hunt you down like an animal, and then I will kill you very slowly. Got it?"

"Si, Si, ho capire," he replied.

Mary Jo trussed him up and thought about cutting his Achilles tendons to be sure. She decided she'd rather hunt him down rather than risk his screaming — she would then be forced to turn him over to the police. Mary Jo headed toward the line of police cars, and, since everyone's attention was focused on the wreckage, even though she was carrying a loaded Uzi, she was able to walk up to the crowd gathered around Giovanni.

When Giovanni saw her approach, he pulled away from the crowd of men and said, "Mary Jo, I'm relieved to see you. I was afraid we'd lost you too."

"Not even close. The RPG guys have gone, but I eliminated one of them, and I captured another one. I didn't bring him in because I didn't want the police to get to him before we could find out just what he knows."

"You don't have to worry about the police; my father owns the locals and has a great deal of influence with the national police. We'll have all the cooperation we need. Right now, we'll handle this within the family, with support from the authorities, if we need it. Someone has made a grave error in judgment. Killing one of Don Ernesto's sons will not go unavenged."

"Oh, I can assure you that Maurice's death will be avenged, Don Ernesto or not. Now, I'm going to bring this bastard in, and I expect you to see that he goes with us, not the police."

"Stefano Grammitti, our number-two security guy is standing over there. Let's give him instructions to get your prisoner to the villa."

The two walked over to a grim-faced man in a leather jacket, and Giovanni said, "Stefano, this is Mary Jo, Maurice's fiancée. She managed to kill one of the attackers and capture another. She'll show you where he is, and I want you to take him to the villa and put him in the old cellar. Make sure nothing happens to him until we get there."

Stefano looked at Mary Jo and said, "Mademoiselle, I am very sorry for your loss. We all loved Maurice; he was the bravest of the brave. We will punish whoever did this. Now, lead me to this dog you captured."

Mary Jo led Stefano up the hill until they found the man exactly where Mary Jo had left him. Stefano untied the prisoner's legs, pulled him to his feet, turned to Mary Jo, and said, "I'm surprised that such a young woman could have subdued a thug like this."

"Well, don't be. I managed to knock one of the RPG guys down just over the crest of the hill, but I'm sure his partner hauled him off, along with the other one whose throat I cut. I heard what sounded like a Range Rover or a Hummer take off."

Mary Jo left Stefano to deal with the prisoner and walked down the hill where Giovanni was comforting Nicole and his sons. The ambulance attendants were loading a body bag, and Mary Jo walked over and said, "May I have just a moment alone with him?" They nodded and stepped away. Mary Jo unzipped the bag and looked at what was left of Maurice's handsome face. She leaned down, kissed his cheek, and wiped away a stray tear. She re-zipped the bag and motioned for the EMTs to come back. She thanked them and walked toward Giovanni, wiping more tears from her eyes.

Giovanni took Mary Jo by the arm and said, "We have to go to the villa; my father is waiting."

"What about the cops? I'd think they'd want to interview us."

"I'm sure they will, but they'll come to the villa when we're ready to talk to them. In the meantime, we've got to make our plans," Giovanni replied.

The five of them were placed in a black van driven by a hard-faced man in peasant clothes. When Mary Jo sat, she remembered that she was still carrying the Uzi. She shifted it across her lap and rode in silence. The van zigzagged back and forth, gaining altitude with each turn, until they pulled through a large gated entrance where four heavily armed men were standing guard.

The van stopped in a circular drive, and Giovanni held the door while everyone stepped onto the gravel. They all climbed a flight of stone steps and were met at the door by a tall, graying man with an agonized but determined look on his face. He hugged Giovanni, Nicole, and each of his grandsons, and then he turned to Mary Jo and held out his open arms. He embraced her and said, "My heart is breaking that our first meeting has to be on such a terrible night. But my son loved you, so you are my daughter now, and this is your home."

Mary Jo hugged him back and said, "Thank you, Don Ernesto. I'm honored and grateful that you would welcome me as your daughter, and, *together*, we will avenge Maurice."

Don Ernesto was somewhat taken aback by her reply but maintained his composure and said, "You must be exhausted; we will show you to your room. A bath has been drawn, and we have borrowed some night clothes for you from one of my daughters, since all of your things burned in the wreckage. Tomorrow, we can have some regular clothing picked up for you. You must also let us destroy the blood-stained clothing you are wearing."

Mary Jo stiffened, looked him in the eye, and said, "Don Ernesto, I realize that you are acting in what you believe to be my best interest, but I have to tell you that I have no intention of bathing *or* changing clothing until we've questioned my captive."

A dark shadow crossed the Don's face, but, before he could speak, Giovanni said, "Papa, you should hear her out. After the attack, Mary Jo took control of the situation and made sure my family was protected before she ran into the night and silenced our assailants. I'm a major general, but she was barking orders, and I was following them. This young woman is someone special, whose voice and participation need to be included."

Don Ernesto frowned for a moment and then said, "Very well. It was clear that Maurice not only loved you but held you in high regard and so, it seems, does another of my sons. Perhaps we need to get to know each other better, Mary Jo. Let's all get a glass of spirits and meet in my office." He turned to a young man standing at the door and said, "See that Jeppe joins us, please."

Mary Jo and Giovanni walked to a small table, and each poured a snifter of brandy. When they were alone, Mary Jo said, "Thank you for your support; I didn't mean to be ordering you around."

"Mary Jo, tonight was not my first firefight, and I instantly recognized you as one of those rare officers who can assess a situation and make the right decisions under stress and incoming fire. You are a natural warrior, and I was glad to have you in command."

"Thank you, Giovanni. I'd like to be able to work together to get the bastards who just killed Maurice. Who is this Jeppe that your father summoned?"

"Think Yoda. Jeppe has the finest strategic mind I've ever known, and he's been with the family for three generations. We'll need his support if we're going to convince Papa to let us handle this."

"I have to say — I'm flattered at the confidence you have in me. Flattered and a little surprised."

"Well, don't be. You're going to do this no matter what we decide, and I'd rather have you in the tent pissing out than out pissing in. Also, I've seen your file from the 902nd, and I've vetted you thoroughly. My good friends Jack Litton and Amy Wilson have assured me that you're a person of serious skills."

"Giovanni, would I be right in assuming that your position with NATO involves intelligence?"

"Probably a good guess. Now, let's go sell Jeppe and Papa."

"Well, good...since we seem to be on the same page about my involvement, I'm right behind you."

The two took their brandies and walked toward the back of the villa. Giovanni stood aside and allowed Mary Jo to enter the Don's private office and then followed. Don Ernesto was sitting beside the fire in a leather wingback chair, and Stefano Grammitti sat facing him. A small man with just a wisp of gray hair stood warming his backside in front of the fire.

Giovanni spoke in a calm, reasoned voice and said, "Mary Jo, you've met Stefano and Papa, but I want to introduce you to Jeppe Corleone. Jeppe has been our family Consigliere for many years."

Mary Jo stepped toward the fireplace and extended her hand. "Signor Corleone, it's my pleasure to meet you."

Jeppe took her hand, gave it a gentle squeeze, and replied, "No, it is my pleasure to meet Shiva. Your prowess in battle proceeds you."

Mary Jo was always amazed when a stranger knew enough about her to use that god-awful nickname, but she shook it off as a compliment and said, "And your prowess as a master of strategy proceeds you, as well. I look forward to working with you to avenge Maurice."

"Revenge will be ours, and it will be swift and complete," Jeppe replied.

Mary Jo decided to push the envelope and get everyone's cards on the table. She smiled at Jeppe and said, "As everyone probably knows, during my army career, I was stationed in Rome. Part of my job required me to study the structure of the Cosa Nostra. I learned that each family has a ruling triumvirate." She nodded in the direction of Don Ernesto and Jeppe and said, "The Don, the Consigliere, and the Capo Bastone. The Don and Consigliere are here tonight, but where is the Capo Bastone?"

Don Ernesto looked up and said, "Giovanni is our Capo."

Giovanni smiled and said, "Before you ask about conflicts of interest, let me assure you that I have been able to use my position with French Army Intelligence to our advantage in my role as family Capo. My first loyalty is, and always will be, to my family, and, should a situation develop in which the interests of France and my family are not compatible, I will resign my commission and protect my family. Does this give you any problem?"

"None whatsoever. In fact, if I sensed that you were struggling with this, I'd simply deal you out of the loop and work on my own. I'd like to ask a question though. Soon your two brothers will be joining us. Are they clear on family loyalty too?"

"Absolutely. Jean is one of our senior merchant captains, and he and Paulo are members of the family leadership.

Paulo's position with the Surete gives us a valuable intelligence source. I've spoken to both of them and advised them of Maurice's murder, and both of them will be here in the morning. We have a Bombardier that left this evening to pick them up."

"Well, that brings up another question. If the family owns a Bombardier, then you weren't stranded in Marrakesh, were you?"

"No, I wanted the opportunity to meet you before we all gathered here. Maurice had told me about your handling of the Broussard murder, as well as your dealings with various diablos. I needed to be sure of anyone who is to be welcomed into our family. It's part of my job as Capo. Now, if you'll allow me, I'd like to move on with the issue at hand."

Mary Jo nodded in agreement, and Giovanni continued: "I want to propose that we include Mary Jo as an equal member when we begin to plan our response to the Castellanos. She'll bring assets that we otherwise could never tap into."

Jeppe shifted in front of the fire and said, "Tell me about these assets."

"Well, for one thing, she's a valued client of the Dalhousie banking firm and has the complete confidence of Emile Dalhousie."

"What else does she bring?"

"She has the complete trust of two legendary members of U.S. military intelligence, General Jack Litton and Admiral Amy Wilson. These give us access to resources we have never been able to use."

"Is there more?"

Giovanni paused, looked at Mary Jo, and asked, "Mary Jo, is there anything I've left out?"

Mary Jo thought for a moment. "If, for some reason, I'm refused participation, then I fully intend to move on my own, and my connections to Roberto and Carlo will be invaluable; however, I believe that the best route to finding Maurice's killers will be working with the family, so I'm going to go all in." She turned to Don Ernesto and said, "Do the names Roberto Morelli and Carlo Baggetti mean anything to you?"

The Don seemed a bit surprised but quickly covered it up and replied, "I am not familiar with Morelli, but I know Carlo very well. We have worked together since his days as commercial attaché to the U.S. Embassy in Rome."

Giovanni said quietly, "I know Roberto Morelli very well; he is at the very top of Italian counterintelligence. I believe we could request his help and get a positive response."

Mary Jo said, "You may know him well, but did you ever save his life?"

"No, of course not."

"Well, I did, and he will do anything that does not harm Italy if I ask him to. Carlo and I have a long history of working together, as well."

Jeppe turned to Don Ernesto and said, "Don, it is my judgment that we should welcome Mary Jo into our inner circle and get on with the business of wrecking the wretched family of Castellanos."

The Don thought for a moment and then replied, "I agree. Shall we proceed to the basement and have a chat with our guest from Sardinia?"

Mary Jo interjected, "Jeppe's remark about a family of Castellanos is the second time I've heard them mentioned as Maurice's killers. Are we sure?"

Jeppe walked away from the fire and said, "We are almost positive, but the man in the basement can give us proof."

TEN

MARY JO FOLLOWED EVERYONE to a small elevator and squeezed in. The doors opened into a well-lit cellar, packed with wine racks and oak casks. The air was cool, and the aroma of aging wine and other spirits almost made her eyes water. Stefano stopped at an iron-clad oak door and removed a heavy padlock. They walked single file down a tunnel carved out of solid rock, until they reached a rusted, iron gate, also padlocked.

Stefano pulled the creaking gate open, and they all entered a large room with stone walls and floors, a bare light hanging from the ceiling. The man Mary Jo had captured was sagging against the far wall, his arms behind his back, secured in chains. He looked at them defiantly and said, "Si sta sprecando il vostro tempo; non ho nulla da dire."

Jeppe stood within a yard of the man and chuckled. "I see that you have a working knowledge of Italian, so I suggest we continue in that language…si?"

The man strained against his shackles and said in a heavy Sardinian accent, "Italian, English, or Swahili, I still have nothing to say. You Corsican bastards don't understand morte."

Don Ernesto shot back, "Oh, before dawn, you'll have a lot to say, and it is you who do not understand morte. Do we look like the damn police?" The Don stood face to face with the man and said, "Tonight, you and your friends murdered my son and two of my best men. I know that you understand that there is no way you live to see morning. You will die tonight, and the only choice you have is when and how. I am going to ask you one simple question. If you answer it truthfully, I will put a bullet in your brain, and you can die without pain. If you lie to me, then the offer is gone, and you will die sometime around dawn in excruciating pain. Do you understand?"

The defiance drained from the man's face. "Si, I understand."

"I'm pleased that you do. Here is the question, and you only need to answer yes or no. Did Giuseppe Castellano order this attack?"

The man raised his head and looked into the Don's eyes. "Si."

Don Ernesto sighed and said, "Is there anything else you'd like to tell me?"

"Only this. Your son was not our target. We were told that it would be you in the lead car, but, Don Ernesto, you must know that this was only business. There was no disrespect intended."

"I do understand. You were only doing the bidding of your Don. What is your name, my son, and what is your village?"

"I am Luigi Buono from Olbia on the northeast coast."

"Luigi from Olbia, your body will be returned to your home and buried with respect. Thank you for your honesty," Don Ernesto replied. He pulled an old revolver from his waistband and shot the man in the head. Then, the Don turned to Stefano. "See that his body is treated with respect and returned to his family. I suggest that we all retire for what's left of tonight and reconvene in the morning." Ernesto looked at Mary Jo and said, "I regret that you had to witness this, but it had to be done."

"I would have gladly pulled the trigger myself," Mary Jo replied.

Don Ernesto's face took on a grim countenance, and he said, "I believe that. I was saving you and your razor, in case he told a lie."

One of the maids led Mary Jo to her room on the second floor of the villa. The maid drew a hot bath and laid out a nightgown and robe for Mary Jo, who peeled off her bloody flight suit and muddy boots. The young woman gathered them up and took them away.

Mary Jo stepped into the steaming hot water and slowly slid in until only her head remained above the surface. She let the heat leach the aches and pains away, and, finally, she acknowledged the portion of her mind that now held only the memory of Maurice. Mary Jo allowed the intensity of their love, the joy of their brief time together, and the pain of his death to flood her mind, and she wept gut-wrenching tears. By the time the maid returned to help Mary Jo to bed, the water had begun to cool, and Mary Jo was exhausted from the exertion of deeply felt emotion and grief — like nothing she had ever experienced.

When Mary Jo awoke in the morning, she looked at her watch and saw that it was 6:30. Her flight suit and her bra and panties had been washed, ironed, and neatly folded at the foot of her bed. Her boots were clean and freshly polished. She walked downstairs and found Giovanni sitting at the kitchen table with a cup of coffee in his hand. He smiled and asked, "Did you manage any sleep?"

"Yes, I was finally able to fall asleep. I won't rest though until we find and punish Maurice's killers."

"I'm about to go back to the airport and meet Jean and Paulo. Would you like to come with me?"

"Yes. I keep an emergency bag packed in my plane, and I'd like to pick it up."

"Good, I want to fill Jean and Paulo in before we get back to the villa. It'll give you a chance to meet them, as well. Later in the day, we'll send someone in to buy whatever you need."

"Thank you. I'll put together a list."

"Pour a cup of coffee and let's head to the airport. The plane is due in at 8:00, and we can get breakfast at the airport café."

Giovanni called for a car, and soon three black SUVs pulled in front of the villa. Stefano stepped from the front van, held the door to the second, and said, "Il mio Capo, there is news from the police. They have arrested two men at the local hospital, both suffering from gunshot wounds. They are in stable condition. Do we want to question them?"

"I don't think so. I suspect they were victims of a hunting accident and should be released to return to Sardinia when they recover. I would like to know when they are released." When Giovanni noticed the questioning look on Mary Jo's face, he said, "You and I might see to their safe passage when they're released. I think we may want to chat with them in private."

"I think we might, indeed," Mary Jo replied.

The caravan of SUVs left the main gate and began the twisting descent into Ajaccio. Mary Jo noticed heavily armed men stationed along the road, while others patrolled the hillsides. She asked, "Damn, Giovanni, how many men do you guys have?"

"There are 37 men in our employ, but some of these men are volunteers from other families and friends."

"Well, it looks like the whole island is out there."

"Not yet, but it will be if we need them. We're all related if you dig deep enough."

Giovanni and Mary Jo were dropped off at the terminal, where they walked to flight operations. Giovanni was greeted and told that the plane was due to touch down in 15 minutes.

Mary Jo said, "That gives me enough time to get my bag. I'll be right back."

Mary Jo told the lady at the flight desk what she wanted, and, soon, a young woman dressed in a mechanic's uniform walked up and said, "Please, come with me."

The two women got in a golf cart, drove across the tarmac to the Capriati hangar, and pulled up next to the Cessna. Mary Jo hopped out, opened the exterior baggage bin, and pulled out an olive-drab duffel bag with "Lt. Col. M.J. Thibodaux" stenciled on it in black ink. She tossed it into the cart, and, as they drove back to the terminal, Mary Jo saw a gleaming-white Bombardier touching down on a far runway. She slung the bag over her shoulder and came back to flight operations.

Giovanni was standing looking out over the flight line, holding a mug of steaming coffee. He looked at the bag and said to her, "Did you find everything?"

"Oh yeah. I'll still need some clothes, but all of my tools are in here."

An airport van pulled in to the terminal, and two men jumped to the ground. One was slightly graying and weather-beaten, wearing seaman's clothing, including an officer's hat. The other was younger, dressed in a business suit, and had that "I've heard it all look" that fills the faces of most policemen worldwide.

When the brothers entered the terminal, Giovanni met them and embraced each. He turned to Mary Jo and said, "Mary Jo Thibodaux, I'd like to introduce my brothers, Jean and Paulo."

Mary Jo extended her hand to both men and then said, "Maurice spoke so highly of you both. I'm saddened that we have to meet under these unbearable and terrible circumstances."

Jean took her hand and replied, "Yes, we too regret the excruciating situation under which we meet."

Giovanni suggested that they move into the small café.

Giovanni said, "Did you have breakfast on the plane?"

The newcomers looked at each other, and Paulo said, "No, just a glass of juice and some coffee. Breakfast sounds good."

Once the group had sat at a table, Mary Jo said in Italian, "Paulo, I know you're with the French National Police, or what we used to call the Surete, and you'll be moving to Marseilles soon?"

"Yes, I am, and, yes, my family is on the way to Marseilles now. The plane will pick them up tomorrow, and, by the way, your Italian is excellent."

"Thank you. I was stationed in Rome for some years. Where did the plane pick you up?"

"We had docked at Mumbai on Monday, and I had plans to go on leave next week. My executive officer will continue to Sri Lanka, and I'll rejoin the ship there, if we have finished the business at hand."

Paulo stirred his coffee and then said, "Speaking of the business at hand, Giovanni sent us copies of your file, and we read it during the flight. Jean and I agree that you should be an integral part of our response to the Castellanos."

"Thank you, Paulo. I believe we'll be more effective working together than stumbling all over ourselves if we work separately," Mary Jo replied.

They all ate a quick breakfast and then rejoined Stefano and the caravan. Mary Jo tossed her bag in with their luggage and sat in the back with Paulo. On the ride back, Mary Jo watched as Paulo took in the lay of the land, and, when they passed the burned-out SUVs, his face hardened, and he looked away.

It was close to 10:00 when they reentered the guarded gate and pulled in front of the villa. Servants unloaded the baggage, and the four of them followed Stefano into the Don's conference room. The room had been converted into an operations center, with extensive military maps of the whole area around Corsica and Sardinia laid out.

A series of aerial photographs lined one wall, and a group of high-resolution mug shots lined the other. There were place tags for each person, and it didn't escape Mary Jo that she had been seated next to Jeppe at the head of the table. Servants brought in coffee and tea, withdrew, and closed the door behind them. Don Ernesto took his seat at the head of the table, and everyone sat and waited for him to speak. He cleared his throat and said, "I'd like us to begin with a moment of silence for Maurice. May he rest in peace." They all crossed themselves as they bowed their heads, and, in a moment, the Don continued. "This morning, we have to take a long look at our current situation and decide what our response is going to be. Jeppe, would you lay out the strategic situation for us?"

"Si, il mio Don. Earlier this month, someone attacked and boarded one of our smaller freighters here in the Med, slaughtered the crew, and left the ship adrift. We suspected the Castellanos, but, until last night, we did not have proof. Now we do. As much as we all want vengeance for Maurice, we must frame our response in a larger strategic sense. I believe we must first understand the Castellanos's motive for starting this war."

Jeppe continued: "I have given this a great deal of thought, and I will share my conclusions. Don Giuseppe

Castellano is a young man, only 27 years old. He only assumed leadership of the Castellano family last year, when his father, Don Tomasso, unexpectedly died. We always had a good understanding with Don Tomasso, and I worked with his Consigliere to resolve any disputes that arose. We had an agreement. We'd stay out of the drug-smuggling business, and they'd leave the gun and cigarette traffic to us. It is my opinion that the new Don is trying to prove himself and sees us as an easy target."

Don Ernesto thought for a moment and then asked, "Jeppe, why would they suppose we are an easy target?"

"I suspect our refusal to enter the drug trade has sent that message."

Don Ernesto asked, "Why should that be considered a weakness?"

"We all know why we do not deal in drugs. First, we believe it to be an evil thing and refuse to do it on moral grounds. The second reason is that it would disturb the delicate balance we have with the French and Italian authorities. They know we don't deal in drugs, and so they allow us a special relationship. Third, it would be a threat to Giovanni's and Paulo's careers. To Giuseppe Castellano, this says that we don't have the stomach for it and that we will give up our business without a fight. Those who do not study history are doomed to repeat it. The last time the Sardinians tried to muscle in on our business, it took them three generations to recover from our wrath."

Don Ernesto shook his head, and Giovanni said, "Jeppe, that is probably as close as we're going to come to the *why* of this thing. The next question is…how do we respond?"

Jeppe said, "Yes, and that's where we must think our actions through carefully. In my experience, there are two factors that can result in a failed plan: ignoring what you don't know and not allowing for the unexpected consequences of your actions. We must try and determine what it is that we don't know and find the answers, and we must examine all possible unexpected consequences. We must do these things before we take even the first step against the Castellanos."

Don Ernesto said, "Logic demands that, first, we determine, to the best of our ability, just what additional information we need before even considering our response. We have nearly a week until Christmas, and, chances are, even the Castellanos will not strike again until after the holidays. I want us to be ready to act by Christmas Eve. I want to hit them when they are least expecting it. I want Giovanni to lead the identification and gathering of the needed intelligence, and Jeppe and I will be considering possible responses. Today is Tuesday, and we will meet again on Thursday morning to check our progress. Are there any questions?"

Don Ernesto looked around the table, and no one responded. He began to leave the room with Jeppe following him to the door, and then the Don turned back to the group and said, "Giovanni, you and Mary Jo are seasoned intelligence officers. Treat this as a military operation, and, remember, we will soon be in a war of survival."

"Yes, Don Ernesto. We'll come up with a sound plan."

After Jeppe and the Don left the room, Giovanni moved to the head of the table and suggested that everyone take a short break to get some tea or coffee. He then asked Stefano if he could stay and help. Stefano said that he would like to check on the security of the villa but that he would return as soon as he could.

Once everyone had filled their cups and taken their seats, Giovanni began. "I believe we can approach this with an overall goal in mind. If you'll pardon the comparison, I'm drawn to the strategy Michael Corleone used in *The Godfather.* He let the baptism of his godson serve as the cover for destroying his enemies. He struck them hard on every front, and his preemptive attack left no viable opposition in place. We must do the same. We have to define the battlefield and annihilate the Castellanos. They must not have the ability to strike back."

When no one immediately responded, Mary Jo said, "I agree with the concept of total war and a preemptive strike, but I want to make one thing clear. Don Giuseppe Castellano is going to die. Any compromise on this is a deal killer for me. If we can't agree on this, then I best pack my bags and leave before we go any further."

Giovanni said, "I understand your feelings. Rest assured, we too want the bastard dead. Strategically, he cannot remain alive after we strike. Tactically, how we kill the little punk is something we'll have to figure out. You have my word on this."

"Thank you, Giovanni. I needed to hear that," Mary Jo said with relief in her voice.

Giovanni stood, walked over to the wall of maps, and used a pool cue as a pointer. He stopped at a map of Corsica, Sardinia, and the adjacent coast of France and Italy. He waved the cue from Gibraltar to the toe of Italy and said, "This is our battlefield. We must identify the most strategic targets in this area and plan to take them out. First, let's concentrate on the head of the snake, Don Giuseppe."

Giovanni pointed to the map of Sardinia and placed the pointer on the island of La Maddalena, just off the northeastern coast of Sardinia. "La Maddalena is the headquarters for the Castellanos's shipping operation. It's the nerve center of the whole enterprise. We know very little about its layout or personnel." He moved the pointer to a dot about 12 miles inland and southeast and said, "This is the village of Luogosanto, where the family home of the Castellanos is located. We don't know the habits of Giuseppe on a day-to-day basis, but he will probably be at one of these two locations."

Mary Jo studied the map for a moment and then said, "I never realized that Corsica and Sardinia were so close to each other. It looks like 10 miles or so between them?"

"Yes, but there are two distinct cultures. There's a ferry that regularly runs between Bonifacio on Corsica to Santa Teresa on Sardinia. It takes less than an hour to make the trip."

"I think it's time for some basic recon work," Mary Jo said.

ELEVEN

MARY JO WALKED TO THE MAP display, thought for a moment, and said, "Do you have any assets in place near either of these sites?"

Giovanni said, "Jeppe has a listening station on La Maddalena that keeps track of the Castellanos's fleet. The men who oversee it are pretty passive though, only reporting what they hear on the radio and in the bars."

Mary Jo said, "I take it that they picked nothing up before the attack on your ships?"

"So it seems, which is kind of strange."

"Is it possible that they have been compromised?"

"There's always that possibility. Let's see what Jeppe thinks."

Giovanni dialed a number into his cell and said, "Jeppe, this is Giovanni. Please give me a call."

In less than a minute, the phone buzzed, and Giovanni put it on speaker. "Jeppe, did you find it strange that our listening station on La Maddalena didn't pick up any suspicious traffic before the attacks on our ships?"

"Yes, I did, and I reviewed the tapes leading up to the attacks. There was nothing indicating any planning or orders to carry out these acts. I carefully studied the transmissions immediately following the attacks, as well, and, again, nothing."

"Do you completely trust our men there?"

"Giovanni, I completely trust no one whose name is not Capriati, but I've found no reason to suspect that my men on La Maddalena have been turned."

"Then we have to assume the Castellanos have another method of communication running parallel to their commercial net. They probably use cell phones that we can't track. Jeppe, do we have any other assets in Sardinia?"

"There is a tavern owner in Luogosanto who has been on our payroll for over 20 years. He has family here, and I have used him to keep an eye on the comings and goings at Castle Castellano. Why do you ask?"

"Mary Jo and I are considering a reconnaissance of the island and the village. We might want to talk to this tavern owner."

"I will let him know to expect you. When do you plan to go?"

"Considering Don Ernesto's time frame, we ought to do it today. Let Mary Jo and me work on it, and I'll let you know."

Jeppe said, "I think it is a good idea, and all I have to do is call his cell. Let me know."

Jean looked at Giovanni and asked, "Whom do you plan to send to Sardinia?"

"I thought Mary Jo and I would go."

"No way...we cannot risk your capture. I know that Mary Jo will insist on going, but I think I should be the one to go with her."

Paulo spoke up. "I agree with Jean. You are too valuable to the family, and we certainly don't need a major general in the French Army arrested on Sardinia. Jean is the logical choice."

Giovanni looked at Mary Jo and asked, "What do you think?"

"I'm fine going alone. I agree that we can't risk you or Paulo getting pulled into this officially, and Jean doesn't have the operational skills needed for undercover work. I used to do this for a living. I'd prefer going in alone. No offense, Jean."

Jean smiled and replied, "None taken, and you're probably right. I'd just get in your way."

Giovanni looked around the table, turned to Stefano, and asked, "How about you, Stefano? What do you think?"

"I had to clean up after Mary Jo's counterattack Monday night, and, judging by the rout of two of the attackers and the capture of the other, I'd say she can handle it. I can assign someone to go with her, but, frankly, I'd rather see her go in alone as an American tourist."

"Okay, then it's settled. Mary Jo goes in alone," Giovanni replied. "Mary Jo, how do you want to handle this?"

"Do you have a motorcycle available?"

"Yes, we have several, including a high-end Ducati."

"Maybe something that would cause a little less interest than a Ducati. Got any Harleys?"

"How about it, Stefano?"

"Yes, we have an older model Super Glide that's in perfect condition."

"That's my bike then. I ride one at home," Mary Jo replied. "Now, let's decide where I'm going."

Giovanni said, "I don't see any need to look at anything on La Maddalena. Jeppe's guys have that covered. If we're going to take out Giuseppe, it will have to be in Luogosanto. We need some hard intel on the layout and his habits. Between Jeppe's tavern keeper and your work on the ground, we should at least be able to find out what we don't know."

Mary Jo said, "How long will it take me to get to Luogosanto?"

"It's 75 miles to the ferry at Bonifacio. That should take an hour and a half...then, add 45 minutes for the ferry, which runs every 30 minutes, and another 30 minutes to get from Santa Teresa to Luogosanto. So, close to three hours, if you don't have a hitch."

Mary Jo looked at her watch and said, "It's nearly noon. I've got a couple of phone calls to make, and there are some things I need from town. If I can be ready to leave by 2:00, I can get there by dark."

Giovanni said, "I'll let Jeppe know to alert the tavern owner to find you an inn as close as he can to Luogosanto. If you give me a list of what you want, Stefano can send someone in to get it."

Mary Jo handed Stefano the list she'd already made and said to Giovanni, "I'd like to use a phone to make a couple of calls to the States."

"No problem. We have international phone service, so you can direct dial. Let me show you the system and you can get started. I'll have lunch sent up to you." Giovanni led Mary Jo down the hall to a private office and said, "This is my office. Make yourself comfortable and let me know if you need anything."

"Thanks, Giovanni. I'll come back to the conference room when I'm done."

Giovanni closed the door, and Mary Jo dialed Allie Burke's cell phone. Allie picked up and said, "Oh my goodness, Mary Jo. I know about Maurice. Are you alright?"

"I'm okay, but I intend to help Maurice's family find who did this, so I have no idea how long I'll be here. Can you tend to the shop till I get back?"

"Of course, take as much time as you need. I can outsource anything that I need to and handle most of the clients myself. You just do what you have to do. Is there anything I can do to help?"

"Yeah, I'd appreciate it if you'll let Alan Brooks and Will Ransom know what's happened and tell them I'll call as soon as I can."

"Is there anyone else you want me to call?"

"I'm going to call Emile as soon as we hang up, but you can give Frank Carcello and Doug Schuler a heads-up and tell them that we'll talk when I get back. Other than that, just call me if you need me."

"I will, and please know that Laurie and I are here for you."

"Thanks. Be sure to tell Laurie I asked about her. She loved Maurice. I'll call and keep y'all up to date."

"Goodbye, boss. Be careful."

Once Allie was off the line, Mary Jo dialed the Dalhousie office, and a woman answered, "Good morning. Emile Dalhousie's office. How may I help you?"

"Good morning, Melissa. I'm glad you still come in early. This is Mary Jo. Do you think Emile can come to the phone?"

"Oh, Mary Jo, we just heard about Maurice. I'm sure Emile will speak with you. Let me connect you to the residence."

In a moment, Emile Dalhousie picked up and said, "Mary Jo, my dear, our office in Paris called late last night with the news. I took the liberty of calling your office and letting Allie know what had happened. Constance and I are so distraught over this and so very sad for you."

"Thanks, Emile. We had just decided to get married, and I planned to call y'all today with that news."

"Oh, Mary Jo, how awful. What can Constance and I do?"

"There's nothing I need at present. I'd like for you to call Collette and Augustin and let them know. We don't have a decision about the funeral yet, but I'm sure it will be a family affair here in Corsica. I'll see that someone calls with the details. I'll be out of reach for a day or so, but you can get a message to me by calling this number and asking for Giovanni Capriati. Giovanni is Maurice's brother."

"We'll certainly contact Collette. Is there anything else? You know all you have to do is ask."

"I do, Emile, and, when all of this is over, I'm sure I'll need to talk with both you and Constance. But, in the meantime, we have to punish the people who did this."

"Mary Jo, I know you well enough to know that you'll not rest until Maurice's murder is solved and the murderers are punished. I also know his family. The Capriatis have been our clients for hundreds of years. Just know that all the resources of the firm are available and assure Don Ernesto and Jeppe that we're here if needed."

"I will, and I won't hesitate to call if we need anything. I'm sure you'll be kept in the loop, so we'll talk when this is resolved."

"Mary Jo, be careful. Trust the Don and Jeppe. They are very capable folks."

"Thanks, Emile. We'll talk later."

Mary Jo finished the salad that the maid had brought for lunch and then walked back to the conference room. When Mary Jo entered, Giovanni was studying a display of aerial photos taped to the wall. He said, "Did you get all of your calls made?"

"Yes, thanks. Where are we on my recon?"

"Jeppe alerted his man, Angelo Abruzzese, the tavern owner in Luogosanto. Abruzzese's bar is on the main square in the village; it's called La Taverna Vite. Abruzzese also rents a room in the Taverna, and it's reserved for you tonight."

"Good. How about my shopping?"

"Stefano's wife just returned. What you asked for is on the bed in your room. One other thing, Mary Jo — the Don has made arrangements for Maurice's funeral. It will be held here in our chapel, and Maurice will be buried in our family plot. The Mass will be at 10:00 Thursday morning."

"I assume you'll let the Dalhousies know about the Mass?"

"Don Ernesto has already talked to the Bordeaux office. Andre Dalhousie will be here representing the firm."

"Andre? I've never heard either Emile or Maurice mention him."

"Andre is the Chief Executive Officer of the firm. He's Emile's uncle."

"Wow, the main guy, huh?"

"I suppose he is. He's also one of my father's closest friends."

Mary Jo checked her watch and said, "It's already after 1:00. I need to pack my gear and get on the road, if I want to get to Luogosanto before dark. Is there anything else we need to go over?"

"Before you leave, I want you to take a look at these aerial photos of Castle Castellano. We had a man fly over the area this morning. You can at least get the lay of the land. While you're studying them, I'll have Stefano get the Harley and a riding jacket ready, as well as prepare a package of local maps for you. You'll also need some euros."

"Thanks, Giovanni. I have several thousand euros, so I'm covered. I'll take a quick look at the photos and get dressed and packed. I'll be ready by 2:00."

"Okay, we'll meet you at the front entrance when you're done."

Mary Jo studied the photos of Luogosanto and located Castle Castellano. The main building, indeed, was a castle, complete with a moat. The building itself was a stone castle keep, three stories tall, with a large, flat roof. Mary Jo could see two entrance gates to the grounds, each with a guardhouse. She estimated the property to be close to a hundred acres, and the castle was in the center. She committed the layout to memory and left the conference room.

When Mary Jo got to her room, there was a brown-paper bundle lying next to her duffel bag. She ripped it open and found four pairs of blue jeans, some underwear, socks, and four plain, gray sweatshirts. When she looked at the clothing, she thought, "I'm glad Collette isn't here to see this. My reversion to my regular wardrobe and the loss of everything I brought from Paris would break her heart."

Mary Jo stripped out of the jumpsuit and put on a pair of the jeans, a sweatshirt, and a pair of new cotton socks. She slipped her passport into her back pocket, pulled her boots back on, slung the duffel over her shoulder, and walked down to the front entrance.

Giovanni and Stefano were standing beside a gleaming Harley Super Glide when Mary Jo approached. Stefano took her duffel, lifted it onto the rack behind the seat, and secured it with bungee cords. He handed Mary Jo an envelope filled with maps and a list of phone numbers and then said, "You shouldn't have a problem if you follow the route that I've laid out. Call me if you do."

"I will. Thanks, Stefano."

Giovanni reached out, took Mary Jo's hand, and said, "Please don't take any unnecessary chances. Just get in, do the recon, and head back here as quickly as you can."

"Unless I just happen to bump into Giuseppe Castellano on the street."

"I shudder to think what would happen if you did."

"Well, this whole thing would be cut short, along with his throat."

"Just be extremely careful."

Mary Jo smiled, started the bike, and drove away from the villa. Following Stefano's directions, she turned east on route 196. The warm sun made the clear, December day pleasant for a ride. The trees had shed their leaves, and she could see several hundred yards into the forest along the winding road. She noticed that she was gaining altitude as she rode away from the coast in the general direction of the mountainous spine of the island.

The higher Mary Jo climbed, the more twisted the road became, and, just after turning south and beginning a gradual descent, she could see the blue sea to her right. She realized that she was glad for the freedom of the ride, which took the haunting memory of Maurice's death away, at least for the moment.

Mary Jo rode to the seaside village of Propriano, and, for a few miles, the road ran along the bay. It turned east again, following the coastal plain, until it began to climb back into the foothills. She passed through the village of Giuncheto and continued to move upward.

Mary Jo pulled to the side of the two-lane road and took the packet of maps from her jacket pocket. She sat on the bike, checking her location, when a white van came up behind her. She had seen the same van near Propriano, and her primal brain had sent a danger signal. She watched the van disappear around the next curve. Then, she folded the map and tucked it back into her jacket.

Mary Jo checked her watch and saw that it was 3:15. She was close to halfway to Bonifacio and the ferry. She pulled the Harley back on the road and continued south. In a mile or so, she passed the intersection of 196 and 859, and she saw a black sedan turn off 859 and drop in behind her. For several miles, the car maintained its position a half-mile back, matching her speed. Again, Mary Jo's primal brain sent a danger signal. Her senses reacted to the message, and she shifted into operational mode. She rounded a curve and spotted the white van pulled to the side of the road, and two men were bending over looking at one of the back tires.

As Mary Jo approached, one of the men stepped into her lane and began waving his arms. She glanced into the rearview mirror and saw the black sedan speed up and start to gain on her. She slowed down as if to pull to the side to offer help, and the man started pointing to the shoulder of the road just behind the van. Mary Jo allowed the bike to drift to the side until she was almost directly behind the van. She checked the black sedan, and then she hit the throttle and zoomed past the van in a shower of dirt and gravel. She heard the big sedan begin to accelerate as she disappeared around the next curve. She knew there was no way she could outrun the car, so she took a narrow trail that led up the side of the mountain. She rode the Harley like a dirt bike until she had gained the strategic high ground. Then, she stopped and cut off the engine.

Mary Jo saw the black sedan speed by, and soon it was out of sight and hearing range. In a moment, the white van came by in pursuit of the sedan. Mary Jo waited until the woods returned to its normal rhythm, and she watched as several vehicles came and went. There was no sign of the car or the van. After she was sure that the immediate danger had passed, Mary Jo pulled the cell phone from her pocket and dialed Giovanni's number.

Giovanni answered immediately. "Mary Jo, are you in Bonifacio?"

"No, I'm hiding in the woods near a place called Giunchete. We've got a problem. Some guys tried to take me about 20 minutes ago. I managed to get away, but they were expecting me. We've got a mole, and I don't want to alert whoever it is."

"I agree. Jeppe and I will get to work on it right away. I don't want you to ride back here. Go into Giunchete and find a landing zone. I'm sending our helicopter to bring you out."

"What about the Harley?"

"Just leave it at the landing zone. We'll send someone to pick it up. Call as soon as you decide on the pickup point. You ought to know how to find a landing zone since you own a Bell Ranger."

"Yes, I do. I'll call as soon as I'm ready. Start the helicopter and I'll direct them in. Have them hover south of Giunchete until I call them."

"Consider it done."

TWELVE

MARY JO EASED THE BIKE DOWN the hillside until she reached the highway. She listened carefully and then headed back toward Giuncheto. She turned off Route 196 and took a narrow two-lane road into the heart of the little village. She noticed a sign indicating a soccer field near the northern edge of town. She found it, and it was deserted this time of the day, so she called the number of the helicopter. They answered right away.

Mary Jo gave them the GPS for her location, and soon she heard the turning of the rotors. The helicopter came into view and dropped into the soccer field, where it sat with its rotors still rotating. Mary Jo pulled her duffel off the bike, stuffed the keys into her pocket, and ran toward the waiting ship. One of Stefano's men climbed out and helped her with her duffel. He said, "Do you have the motorcycle keys?"

Mary Jo nodded and handed them to him, and he trotted toward the bike as she climbed into the ship. She strapped in, and the pilot lifted off and headed northwest back toward Ajaccio. They sat down in front of the villa, where Mary Jo saw a group of men waiting just outside the rotor wash. She climbed out, carrying her bag, and Paulo came running toward the helicopter. He ducked under the slowly rotating blades and said something to the pilot.

Mary Jo walked up to Don Ernesto, Giovanni, Jeppe, and Jean. They all had grim, determined looks on their faces.

Mary Jo asked, "What's going on?"

"Paulo is telling the pilot to fly to Luogosanto to evacuate Angelo Abruzzese and his family. We managed to get a message to him to take everyone to a remote landing zone in the hills above the village. I just hope we acted in time," Giovanni responded.

"I agree. That's the prudent thing to do. If there's a mole, then Angelo's life is in danger."

Don Ernesto shook his head. "Oh, we *had* a mole, but he has been flushed out of his hole. As soon as you told us about your near-ambush, we knew who it had to be. Stefano was just too eager to have you go to Sardinia alone and to follow his suggested route. Stefano broke and spilled his guts before we could even get him to the dungeon."

"How about the guys in La Maddalena?"

"Jeppe alerted them to keep a low profile until all of this is over. They are natives of La Maddalena, so they can blend into the background."

The helicopter lifted off, and Paulo trotted back and joined the group as Don Ernesto led everyone to the conference room. On the way in, Mary Jo walked next to Giovanni and asked, "What will become of Stefano?"

"What do you think should be done?"

"Leave it to me. The son of a bitch helped kill Maurice. I have no compunction about cutting his fucking throat."

"His body has been turned over to his wife's family. He died quickly."

"Okay, then," Mary Jo said with a placated look on her face. "Now we need to assess the damage he did."

"I suspect that's exactly what we're about to do. That, and figure out our next move."

When everyone had gathered around the conference table, Jeppe said, "The death of Charles Carbanno in Monday night's attack pushed Stefano to the top of our security. This was his first time to be fully engaged in our planning, and, regrettably, we didn't think to vet him further. I'll have a word with Antonio to see that a complete background check is run on the whole security office. In the meantime, Antonio will be in charge of security, as well as continuing his job running the shipping operation. He'll be joining us shortly. The loss of Abruzzese's eyes and ears leaves us without anyone we trust in Luogosanto and makes any on-site recon much more difficult. When Angelo gets here, we can see what he thinks about any further effort in that direction. I'd like to stay with this until we have a general plan and then adjourn until tomorrow morning. We all need a hearty meal and a good night's sleep."

Mary Jo glanced at her watch and saw that it was nearly 5:00. Antonio Vincentia knocked on the doorframe, and Jeppe motioned for him to join the group. Jeppe looked at Vincentia and asked, "Have you heard from the helicopter?"

"Yes. They have picked up Angelo and his family and should be landing about now. I have one of my men bringing Angelo here and getting his family settled in the guest wing."

There was a ding as the elevator opened, and a man wearing chef's whites came to the door. Jeppe walked over, hugged the man, turned to the table, and said, "Don Ernesto, this is our faithful friend Angelo Abruzzese. Angelo has kept a watch on the Castellanos for the past 20 or so years. He and his family will be relocated to his village here on Corsica, and he will have a new tavern and inn to run. For now, he is here to help us plan our next move."

Jeppe looked at his friend and said, "Angelo, we have decided to hit the Castellanos multiple blows during the Christmas weekend. Christmas Eve is this coming Sunday, and we feel they will be most vulnerable then. What do you think?"

Angelo said, "I can only speak for Luogosanto. I have no information about their business interests. It is traditional for the Don and his whole family to attend Mass at the village church and then to return to the castle to celebrate Christmas with the children. Don Giuseppe is not married and, of course, has no children, but his brothers and sisters do. I can't imagine that he'll want to disappoint them. So, I believe he will comply with the family tradition."

"Have you seen an increase in security at the castle since the attack on our ships?" Giovanni asked this with concern in his voice.

"Yes, and in the whole village, as well. It has escalated even more since the death of Maurice. The Don has moved men in from the provinces, and the village is an armed camp. I'm grateful to have been extracted before they came for me."

Giovanni said, "Antonio and his men are working on a plan to hit their business interests all around the Med. We are concentrating on taking Giuseppe out, and we want the whole thing to be coordinated."

Angelo said, "The only time he will be exposed is to and from the church, but he will be heavily guarded the entire time."

Jeppe thought for moment and then said, "It is in our long-term interest to be able to work with the Castellanos after Giuseppe is gone. We don't want a bloodbath where many family members are killed. Whatever we do must minimize the collateral damage."

"I agree with Jeppe," Don Ernesto added. "Giuseppe must die, but we don't want to turn a commercial rivalry into a long-term family war. That would be bad for both families and would bring the French and Italian authorities down on both of us. We need to strike them hard to get their attention and then offer a generous solution to the Don who replaces Giuseppe."

Mary Jo asked, "Do we know who that will be?"

The Don said, "Giuseppe's brother, Dano, is the logical candidate, but you never know what may happen to fill a power vacuum. Jeppe, do you think we can deal with Dano to make peace after this is over?"

"Only if we damage them badly. We would want the new Don, whoever he is, to be too busy trying to salvage his business to have the resources for an all-out war."

Giovanni stood and walked to the maps. "I agree. First the stick and then the carrot. The death of Giuseppe doesn't have to be dramatic, just final, and I don't think we should hit them during the Christmas Eve services."

"Whatever we decide, we must take Giuseppe out while we are hitting their business interests. We can't risk him going to ground and waging a retaliatory campaign against us," Antonio added.

Mary Jo asked, "Just how secure are the grounds surrounding the castle?"

Antonio said, "The entire estate is surrounded by a ten-foot stone wall with razor wire on top. The grounds themselves have heat and motion sensors positioned throughout, and there is a laser system covering the whole property. All of this is backed up by a pack of Doberman Pinschers that are turned loose at night. There are high-powered lights mounted on towers that allow for the illumination of every foot of the grounds."

Giovanni made a face and said, "I think we can rule out any attack on the castle. They have covered every possible route of attack, and it would take a battalion of trained troops and heavy weapons to take it."

Mary Jo walked to the aerial photos and looked at them for a full minute. Then, she said, "I agree with Giovanni. The castle is too well guarded to be taken by any ground action, but it may be exposed to an airborne operation. I don't see any defensive positions on the roof or any radar antennas. They may have left the door open for us."

Jean laughed and said, "Great, now all we need is a company of paratroopers and some transport planes."

Mary Jo grinned at him and replied, "We don't need paratroopers or planes. I can get on the roof without any trouble. Give me a few hours in the morning to put a plan together, and I'll be ready to present it tomorrow afternoon. In the meantime, we can concentrate on their business operations."

Everyone looked at Don Ernesto, and he said, "I suggest that we call it a day. We'll have dinner in the main dining room at 7:00. That gives everyone an hour to get ready. Angelo, you and your family are welcome to join the family for dinner. We owe all of you a great debt for your years of loyalty."

Abruzzese smiled and said, "Thank you, Don Ernesto, but I believe we will eat in the kitchen with the staff. It's been a long day, and my daughter and her children need to get to bed."

Everyone filed out of the conference room, leaving Mary Jo and Giovanni behind. They stood looking at the aerial photos, and Giovanni said, "I don't think I'm going to like your plan."

"Don't jump to any conclusions until you've heard it. Now, let's go get ready for dinner."

Mary Jo stowed her duffel bag, slipped on fresh jeans, left her room just before 7:00, and went directly to the small dining room. To her surprise, it was dark and empty. She realized that everyone must be in the large formal dining room down a short hallway. She entered the room and found at least 20 people sitting around a long trestle table. The table was set with gleaming-white linen, china, crystal, and heavy sterling silver. Mary Jo recognized Giovanni's family — Nicole and the boys.

Giovanni stood when he saw Mary Jo and took her arm. He introduced her to everyone. All of Don Ernesto's daughters and their families were there, along with Paulo's family, just in from Marseilles. After the introductions were done, Giovanni led Mary Jo to an empty seat next to Nicole. As Giovanni held her chair, the boys stood and greeted Mary Jo politely. When everyone was in their place, Don Ernesto tapped on his wine glass. "It is with great sadness that we're gathered here tonight. On Thursday, we must bury our son, brother, and uncle, Maurice Capriati. Our loss is shared by Maurice's fiancée, Mary Jo Thibodaux. I ask that everyone keep Mary Jo in your prayers. Now, if Jeppe will say grace, we'll begin our meal."

Jeppe said a short grace in Corsu, and the servants began serving the meal. Mary Jo made small talk with Nicole and Ernesto, while looking around the table. She recognized the daughter who had given her the gown the night before, and she decided to thank her before the evening ended. The meal was five courses, with wine served with each one. Mary Jo noticed that even the older children were allowed to have a small glass. The talk was subdued, obviously, out of respect for Maurice, but the children laughed and kept it from becoming too somber.

Dessert was served, along with rich, dark coffee, and, just before 9:30, Don Ernesto said, "These last two days have been hard on us all. I suggest that we go to our rooms and try to get a decent night's sleep. After breakfast tomorrow morning, the men will convene at 7:00 in my conference room. Mary Jo will join us."

Mary Jo could see the look of shock on some of the women's faces. It was unheard of for women to be included in the affairs of the family, and Don Ernesto offered no explanation. As she rose from the table, Mary Jo asked Giovanni the name of the girl who had lent her the gown. Giovanni answered, "That's Anna Marie, my oldest sister. The man on her right is, Tomas, her husband, and those are their five girls."

Mary Jo made her way across the room and touched Anna Marie's arm. "Anna Marie, I'm Mary Jo. I just wanted to thank you for the lingerie. I lost everything I brought with me in the attack."

Anna Marie took Mary Jo's hand and said, "Oh, Mary Jo, I can't imagine how you feel. Maurice was one of God's good people: kind, generous, and caring. I'm so sorry for your loss." She pulled Mary Jo to her and held her tight. "You are now a member of our family. If there is anything that we can do for you, you have only to ask."

When Anna Marie released her, Mary Jo thought, "I've never seen such an open, loving family. No wonder Maurice adored coming home."

***

Mary Jo was the first one down for breakfast the next morning. She ate freshly made buns and an assortment of fresh fruits. She was pouring a cup of coffee when Giovanni came through the door. He poured himself a cup and sat next to Mary Jo.

Giovanni asked, "Did you sleep at all?"

"Actually, I was able to sleep through the night; how about you?"

"Not so well…too many loose ends running through my mind."

"Heavy is the head that wears the crown."

"Don Ernesto wears the crown, and I suspect he slept like a baby, but it's the Capo who bears the responsibility to handle situations such as this."

"What part of this is weighing the heaviest on you?"

"Taking care of Giuseppe worries me the most. We can handle hitting the Castellanos's business interests, but I'm not so sure we can get to Giuseppe."

"Then let me ease your mind. I'll take Giuseppe out, and, if I'm successful, no one will be able to figure out how I did it."

"I take it that you have a plan?"

"I've got the basic strategy in place. I just need to fine-tune it."

"I look forward to hearing it."

"All I'll be able to share is that Don Giuseppe Castellano will not live to see Christmas morning. It will be impossible to share the details because there will be too many sensitive components. I also want to lessen the likelihood of any more leaks."

"Don Ernesto will never agree to this."

"He will if you agree and support me. Besides, I'm not asking for permission."

"I'll have to know exactly what you plan to do before I commit to supporting your idea."

"Fair enough, but you have to swear that you will tell no one the details, only that it will be taken care of."

"Okay, you have my word. Give me as much as you can before the meeting starts."

Mary Jo told Giovanni the general strategy of her plan and assured him that she'd keep him in the loop as she modified the details. When she finished, he shook his head and said, "Mary Jo, I know your background, and I believe you have the tradecraft to pull this off. And I agree that if you're successful, it'll drive the Castellanos crazy trying to figure it out. That's the good news; the bad news is that it's incredibly risky, and, if anything goes wrong, we'll be powerless to help you."

"I understand that I'll be on my own, but that's the way I like to operate. If I'm working alone, I don't have to worry about someone else's safety. You have to admit that this would send a message that there is no place to hide if you cross the Capriatis."

"Yes, and that'll be the best way for me to sell the plan to my father and Jeppe."

"So, I can count on your support?"

"Yes, let's go to the conference room and start the process."

THIRTEEN

MARY JO AND GIOVANNI were the first in the conference room, and, as they sat discussing her plan, the others drifted in from breakfast. When the Don came in and took his seat at the head of the table, he began by thanking everyone for beginning so early, and then he turned the meeting over to Giovanni.

Giovanni looked around the table and said, "First, I'd like to set the order of business this morning. We have two projects to deal with: the retaliatory attacks on the commercial interests of the Castellanos and the elimination of Don Giuseppe Castellano. Let's begin with the Don's elimination. I'm going to ask that everyone here trust me on what I'm about to suggest. I'm a major general of intelligence in the French Army. I have in-depth information on Mary Jo Thibodaux that I can't share with everyone, but — I believe you will all agree — I'm not a neophyte in this area."

Giovanni continued: "So what I'm about to tell you is something I'm professionally comfortable with. I'm also speaking as Capo of the family, and I have considered this from all aspects of our interests. Again, I am comfortable." He looked around the table and could see the growing curiosity in each face. He paused for a moment and then said, "Mary Jo has devised a plan to take out Don Giuseppe. This plan will not require our further involvement. We will be free to focus on our attacks against the Castellanos's commercial interests, and Mary Jo assures me that Giuseppe will not live to see Christmas morning."

Giovanni added, "This plan will mean that Mary Jo will be leaving us this morning, and, except for Maurice's service tomorrow, we won't see her until Christmas Day. She and I will be in constant contact, and, if something happens to change her timetable or causes her to abort her plan, we'll have time to react. I'm asking that everyone trust my judgment and Mary Jo's skills. Let's allow her to execute her plan. One of the most appealing aspects of this plan is, if she is successful, it will send a message to all of our enemies that they cannot escape the long arm of Capriati vengeance. This will give pause to any who might want to cross us in the future."

Giovanni paused again, looked around the table, and then said, "I'd like everyone to speak up now or allow us to start the necessary preparations."

Paulo was the first to respond. "I have to look at something open-ended like this as if I'm examining a crime scene. What happens if Mary Jo fails in her attempt to kill Giuseppe? What will be the unintended consequences?"

Giovanni said, "Let's just say that there will be no connection to the family. Others will be blamed, and, if she is unsuccessful, she will probably be dead."

Jeppe immediately spoke up. "It is not like we're farming out Giuseppe's assassination to an outside contractor. Mary Jo is family now, and she will be acting on our behalf. I, too, have done my homework on Mary Jo, and I believe she knows what she's doing. I particularly like the possibility of achieving this task while leaving everyone wondering how we did it. I'm in favor of allowing Giovanni and Mary Jo to take care of Giuseppe."

Giovanni searched the table for other comments, and, when no one said anything, he turned to Don Ernesto. "How about you, Papa? What do you think?"

"I'm still old-fashioned when it comes to the family honor. I'd like to stick my blade between Giuseppe Castellano's ribs and watch him die. It is difficult for me to allow a female member of the family to take an equal role in such things. I also know that times and traditions are changing. If people, like Carlo Baggetti, have trusted Mary Jo, then I'm prone to agree to this plan."

"Don Ernesto, I will have Carlo call you to reassure you further, if you'd be more comfortable. He and I have worked on many similar missions successfully," Mary Jo said.

"That won't be necessary, my child. You are family, and I know you want to punish Maurice's killers as much as any of us. If you are willing to take on this defense of our family's honor, I'll support you."

Giovanni looked around the table and then said, "Okay. That makes it official. Mary Jo and I will be responsible for Giuseppe, and the rest of our energies can be focused on the Castellanos's businesses. There is one more thing I'd like to report. The two men injured in the ambush Monday night recovered from their wounds enough to be released from the hospital here and transferred to Sardinia. Unfortunately, the ambulance sent to take them back ran off a mountain road. There were no survivors."

Jean smiled. "I knew they should have gone by sea. Driving is just too dangerous."

Don Ernesto laughed and added, "Yes, tragic accidents happen. Now, I suggest that we bid Mary Jo goodbye until tomorrow morning and leave her to her task."

Mary Jo walked around the table and told everyone goodbye. When she reached the Don, she bent and hugged him and kissed him on both cheeks. "Thank you, Don Ernesto. You won't regret this decision. When we meet on Christmas morning, Maurice's death will have been avenged."

The Don returned her hug and said, "Si, andare con Dio, mio figlia."

Giovanni asked, "When do you plan on leaving?"

Mary Jo said, "As soon as possible. I'll return tomorrow for Maurice's funeral and then leave immediately after it's over."

Giovanni said, "I'll have Antonio take you to the airport when you're ready, and he'll be waiting at the airport when you return in the morning."

"Giovanni, I'll be forever grateful for your support. You won't be sorry."

"As Papa said, 'Andare con Dio.'"

Mary Jo left the conference room and took the elevator down to her room. She placed her few belongings in her flight bag, changed into a flight suit, and took her bags to the front door. Antonio was waiting outside beside one of the black SUVs. He took her gear and held the passenger door for her. As they drove through the heavily guarded gate, he said, "I've called ahead; they will have your plane fueled and ready to go when we get there, and I told them that you would file a flight plan before you leave. Giovanni asked me to give you this before we parted." Antonio handed her a small gun case, and, when Mary Jo opened it, she saw a well-cared-for Colt .45 automatic and four boxes of cartridges.

"Send him my thanks, and I'll see you in the morning," Mary Jo said.

Antonio dropped Mary Jo off at the Capriati's flight operations, and she filed a flight plan for Rome's Urbe airport. When she'd finished submitting the plan, she moved to a private office and dialed Carlo Baggetti's private number.

Carlo picked up and said, "Let me guess…you've dumped the Corsican and are coming to Roma to live happily ever after with your Carlo?"

Mary Jo realized that he had no way of knowing what had happened and said gently, "No, Carlo. Something terrible has happened. Maurice was killed in an ambush Monday night as we were driving to his family's villa in Ajaccio."

"Oh, Mary, Mother of God! Mary Jo, I had no idea! I'm so sorry. Were you injured?"

"No, Maurice was in the first car talking with the family's head of security when they were hit with an RPG. It was a classic ambush: knock out the first vehicle and block the road."

"Was there any attempt to complete the ambush?"

"Yes, both cars were shot to pieces, but I was able to get the people in our car into a defensive position, and I broke up the attempt to finish us off."

"What can I do to help?"

"I'm about to leave Ajaccio to fly into Urbe. Could you meet me? I need your help."

"Of course. I'll be there when you land. Plan on staying at my home. I have several extra bedrooms. What else can I do?"

"Contact Roberto and see if he'll meet with us this afternoon. I'll need to fly back to Ajaccio tomorrow morning for Maurice's funeral. Then, I'll fly back to Rome, but I'd like to meet today, if possible."

"I'll call Roberto right away. If he can come this afternoon, then we'll meet at my home. It's completely secure. So, you have a plan. Am I right?"

"Absolutely, and I'm going to need help from both you and Roberto."

"You know you can count on me, and I also know that Roberto will do everything in his power to help you. I'll be waiting when you land. What's your tail number?"

"I'm flying a Cessna CJ4, tail number N98476. It's 9:15, and I'm about to leave. I should be on the ground no later than 10:15."

"I'll head to Urbe right now and talk to Roberto while I'm driving. I'll meet you at customs."

"Thanks, Carlo."

"No problem. Mary Jo, I'm so sorry about Maurice. I believe he truly loved you."

"He did, and I loved him, as well. I intend to kill the son of a bitch who ordered his death."

Mary Jo stowed her gear in the outer baggage compartment and completed her preflight inspection. She moved into the takeoff pattern behind a twin-engine Piper and took off out over the ocean. She was instructed to level off at 6,500 feet and to fly northeast. She crossed the coast of Italy, just south of Porto Santo Stefano, and turned south to line up on a runway at Urbe.

After touching down at 10:03, Mary Jo followed the ground guide to the private aviation terminal. She pulled her bags, and the attendant took them to the customs area. Mary Jo left the .45 in the plane and slung her flight bag over her shoulder. Carlo met her as she approached the customs line and picked up her bags. They skirted the formal customs line and entered a small office where an immigration officer checked Mary Jo's passport and waved them through.

Once the two were clear of customs, Carlo said, "Roberto was tied up in a meeting this morning, but he'll meet us at my house at 3:00 this afternoon. That'll give us a chance to talk and think through whatever it is that you're planning."

"That's great; I don't have a lot of time. I need to execute my plan on Sunday night."

"Mary Jo, you do realize that Sunday is Christmas Eve, don't you?"

"Yeah. I'm gonna come down a scumbag's chimney with my straight razor."

"Well, Merry Christmas. I can't wait to hear the rest."

The friends put the bags into the trunk of Carlo's Jag, pulled out of the airport, and turned toward Rome.

"I took the liberty of calling ahead to Cacio e Pepe and reserved a private room for lunch. Is that okay?"

Mary Jo laughed. "I've been gone from Rome too long. I forget that the next meal takes precedence over anything else."

"Hey, we gotta eat. It's important to keep our strength up as we approach a new operation."

"Then, eat we shall."

Carlo gave his keys to the valet at Cacio e Pepe, and Cosimo met them with a smile. He took them to a private dining room and closed the curtain. A waiter immediately came and asked if they would like wine, and Carlo ordered a bottle of Zenata Valpolicella and an antipasto. When the waiter withdrew, Carlo took Mary Jo's hand. "Start at the beginning and tell me exactly what happened."

Before Mary Jo could begin, the waiter returned with the wine. He pulled the cork and handed it to Carlo, who examined it and gave it a sniff. The waiter poured a sip or two of the dark red wine into Carlo's glass, and Carlo swirled it for a moment, sniffed it, and then took a sip. He nodded that the wine was satisfactory, and the waiter poured each of them a generous amount.

Mary Jo tasted her wine and then began to fill Carlo in on everything that had happened from their arrival in Ajaccio through this morning's meeting. Several times, he stopped her and asked for details, forcing her to relive the entire chain of events. When she finished, Carlo said, "Give me a moment to think this through. We'll continue once we've ordered lunch." He pulled the bell tassel, summoned the waiter, and ordered for both of them. Once the waiter had withdrawn, Carlo continued. "Mary Jo, you've got your Shiva on. I observed you as you described what happened, searching for some sign of personal loss. All I saw was anger and determination. I've seen this before, and I know you're completely in operational mode."

"Yes, I'll grieve Maurice's death when the time is right. Now, I need all of my concentration focused on killing the man responsible."

"I would think that Don Ernesto would decide how to do that."

"He and Giovanni did, and they chose me to carry out this defense of family honor."

"Mary Jo, do you have any idea what an honor they've given you?"

"Yes, I do — a great honor and even greater responsibility."

"Did Jeppe agree?"

"He not only agreed, but he also advised the Don to allow me to do it."

"Okay, but I would have thought the Don would have the resources to do this far better than you."

"No, I'm probably the only resource that has the training and experience to pull off what I have in mind. Let's finish lunch and wait until Roberto joins us. That way, I'll only have to tell it once."

Carlo smiled and lifted his wine glass. "Buon appetito."

The friends finished their meal with small talk, and, just after 2:00, Carlo signaled Cosimo that they were ready to leave. Cosimo led them to the front entrance and said, "Thank you, Signor Baggetti. Please come again and bring the lovely Mary Jo with you."

Carlo said, "We'll be back very soon. You and your family have a happy holiday."

The parking valet brought the Jag around, and the two pulled out, heading toward Carlo's neighborhood.

Mary Jo asked, "Do you still live in the house you bought with the interior decorator, Gina?"

"Yes, everything is the same except that she's moved on."

"Do you miss her?"

"Not so much. She was getting a little clingy there at the end."

"That's the best way to fall victim to Carlo's recycling plan. Got anybody in the wings?"

"There are a couple of candidates competing to replace Gina, but nothing has really firmed up. I'm enjoying the casting call."

"One day, you're going to meet someone, and the shoe's going to be on the other foot."

"You can't wait to see me meet my match, can you?"

"Oh, yeah, and it'll be worth the wait."

While the friends bantered, Carlo expertly maneuvered through the traffic until they reached the large open space surrounding the Villa Borghese. Mary Jo had been to Carlo's town house only once during a cocktail party, but she recognized the neighborhood. Carlo noticed her eyeing the street signs.

"We'll soon be coming into my neighborhood, the Gianicolense. I live in a section known as Monteverde Vecchio or the old section of Monteverde."

"Sounds impressive. I'm sure it's beautiful."

"It really is a pretty area. I fell in love with it the first time I saw it."

Finally, Carlo entered a circular street, Via Innocenzo X, a quiet cul-de-sac of town houses set behind stone garden walls. Carlo paused in the street while an iron gate slid open, and then he drove into the courtyard of a handsome, small villa. He pulled the convertible into a parking area, went around, and opened Mary Jo's door. He grabbed her bag and used an electronic key to unlock the villa's front door.

Carlo pushed the leaded glass door open, and they stepped onto a marble-floored entranceway, flanked on one side by a walnut-lined library, and on the other by an elegantly decorated dining room. They faced a wrought-iron circular stairway, leading to an upper floor with doorways on either side.

"Oh, Carlo, it's just wonderful. I had no idea you had such exquisite taste. You might have a career in interior design when you decide to quit the spook stuff."

"I wish I could take credit for it, but the truth is that I had some pretty good professional help. Gina was very talented in the arts. This is what she left me when she split."

"I see," replied Mary Jo. She *thought*, "I'll let that comment go unattended until later. I may have detected just a touch of bitterness."

Carlo motioned Mary Jo onto the stairs and then carried her bag to the second floor. He opened the door to a large bedroom suite, with French doors leading to a balcony that overlooked an interior courtyard. There was a king-sized bed and a seating area that fronted a large granite fireplace. An enormous marble bath area could be seen across the room. Mary Jo said, "How very elegant. I don't know that I've ever seen such a lovely guest suite. I imagine your master suite must be quite something else."

"My rather humble bedroom is on the third floor," Carlo said and led Mary Jo down the stairs where they were met by an extremely tall man with just a wisp of white hair and a long, sad face.

The man bowed to Carlo and said in perfect English, "I'm sorry that I didn't meet you at the door. I was in the backyard and didn't hear you drive in."

"No problem, Malcolm. This is our guest, Mary Jo Thibodaux. She'll be with us for several days."

The tall man stooped and took Mary Jo's hand. "I'm Malcolm Powell, Mr. Baggetti's factotum. Please let me know if there is anything you need."

When Malcolm disappeared into the back of the house, Mary Jo looked at Carlo and asked, "Factotum?"

"Yeah, well, Malcolm came up with that. He didn't like butler or valet — too common for him. Malcolm holds a doctorate in classical literature from Cambridge, and he's a stickler for protocol."

"Baggetti, you live an interesting life. You're the only guy I know with a factotum."

The doorbell chimed, and Carlo said, "That must be Roberto. I guess it's time to get to work."

FOURTEEN

MALCOLM ANSWERED THE DOOR and led Roberto Morelli to the den. Carlo extended his hand and said, "Roberto, welcome. I regret the unfortunate circumstances."

"As do I," replied Roberto.

Roberto held out his arms and took Mary Jo in a bear hug. "I heard late last night about Maurice's murder. I also read the after-action report filed by the police in Ajaccio, including the part about the mysterious woman who fought off the attack and captured one of the attackers. I recognized Shiva's work at once."

"I only allowed him to live so he could be questioned. I wounded two others who, unfortunately, got away."

"Yes, so I read. There was also mention of the captured man's dying while trying to escape and the two who died in the tragic crash of their ambulance."

"It's been a busy couple of days," Mary Jo replied. "I hope you're here as my friend, not in your official capacity."

"I'm a simple citizen visiting with friends."

"Good, because I'm going to share my plans with this simple citizen who may find them interesting but choose to leave them here."

"That will always be an option. So, tell me what you're planning."

"First, let me set the background for you."

Mary Jo spent the next 30 minutes laying out everything that had happened, including her analysis of the defenses surrounding Castle Castellano. When she'd finished, Roberto said, "Did you bring the aerial photos with you?"

"Yes, I have them on my phone."

Carlo spoke up and said, "Email them to me, and I'll put them up on the big screen in my office."

Mary Jo and Roberto followed Carlo to the elevator and gathered around the 72-inch display. He pulled the email up, and the screen was filled with views of the rooftop of the castle. The vertical angle of the photos made it difficult to see details.

Roberto said, "These are not clear enough to focus on the equipment and structures on the roof. We'll need photos from an oblique angle and with much higher resolution. I agree with your assessment of the ground attack. Anything short of a battalion-sized assault would be repulsed with heavy losses. The castle will have to be taken from the air. How many men do you intend to land on the roof?"

"Just one. I'm going to do it alone."

Roberto looked intently at her. "Just how do you plan to get on the roof?"

"I'm thinking a low-level parachute landing."

Carlo shook his head and muttered, "Aw shit, I was afraid of something like this."

Roberto nodded in agreement and said, "You don't have the equipment *or* flight support to do this, and you don't have time to bring it in from the States."

"No, you're right, but, since the security and well-being of Italy will be served, I was hoping for your unofficial support in those areas."

"Maybe you'd better explain how the security and well-being of Italy is to be served," Roberto suggested.

"I thought you'd never ask. It's pretty simple. Both the Capriatis and the Castellanos are involved in smuggling into and out of Italy. That has been a tradition for both families for centuries. The Capriatis have been given the protection of both the French and Italian authorities in return for services rendered from time to time."

Carlo agreed. "Roberto, this is true. Don Ernesto has always been a friend of the U.S. and Italy. Mary Jo, do you remember the fishing boat that extracted you from Thessaloniki?"

"I do."

"Do you remember the captain of the little vessel?"

"Yeah, his name was Paulo."

"Whom do you think he worked for?"

"I'm gonna take a guess and say Don Ernesto."

Carlo said, "The same. The Don supported many of our operations all through the Med. I may be able to get you some of the equipment you'll need. My former colleagues have warm memories of the Capriatis."

Roberto asked, "Mary Jo, I'm well aware of the activities of both the Capriatis and the Castellanos, but how does this affect Italian security?"

"Roberto, Don Ernesto refuses to deal in drugs, but, since Giuseppe became Don, the Castellanos have become the major source of drugs coming into Italy. If we're successful between now and Christmas morning, they'll be blasted out of the drug business for a long time. I'd think this would be a good thing for Italy."

Roberto sat in silence for almost a minute. He finally said, "We've been aware of a new source of drugs over the past year. We're seeing an increase in the more dangerous drugs, particularly the synthetics. I don't believe we've discovered the source. Are you sure about this?"

"From Don Ernesto's lips," Mary Jo answered.

"If this is indeed the case, the elimination of this scourge will certainly be in the interest of my government. Let's assume you're right; what sort of support do you want from me?"

"As you pointed out, we're going to need much better aerial photos. Would it be possible for you to arrange that?"

"If the weather holds, yes, I can arrange such a thing."

"Speaking of the weather, we'll need hour-by-hour updates of the weather conditions over northern Sardinia."

"That, too, I can arrange. What else?"

"I'll need a ride in and out. I plan to make a low-level exit from a hovering helicopter — from about 5,000 feet."

Roberto thought for a moment. "Why are you jumping from 5,000 feet? Doesn't that increase your margin of error?"

"Yes, but I'm up to date on making HALOs[1] from 20,000 feet, and I can consistently hit my landing zone dead on. I'd rather have the height and lessen the chance of someone on the ground wondering why a helicopter is hovering overhead."

"How about the weather?"

"I can handle anything but a storm. Light rain or steady winds are manageable, but I can't do it in a thunderstorm. I've checked the flight info on the weather for Christmas Eve; it's broken clouds and a quarter moon. Perfect, if it holds."

"So far, we've talked about just how to get you on the roof. What happens next?"

"I find Don Giuseppe sleeping in his bed and slit his throat; then, I get picked up from the roof. The obvious way is to have a helicopter pull me out."

"Doesn't that increase the risk of being detected?"

"Yeah, it's the weakest link in my plan. I could rappel down the side of the castle and try to sneak out, but the dogs and the electronics make that very difficult. Then, there's the problem of leaving the rappelling rope behind; I'd like to do this *without* leaving any evidence."

Carlo rubbed his chin and asked, "How much equipment are you planning on bringing in with you?"

"Not a lot. I'll have my small equipment bag with personal gear and the standard Ram Air chute. I'll bring a handgun and my razor — no other weapons."

"How much will all of that weigh?"

"I'd like to use a lightweight chute, with no reserve. The system will probably be about 35 pounds, and my bag will be another 25; so, call it 60 pounds or so."

"I'm guessing you weigh in at 120 or so."

"127 the last time I stood on the scales."

"So, we're talking about a total of fewer than 200 pounds."

"Yeah, why?"

"There may be a better and safer way to get you on and off that roof. I've been consulting with a French firm that has developed a tactical ultralight helicopter for military use."

"No kidding? Have you ever seen it demonstrated?"

"Better yet, I've actually flown one. I have a contract with Joliette Aerospace in Marseilles to help with the field-testing."

"Really? I never knew you were a pilot."

"If it weren't for carrier landings, I'd be flying F-18s instead of doing this spook foolishness. I washed out when the navy realized that I could take off but could never land."

"Tell me about the ultralight. I've never flown one."

"The latest model is called an X-14, which weighs less than 200 pounds. It can carry a fully equipped infantryman and all his gear — up to 300 pounds. They're easy to fly, sturdy, and dependable."

"Could it land and take off from a rooftop?"

"Yes, if the roof has a clear space of 25 feet in diameter."

"How's it powered?"

"There's a small, but very efficient, electric motor — powerful and all but silent. You're barely aware of its sound."

Roberto had been listening, and, finally, he said, "Carlo, do you think the X-14 would get Mary Jo in and out?"

"I'm sure it could, and it would be a lot less risky."

"Well, how do we get our hands on one?"

"Getting one from France would be difficult, but I think we could use the one I have here in Italy."

"You've got one here?"

"Yeah, it's at a flying club out at Urbe."

Mary Jo said, "I think I like the ultralight plan better than a parachute. If it all goes well, I can be in and out without attracting attention. The only problem might be getting checked out in it by Sunday."

Carlo asked, "Mary Jo, don't you have a Bell Jet Ranger?"

"Yeah, but I've never flown anything like an ultralight."

"If you can fly a Jet Ranger, flying the X-14 will be a piece of cake. Besides, if something goes wrong, you have some time to recover. The X-14 has a 12 to 1 glide ratio."

"That's plenty of ratio. How about the winds — can it fly in high winds?"

"Anything 20 MPH or less is considered normal. I've been up with 40 MPH, and that was a little tricky."

Roberto said, "So far, the riskiest part of the ultralight plan is getting airborne coming off the roof. Mary Jo will have to restart the motor and build up sufficient RPMs to get airborne. Could be a problem if someone is shooting at her."

Carlo smiled. "Well, there may be a solution to the takeoff problem too. There's an experimental vertical takeoff kit undergoing testing at the company's headquarters in Toulon. It's a pretty simple concept. Four canisters are attached to the skid assembly. They weigh about 20 pounds apiece and contain highly compressed air. When activated, they act as a jet-assisted takeoff device."

Mary Jo parried, "Whose idea was that, Rube Goldberg's?"

"You'd think so, but I've seen it tested. When you get ready to take off, you activate the canisters, and you're lifted straight up until you have sufficient altitude and RPMs to gain airspeed. Once you start the engine, you can deactivate the canisters and resume normal flight."

Mary Jo asked, "How high can the system carry you?"

"You could probably get up to around 500 feet if you needed to, but a boost to between 50 and 75 feet should give you time to build sufficient lift and airspeed."

"Carlo, do you think Mary Jo could master flying this contraption by Christmas Eve?" Roberto was concerned.

"Mary Jo has thousands of hours flying all sorts of aircraft, not to mention being a skilled HALO jumper. The controls are simple and intuitive, and, yes, I think she can master the X-14 in a day. The problem is getting the company to give me the vertical takeoff kits and getting it here in time."

"Can we get more than one set? I need to try it out before I attempt to exit the castle roof," Mary Jo added.

"That won't be a problem. The canisters can be recharged. All we need are the units, and the flying club has an air compressor. The problem will be convincing the company that I need them. They're highly sensitive to security issues."

Mary Jo said, "If you'll give me their contact information, I might be able to help on that front. I'll make a call and see what I can do."

Roberto said, "It's close to 6:00, and I have one more meeting before the day is done. I'll arrange for new aerial photos and have them sometime tomorrow, and I'll see that you get regular weather reports, starting in the morning."

Mary Jo said, "Speaking of tomorrow, I'll be leaving at 7:00 in the morning to fly to Maurice's funeral. I'll be back about noon."

Carlo spoke up and said, "I've meant to ask if I can go with you. I would like to show my respect and see the family."

"Of course. How about you, Roberto? Would you like to come with us?"

"Yes, I actually would. I'd also like to pay my respects, and it'll give me the opportunity to visit with Giovanni in an unofficial situation. I'll meet you and Carlo at Urbe in the morning, but now I've got to be on my way."

"Roberto, thank you for coming and thank you for your help."

"You're welcome. Let me know if you think of anything else."

After Roberto left, Mary Jo placed a call to Giovanni and put it on speaker. When he answered, she said, "Giovanni, its Mary Jo. I have Carlo Baggetti on the speaker. I need you to make a call."

"Hello, Carlo, it's been awhile. Mary Jo, tell me what you need."

Mary Jo explained the plans to use the ultralight and the need to secure the vertical takeoff package from the factory in Toulon.

Giovanni said, "I'll get right on it. Give me the contact information and I'll call you right back. Is there anything else you need?"

"Just to give you a heads-up that Carlo and Roberto Morelli will be coming to the funeral with me."

"That's good. I'll enjoy seeing Roberto, and Papa and Jeppe always look forward to seeing Carlo. Give me a few minutes to check on the equipment you need. How soon do you need it?"

"Ideally, we'd like to have it tomorrow. I need a day to check out in the X-14."

"If I can arrange it, could you fly to Toulon to pick it up after the funeral tomorrow?"

"That would be great."

"You'll hear from me within the hour."

"Call me back on my cell. Carlo and I are about to run an errand."

When Giovanni left the line, Mary Jo placed a call to Collette's home phone. Judson answered, and Mary Jo asked to be connected to Collette.

"Oh, Mary Jo! Augustin and I were so sorry to get the horrible news about Maurice! You must be devastated," Collette immediately said when she picked up.

"Thanks to both of you. Yes, it's been awful."

"I can only imagine. Is there anything I can do?"

"Yes, I lost everything I packed, and I don't even have a dress to wear to the funeral tomorrow. I'm hoping that you know someone here in Rome who would be willing to help me find something. I know it's late, but I really want to look decent in the morning."

"I don't know a soul in Rome, but I bet Carine does. Let me track her down and I'll call you right back."

"Thanks, Collette; call me on my cell phone."

Carlo smiled and teased, "I guess our errand involves a visit to a clothing shop?"

"Yes, let's head into Rome and get a jump on the traffic. I suspect wherever Collette sends us will be in the center of the city."

"If it involves high-end fashion, it will be in what is known as the Trident. It's the area bordering the Spanish Steps. I know a neighborhood inn with a cozy little bar. We can have a drink, and I'll guarantee that we'll be close to your shop. Later, we can return to the inn for dinner."

"Sounds good; let's head that way."

Carlo's home was located within a 15-minute drive of the posh shopping area behind the Spanish Steps, and soon they pulled in front of a boutique hotel, the Condotti. Carlo double-parked in front of the inn and took the front stairs two at a time. He returned just as a wrought-iron gate began to open. He drove the Jag into a small parking area, and the two entered the inn through a side door. Carlo waved at the pretty young woman at the desk and led Mary Jo into a small alcove just off the lobby. There were four small tables for two, and four stools at the copper-sheeted bar.

There was only one other couple sitting at a table, and there were two men at the bar. Carlo chose a table near the fireplace and held Mary Jo's chair. They were just getting settled when the bartender came over and said, "Signor Baggetti, may I bring your regular?"

"Yes, Neri, and this lovely lady will have a Jack Daniel's neat."

Mary Jo smiled and said, "I'm impressed that you still remember what I drink. It's been a long time."

"Well, you're pretty memorable."

Mary Jo was saved from the uncomfortable moment by the chirping of the LSU fight song from her phone. She pulled it from her jeans and said, "Giovanni, what did you find out?"

"It took a bit of arm-twisting, but there will be a package waiting for you at the private aviation terminal in Toulon. I told my contact that you'd pick it up around noon tomorrow."

"That's great. Thanks, Giovanni; this will help reduce any chance of failure."

"I hope it does, and, Mary Jo, make sure you're still around when we sit down to Christmas breakfast."

"I plan to be there. Thanks again. See you in the morning."

[1] High-Altitude, Low-Opening Parachute Jumps

FIFTEEN

B Y THE TIME THE CALL ENDED, the awkward moment had passed, and the friends sipped their drinks while Carlo talked in detail about flying the X-14. Mary Jo's phone sounded again, and she answered. "Hello, Collette. Did you have any luck?"

"Indeed, I did. It's a long story, but the bottom line is this: An outfit is being assembled for you at a shop called Sorelle Fontana. It's located at 5 Via San Sebastianello. The owner is Micol Fontana, and she will be expecting you before 8:00."

Mary Jo looked at Carlo and said, "I can pick the dress up at 5 Via San Sebastianello; can we make it there by 8:00?"

"No problem. It's actually within walking distance, and it's only 7:20 now."

"Collette, we are very close, and we'll have no problem with 8:00. I'll never be able to thank you enough for your help."

Collette chuckled and said, "Since I've been put in charge of keeping you presentable, Carine and I will see that everything you lost in the attack will be replaced and waiting for you in Paris. It's a good thing you allowed me to choose what you took with you."

"I hadn't even thought about that. Thank you, and please thank Carine for me, as well."

"I'll do that and know that our thoughts will be with you tomorrow."

When Mary Jo finished talking to Collette, she said, "Let's get the car and head to the shop."

Carlo replied, "I wasn't kidding; it is just an easy walk. We can be there by the time we get the car out. It's a little nippy tonight, but this is a beautiful part of Rome."

"Sure, I need a walk anyway."

Carlo held Mary Jo's chair and put her jacket around her shoulders. As they walked by the bar, he stopped and said, "Neri, we're going to take a walk and return for dinner. Put our bar bill on my account and let Theresa know that there will be two for 8:30."

"Si, Signor Baggetti, I will take care of it."

The two friends walked out of the inn and joined the crowded sidewalk filled with holiday shoppers and tourists. They passed shop after shop with names like Hermes, Gucci, and Hugo Boss. Soon, they stood in front of the shop known as Sorelle Fontana. There was a closed sign on the door, but they could see a bright light near the back. Carlo tapped on the glass, and a small lady came walking to the entrance. She opened the door and said in Italian, "Please come in. You must be Signorina Thibodaux. I am Micol Fontana."

Mary Jo and Carlo entered the shop, and Mary Jo replied, "Yes and I will never be able to thank you adequately for accommodating me tonight."

The woman chuckled. "You will have to thank Carine Gilson. Carine, my sisters, and I studied together at the ESMOD School in Paris and have been great friends since. Carine is the only person in the world who could convince me to miss my aperitif and come back to work the week before Christmas."

Micol led them to the back of the shop and pointed to a black A-line dress hanging on a peg. "I think this will do very well for a funeral. I have added shoes and accessories.

Considering the time of year, I have included a wool cloak, as well. I also suggest a black hat and veil."

"Do you want me to try on the dress?"

"No, that won't be necessary. Carine sent me your image, and I've already made a few adjustments. It will fit perfectly."

"Again, I thank you for doing this on such short notice."

"Carine told me of the tragic circumstances that made this necessary. I also had a love who was taken in the prime of his life."

"Oh, I'm so sorry."

"He was killed in North Africa fighting with Rommel, and I grieve for him every day. Now, you youngsters need to be getting on with your lives. You should be well dressed for the funeral of your love. Bury him and then hold him in your heart, but don't let his memory steal the rest of your life."

Carlo began to pick up the bags and hat box, while Micol placed the dress in a vinyl garment bag. She handed the bag to Mary Jo and said, "Go with my prayers, my child, and remember what I said."

Micol began to lead them to the front of the shop, and Mary Jo said, "I assume you will take a credit card."

Micol Fontana smiled and replied, "You'll find all of this on your account with Carine. Now, go."

Carlo and Mary Jo returned to the Condotti and left the bags and boxes in the Jag. They entered the hotel through a side door and went to the café. A handsome woman with streaks of white in her hair greeted them. She kissed Carlo on both cheeks and said, "Ah, Carlo, where have you been?"

Carlo returned the woman's smile, gestured to Mary Jo, and said, "This vision of loveliness is Theresa Fadduci. Theresa is the owner of the Condotti and my ideal of feminine charm. Theresa, I want you to meet my good friend Mary Jo Thibodaux."

Theresa took Mary Jo's hand and said, "I am always amazed at the beauty of Carlo's friends. He's such a charmer."

Mary Jo laughed and said, "Oh, he's a charmer for sure, and he knows it."

Theresa chuckled and replied, "Indeed, he does. Now, if you will follow me, we'll address dinner tonight."

Carlo ordered dinner for the two of them and a bottle of crisp, white Pinot Grigio. After dinner, they each had an espresso, and, finally, Carlo said, "If you want to be in the air by 7:00, we'll need to leave my house no later than 5:30. The traffic will be impossible if we wait."

"Yeah, I want to get there in time to shower and change clothes."

The friends said goodnight to Theresa, and Carlo eased the Jag out of the parking lot and into the busy street. They left all of the new clothes in the car, and Carlo followed Mary Jo to the guest room. He stood, leaning against the doorframe, watched her unpack her bag, and then said, "You know that we still have unfinished business between us, don't you?"

"Yes, but now's not the time to delve into it."

"Yes, of course…have a good night. See you in the morning. I'll have some toast and coffee ready for breakfast at 5:00."

"Sounds good; I'll be ready by then."

After Carlo went to his room on the third floor, Mary Jo took off her jeans and slipped into bed. The temperature outside had dropped to near freezing, and the heavy comforter felt warm and snuggly. She thought about Maurice and how much had happened in the last three days. She found herself feeling terribly alone.

Mary Jo's mental alarm went off at 4:30 the next morning, and she noticed that the heat was on, indicating that Carlo was already up. She took a quick shower and changed into a fresh flight suit. She could smell the aroma of freshly brewed coffee when she stepped out of the little elevator.

Carlo was dressed in a dark suit and sitting in the breakfast nook, buttering a hot piece of toast. When Mary Jo came in, he said, "Good morning. Hope you slept well."

"I suppose I did. The reality of Maurice's death is beginning to set in."

"I know this morning is going to be difficult for you."

"Yeah, the worst part will be seeing his family grieve."

"I agree. Don Ernesto felt a special relationship with Maurice. He bragged about his success in the Legion every chance he got."

Mary Jo drank the small glass of orange juice and ate a piece of toast. She ate just to refuel, but the coffee was a necessity. When the two finished eating, Carlo poured coffee into two Styrofoam cups and said, "We better get going; we don't want to keep Roberto waiting. He's the very definition of dependability and will be right on time."

Carlo navigated the rapidly growing, early-morning traffic skillfully and then parked in the private terminal lot at 6:35. He brought a baggage cart and began loading, while Mary Jo went into the flight operations office and filed a flight plan to Ajaccio, then to Toulon, and, finally, a return to Urbe. When she reentered the lobby, Carlo and Roberto were waiting. They stood, and Roberto took her hand. "How are you holding up?"

"So far, so good."

Carlo followed Mary Jo as she did her preflight walk-around, while Roberto stowed the bags and boxes. As they examined the little jet, Mary Jo asked, "Are you checked out in twin-engine jets?"

"Yeah, but it's been years since I've flown one."

"Want to fly in the left seat this morning?"

"You know I would."

"Good, we shouldn't have to make a carrier landing between here and Ajaccio."

"If we do, you'll have to take the controls. You couldn't mess it up any worse than I would."

They all came aboard. Mary Jo smiled at Roberto and said, "Carlo is going to be our pilot this morning; you may want to try a commercial flight."

"Oh, what the hell. Nobody lives forever, and there probably aren't any carriers nearby."

Carlo shook his head and sputtered, "Damn, Morelli, do you have my file memorized?"

"Yeah. Wasn't all that much of interest in it."

Mary Jo let Carlo slip into the pilot's seat, and she watched as he ran through the preflight. When he was ready, he called the tower for takeoff instructions. Soon, they were wheels-up and climbing to the north. They turned west and then south and began getting landing instructions from the Ajaccio tower.

Carlo set the CJ4 down without a bump and followed the ground guide to the Capriati Aviation hangar. Mary Jo noticed a gleaming-white Gulfstream 650 parked on the tarmac. Apparently, Andre Dalhousie had arrived earlier. Antonio was waiting, and, after the introductions and loading of Mary Jo's bags and boxes, they drove to the villa. They pulled up to the front door, where they were met by Don Ernesto and Jeppe. Don Ernesto hugged Mary Jo and then grasped Carlo by the hand. "Carlo, I'm glad you could come this morning. It's good to have old friends at a time like this."

Carlo said hello to Jeppe and then turned to Roberto. "Don Ernesto, this is General Roberto Morelli. He is a good friend of Giovanni."

Roberto shook the Don's hand and said, "Don Ernesto, today I'm not a general, just a concerned friend."

Jeppe smiled and said, "Giovanni and some of your other friends are waiting for you in the library. Follow me and we'll join them."

Jeppe led the way to the library, and, when they walked in, the room was filled with Mary Jo's and Maurice's friends. She walked over to Emile and Constance Dalhousie and hugged them tightly. Mary Jo brushed aside a tear and said, "I'm so glad you came. Maurice loved you both."

Emile motioned around the room and said, "Since we brought the Gulfstream, we invited some people to come with us."

Mary Jo looked around and caught the eye of Allie Burke, her office manager, talking to Amy Wilson, her counterpart at Brooks Capital. Mary Jo crossed the room and hugged them both. "Thank you so much for coming."

Amy held her hand and said, "Mary Jo, my heart goes out to you. I, too, lost the love of my life, so I have some idea what you're going through."

Mary Jo thanked them again and then walked to the fireplace where Alan Brooks stood talking to Pete Corelli. Pete took her by the hand and said, "Mary Jo, we just wanted to be here today. Maurice was one of God's good people, and we'll all miss him."

Alan nodded in agreement and added, "We want you to know that we're here for you. If there is anything we can do, just ask."

"I can't tell all of you how much this means to me. I have some things I have to do here before I come home, but I'll be calling on your help when I do. Besides, we have projects to complete, and I haven't forgotten them."

Emile came over, touched Mary Jo's elbow, and said, "Gentlemen, I'm afraid I must steal Mary Jo from you."

Mary Jo hugged them all again and said, "Maybe we can visit after the service."

Emile shook his head and said, "Only for a moment. We'll be leaving as soon as the service is over. I promised everyone that we'd be back in the States tomorrow."

Emile led Mary Jo across the room to join Don Ernesto and Carlo. On the way, Emile said, "I talked to General Litton before I left, and he and Karen send their deepest sympathies. He just was not up to the flight."

"No, he and Karen have no business flying anywhere. I'll see them when I get back to Mobile."

"Speaking of that, what are your plans?"

"I'll be here through Christmas, but I think I'll come back the next week. I don't want to miss Maria's New Year's ball."

"Constance asked that I invite you to go to the ball with us."

"That sounds wonderful. Maurice and I were looking forward to it."

"I won't pry into things that don't concern me, but, if I know you and the Capriatis, I suspect you will be busy this Christmas."

"You might be right about that," Mary Jo replied.

When the two approached the Don, he took Carlo by the arm and said, "Carlo, why don't we go to my office and visit while Mary Jo dresses. I want you to meet my good friend Andre Dalhousie. Have you had breakfast?"

"Yes, but a cup of strong Corsican coffee would be welcomed."

"I can make that happen. Mary Jo, would you care to join us?"

"No thanks. You were right; I need to get ready."

SIXTEEN

ALL OF MARY JO'S BAGS HAD BEEN carried to her room, and everything was laid out when she got there. She stripped and stepped into a hot shower. When she got out, she opened the bag marked lingerie and took out a pair of black Gilson pantyhose and a matching bra. Normally, Mary Jo wouldn't be caught dead in pantyhose, but, today, they seemed appropriate.

Micol Fontana had also been proven right. The black dress fit perfectly, and the low-heeled black, leather shoes were stylish and comfortable. Mary Jo began to understand what Collette meant about clothes boosting a girl's confidence.

Mary Jo stood in front of the full-length mirror, placed the simple, black hat on her head, and adjusted the veil. She put the wool cloak around her shoulders, and she felt strangely at ease. The only thing left on the bed was a package containing a pair of black gloves. She slipped them on and descended the stairs. She was almost to the foyer when Giovanni and Roberto came from the library. As she stepped into the room, they stood still, with their mouths hanging open.

Giovanni regained his composure and said, "It's time to go to the chapel; I've asked Roberto to be your escort."

Roberto took Mary Jo's hand and said, "It will be my honor to escort Signorina Thibodaux."

Giovanni left to get Nicole and the children, and Roberto led Mary Jo to a covered walkway connecting the main villa with the small family chapel. Even in the walkway, the

December winds blew cold, and Mary Jo pulled the cloak closer around her shoulders. They came to the chapel doors, which were held open by an altar boy wearing a black cassock and surplice.

The interior of the chapel was dimly lit by the altar candles, and Maurice's casket stood by the altar rail. Roberto led Mary Jo to the coffin and stepped back while she approached. She raised her veil, bent over, and softly kissed the top.

Roberto gently touched Mary Jo's elbow and guided her to her pew. A Legion officer in full dress led a color guard up to the casket. The guard spread the French tricolor across the casket, and then they took their seats in the apse of the chapel.

When Mass began, Mary Jo joined in the familiar liturgy, but her thoughts were not really connected to the words. The priest was a senior man who had been the Capriati family chaplain since Maurice's childhood, and, during the homily, he related stories about Maurice as a boy.

Mary Jo and the family took Communion first and were back in their seats when the rest of the mourners moved to the altar rail. Carlo and Roberto went up together, trailed by a tall, lean man with salt and pepper hair. Mary Jo guessed him to be Andre Dalhousie, and Emile and Constance followed.

As the chapel emptied, the family was escorted to the covered walkway. Maurice's casket was carried by his three brothers and three of his sisters' husbands. The family followed the casket to the small graveyard next to the chapel and walked to the open grave. The Legion color guard stood at attention on the opposite side of the casket.

When everyone settled into place, the priest stood, made the sign of the Cross, and said, "In the name of the Father, the Son, and the Holy Spirit, we gather here to commend our brother Maurice to God, our Father, and to commit

Maurice's body to the earth. In the Spirit of faith in the resurrection of Jesus Christ from the dead, let us raise our voices and offer our prayers for Maurice. Let us pray. 'This is the will of the One who sent me,' says the Lord, 'that I should not lose anything of what He gave me, but that I should raise it on the last day.'"

After several more prayers and scripture readings, the priest blessed the assembly with shakes of holy water and said, "From dust we have come and to dust we shall return. In the name of the Father, the Son, and the Holy Spirit."

The color guard assumed the firing position, and three volleys rang out. The guard returned to attention and then marched to the casket, removing and folding the flag. The senior officer placed the folded flag in Don Ernesto's hands, as a single tear rolled down the Don's cheek.

The casket was lowered into the open grave, and each of the mourners filed by and tossed a white rose onto it. When it was Mary Jo's turn, she gently dropped the flower and said quietly, "Goodbye, my love," and then she allowed Roberto to take her arm and lead her back to the villa.

The staff had prepared a buffet lunch, and the dining room was filling with family and friends. Roberto led Mary Jo to the Foreign Legionnaires and said, "Colonel Feres, I'd like to introduce Maurice's fiancée, Mary Jo Thibodaux. Mary Jo, this is Colonel Marc Feres, Maurice's last commanding officer."

Colonel Feres extended his hand and said, "Mademoiselle, may I offer the sympathy of the Legion to you. Maurice was a brave soldier and a treasured friend. He will be mourned by his comrades."

Mary Jo squeezed the colonel's hand and replied, "Maurice loved the Legion. One of his last wishes was to take me to the Legion's museum."

"I would be honored to escort you if you should ever visit Aubagne."

Mary Jo smiled and thanked the colonel. She then noticed Andre Dalhousie walking toward her. He held out his hand and said, "Mademoiselle Thibodaux, I am Andre Dalhousie, Emile's uncle. The Dalhousie firm is prepared to offer you any assistance during this time of tragedy."

"I'm very pleased to meet you. Emile is like a father to me, and your firm has been a great support over the years."

Andre smiled and then said, "Colonel, before you return to Aubagne, I'd like a word in private if I may."

Andre Dalhousie was walking away with the colonel when Carlo came up and said, "We'll be in the Don's conference room, Mary Jo, when you're ready."

"Of course," Mary Jo said. "But I do need to change."

Mary Jo looked around the room and found Alan Brooks at the buffet table. "Mind if I join you?"

"Of course not, I'd be delighted," Alan said.

The friends carried their food to two chairs near the fireplace and sat, holding their plates on their laps. Mary Jo took a bite and said, "I just wanted to reassure you that we're on top of the Tesla test site on Will's place in Mississippi. Allie and I speak regularly, and all is on schedule to run the first test after New Year's."

"Mary Jo, of all the things you need to be concerned about, Will's project should be way down the list. There's no urgency involved, and it will all work out as planned."

"Yes, I suppose that it will. How are you and Amy doing with Brooks Capital?"

"The system continues to garner as much cash as we need, and, until we're certain that the Tesla project is working right, we're on hold. The NRC has yet to approve the final design of the pitchblende processing plant for the reservation, so that's on hold for now too. When do you plan to return?"

"Shortly after Christmas. I'll need to stop over in Paris and pick up some things, but the flight back will be a lot quicker. I traded my Mustang for a Citation."

"Couldn't take the heat after Pete and I got one, huh?"

"Mine's a used CJ4, so you've still got me out-planed, but I wanted the longer range and additional seating."

"Pete and I have really enjoyed flying on the Dalhousie Gulfstream. That's some airplane."

"What the hell, Alan...they don't cost but $65,000,000. Run the system for a day and pick one up."

"Yeah, it's tempting, but, unless we begin to need to travel internationally, we're good with the Citation. Speaking of the Gulfstream, I see Emile signaling that it's time to go to the airport."

"Be sure to tell everyone how much I appreciate y'all coming."

"I'll tell them. You just be very careful between now and Christmas, okay?"

Mary Jo walked with Alan and said goodbye to everyone as they loaded into the line of SUVs. Then, she returned to the villa and said goodbye to all of Maurice's relatives. After making sure she spoke to everyone, Mary Jo made her way to her room. She took off the funeral outfit, carefully repacked it, and put it in the closet. She put on her flight suit and boots and took the elevator to the Don's office.

When Mary Jo entered the conference room, she saw Giovanni bent over the table pointing at some blueprints and land photos. Carlo, Roberto, and Jeppe were looking intently at them. Giovanni looked up and said, "Come in, Mary Jo. I think you'll find this interesting."

Mary Jo walked to the table and saw what appeared to be plans for the Castle Castellano.

"It seems that Angelo, the tavern owner, has a niece working as a chambermaid at the castle," Giovanni said. "Jeppe was able to have one of his men from La Maddalena visit with her, and she was able to give us the complete layout of the castle. Roberto used his influence to obtain a set of the drawings used when the castle was renovated 10 years ago. The plans, plus the maid's descriptions, have allowed us to get a pretty good layout."

Mary Jo studied the material and then said, "The plans give me a clear idea of how to get from the roof to Don Giuseppe's bedchamber, but I suspect I'll encounter locked doors at some point. There's not a commercial lock I can't pick, but the time it takes worries me."

Giovanni held up a single key and replied, "All of the interior locks are keyed to use this. The maid gave hers to us, and we made you a copy."

"That's really going to help, but I'd still like additional castle-roof photos in better resolution. I need to locate a landing spot."

Roberto smiled and said, "They will be at Carlo's house by the time you both return from Toulon."

"Will you be able to do this while we're flying back?"

"I won't be with you on the trip to Toulon; Don Ernesto has offered to fly me back to Rome on his Bombardier. I have to arrange transport for you and Carlo on Christmas Eve."

Carlo seemed a bit surprised, and Roberto continued, "Don't look so shocked, Carlo. She's got to have a ground crew, and who'd be better?"

Carlo laughed and said, "I should have seen that coming. Of course, I'll be glad to come along."

Mary Jo studied the plans for a moment and then asked, "Can we take these with us?"

"Of course," replied Giovanni.

Mary Jo began to gather the material into her flight case. When she finished, she said, "Carlo and I will pick up the VTO kits and return to Urbe. I want to have everything ready to begin my ultralight crash course in the morning."

Carlo chuckled and said, "You might have chosen a different phrase rather than crash course."

"Yeah, maybe I should have. Let's call it my check-out flights. My instructor couldn't land on a thousand-foot aircraft carrier, but he's going to teach me to land on a fifty-foot roof. What was I thinking?"

Carlo grinned and said, "Don't do as I do — do as I say."

Mary Jo snapped the flight case shut and muttered, "Whatever...let's just get this show on the road."

SEVENTEEN

CARLO TOOK OFF FROM AJACCIO and leveled out at 8,000 feet for the 160-mile flight to Toulon. After he landed, he was directed to follow the guide truck to the military side of the airport. He taxied to the tie-down area, lowered the stairs, and was greeted by a scholarly looking gentleman, carrying four large boxes. When Carlo stepped onto the tarmac, the man said in French-accented English, "Good morning, Carlo. I have to say…you certainly have friends with a great deal of influence. I can't believe you're able to get some of our top-secret work."

"C'mon, Gerald. I've already got a prototype of the ship. I just want to try its vertical takeoff capabilities."

"I trust you will keep careful notes regarding the unit's performance in an operational mode?"

"You can expect a thorough report."

"Any chance of filming your test?"

"Afraid not, but I'll include as many details as I can in my report."

"Since all of this has been approved at levels far above my pay grade, I'll just wish you good luck and Godspeed. Try to bring my baby back in one piece."

"Will do. Thanks for the help. I'll talk to you after the holidays. Merry Christmas."

"Joyeux Noel."

Carlo stowed the boxes in the exterior baggage compartment and then returned to the cockpit. Mary Jo asked, "Everything go okay?"

"Yeah. He was less than thrilled, but we got what we need."

Carlo flew back to Urbe and taxied to the hangar area. After the friends had each gotten a cup of coffee at the café, Carlo looked at his watch and said, "It's after three, so we won't have enough daylight to do much today. Let's go to my house, get a good night's sleep, and start fresh in the morning. I'll pop a pizza in the oven, and we can have a simple dinner before we turn in."

The two beat the rush-hour traffic and pulled into Carlo's home just before 5:00. Mary Jo went straight to her room, peeled out of the flight suit, and hung it in the closet. She pulled on a pair of jeans and a warmup top and met Carlo in the kitchen. He was taking a frozen pizza out of its box and reading the instructions. When he set the box down, Mary Jo picked it up and said, "Here we are in Rome, the home office of pizza, about to eat a DiGiorno's made in Chicago. I'm surprised you can even buy this in Italy!"

"I still have access to the commissary at Camp Darby up near Florence. I make a monthly trip up there to buy stuff. You can take the boy out of Boston, but..."

"Yeah, I remember having Krispy Kreme donuts flown in when I was stationed here. I can't live without Krispy Kremes and Krystals for too long," Mary Jo retorted.

"I've never tried either of those, but I don't need any new addictions."

Carlo put the pizza in the oven and set the timer. Then, he pulled a bottle of Valpolicella from the wine rack and opened it. After he'd poured two glasses, he said, "Let's take our wine into the living room and put some music on."

Mary Jo followed Carlo as he opened a door by the audio equipment and asked, "What are you in the mood for? I've got everything from Willie Nelson to Mozart."

"I have to admit…I'm not much of a music aficionado. Why don't you pick something?"

"When in doubt, you can always go with opera. How about *La Boheme*?"

"Sounds good to me. The pizza might be from Illinois, but the music will be Italian."

Carlo put a CD into the machine, and the opening fanfare of Puccini's classic tale of 19th-century Paris filled the room. They sat listening, each deep in their thoughts (Mary Jo fondly remembering the performance she and Maurice attended in Paris), until the timer sounded that the pizza was ready. Carlo brought two plates and the hot pizza to the coffee table, put a slice on one of the plates, and handed it to Mary Jo. He refilled their wine glasses and sank back into Rodolfo and Mimi's struggle for love.

By the time Mimi had succumbed to tuberculosis, Mary Jo was fast asleep on the sofa. Carlo allowed the opera to end, covered her with a blanket, and closed the house for the night.

Mary Jo awoke to the smell of coffee brewing and snuggled under the blanket for several moments before realizing where she was. She wrapped the blanket around her shoulders and walked into the kitchen. Carlo was standing at the stove frying bacon and didn't see her come in, so she sat down at the table in the breakfast nook and poured a cup of coffee.

Mary Jo looked out the window and saw the sun creeping over the garden wall, lighting a bright, cold, winter morning. Carlo turned to put the bacon on the table and finally saw her. He smiled and said, "Hope you slept okay. I hated to wake you."

"Like a rock. Guess I was pretty beat. Thanks for the blanket."

"There was a frost last night, and I want to let the sun warm things up a bit before we get started. Thought we'd have a hearty breakfast to get us going. I'm just about to make some of Carlo's famous pancakes."

"Well, I better go freshen up a bit before such a treat. Give me a couple of minutes to wash my face."

"Take your time; I won't put them on until you come down."

Mary Jo did her morning toilette and then slipped into a flight suit. She came back to the kitchen in time to eat a stack of six of Carlo's pancakes and four pieces of bacon. She was starting on her third cup of coffee when he said, "Thought we'd spend the morning getting you familiar with the X-14 and let you take it on a cross-country after lunch. You can fly all afternoon, and, this evening, I'll have our mechanic mount the vertical takeoff kit so that you can work on that tomorrow morning."

"Good, I'd like to be fully checked out by noon Saturday. We'll need to meet with Roberto to see how he plans to get us in and out of Sardinia. I also want some time to study the photos and building plans."

Carlo walked to the counter by the back door, picked up a manila envelope, and said, "Speaking of photos, Roberto sent these over this morning."

Carlo handed the envelope to Mary Jo and sat down. She used her place knife, slit it open, and found a dozen or so high-resolution black and white photos of the castle roof. She shuffled through them, passed them on to Carlo, and said, "Perfect — there's plenty of room to land on the roof, and I don't see any security cameras covering it. I wish we had a mock-up of the rooftop. I'd like to make a couple of test runs."

"There's an abandoned tennis court behind the old terminal building at Urbe. It should be perfect," Carlo replied.

"What time do we need to leave?"

"About 9:00 should be early enough. Why'd you ask?"

"I'd like to pick up an insulated black flight jacket and a motorcycle helmet. I suspect it's going to be pretty chilly flying around on Christmas Eve."

"No problem. There's a large Carrefour on the way to the airport. They'll have the jacket. I've got a helmet with built-in Bluetooth for my occasional female companions."

"Yeah, I remember Carrefour — sort of an Italian Walmart."

"This one has a large clothing section, so you'll be able to find something. If not, there's a shop in the main terminal at Urbe, but it's very expensive."

"Let's try Carrefour, and, if they don't have it, I'll spring for the airport."

Mary Jo thought about calling the office to check in, then did the math, and realized that it was just around midnight in Alabama. She'd maybe wait until after Christmas to call.

Carlo finished cleaning the kitchen and joined Mary Jo at the table. She gave him an impish look and said, "I see you doing the cooking and cleaning, and it makes me wonder if you might consider trading in your factotum for a cook and a maid."

"Malcolm will gladly prepare a gourmet dinner for 12 or power-wash the whole damn house, but there's no way he's going to fix breakfast or wash a dish. He thinks we need additional staff so that he can do more 'factotuming.'"

"Doesn't he work for you?"

"We've never really been clear on who works for whom. I find it easier to do some stuff myself rather than debate it with him."

"Does the term 'wuss' come to mind?"

"It occurs to me from time to time, but enough about me! Let's go to the airport and teach you to fly the X-14."

When the two entered the garage, Carlo walked past the Jag and climbed into a Toyota pickup. Mary Jo slid into the passenger seat and said, "Not a day for a sports car, I see."

"Think about it as a recovery vehicle. The X-14 will fit in the bed if needed."

On their way to Urbe, Carlo stopped at the Carrefour, and Mary Jo found a black, nylon flight jacket with Gore-Tex insulation and some thick, wool socks. She put them in her equipment bag with all of her other gear, and Carlo parked in front of a WWII vintage hangar. A sign read as follows: "Il Volo Sportive Club di Roma."

Carlo took a key from his pocket. He unlocked and removed a large padlock. He raised the overhead door, and they walked into the dark interior. When he hit a light switch, fluorescent light fixtures flickered to life. Once the light came on, Mary Jo could see all sorts of airplanes parked wing to wing, filling the building. There were gliders, ultralights, and single-engine stunt planes. Carlo weaved his way between them until he stopped in front of what looked like the world's first helicopter. It stood on two narrow spring-steel skids attached to a tubular and fiberglass frame. A small electric motor was mounted beneath the rotor housing, and a hinged tail section was raised for storage. There were two 10-foot polycarbonate rotor blades strapped to the seat assembly. Mary Jo expected to see Igor Sikorsky step out of the shadows with a wrench in his hand.

Carlo stood back and said, "This allows the X-14 to be stowed in a truck or trailer for transport. If you'll grab the frame on your side, we can move it outside."

Mary Jo took the frame as instructed, and the two lifted the helicopter a foot off the hangar floor. They threaded through the other ships and sat the X-14 on the open tarmac in front of the hangar. Carlo unstrapped the rotor blades and laid them across the frame. He crawled around, loosened two toggle switches, and lowered the tail with the small tail rotor into place.

"Getting into flight mode couldn't be simpler. Mount the rotors and lower the tail section, and you're ready to go," Carlo said as he stood on a small ladder built into the airframe, loosening four nuts that allowed him to mount the rotor blades to the rotor housing. While Carlo worked, he said, "She doesn't have much in the way of instrumentation. There's a GPS system with a high-resolution screen that will give you altitude, ground speed, and location."

Mary Jo stood close and checked out the GPS screen, which was blank. Carlo then pointed to the small fiberglass seat clamped to the airframe. "The pilot sits here, and the collective and cyclic are in their normal positions, as are the pedals that control the tail rotor. You'll be right at home once you get the feel of how she handles. Why don't you sit in her for a bit? I'll go get you a helmet and bring the como gear."

Mary Jo touched the collective with her left hand and held the cyclic with her right. The rear rotor pedals were uncomfortably out of reach.

Carlo walked up carrying the helmet and what appeared to be a walkie-talkie. He was pulling a small handcart with a battery. He grinned and asked, "Well, how does she feel?"

"Is there any way to adjust the seat?"

"Yeah, it can go up and down and back and forth. What do you need?"

"It could be a little lower and closer to the bow."

"Hop out and I'll show you. You don't even need tools."

Carlo made the slight adjustments that Mary Jo had suggested and lifted the hinge to reveal a battery compartment. He placed the battery in the housing under the seat and hooked it up to the cables from the electrical system. He flipped a toggle switch near the GPS, and the screen came to life, as did red and green running lights. He moved it a notch higher, and a high, candle-powered landing light flashed on. He stood back and said, "We're ready to roll. Want to give her a go?"

"Sure. She looks fully equipped, but bare-bones simple. I shouldn't have a problem, but I'm not sure I'll be needing all those lights."

"Of course not. We'll disable them."

Mary Jo climbed into the seat and pulled the flight harness tight. Once she placed the helmet on, Carlo clicked on the radio and asked, "Do you read me?"

"Loud and clear. What frequency are we using?"

"Ah," Carlo answered. "Another secret feature of the X-14. We have a low-frequency channel that has been reserved for battlefield communication. It has a range of five miles, and it's not affected by weather or topography. We don't want to be picked up on a police scanner or by some trucker on his CB."

Mary Jo moved the collective and allowed the ship to hover a few feet from the tarmac. She held the hover for a minute or so and then pushed the cyclic, allowing the aircraft to move forward while gaining airspeed. After she cleared the treetops and power lines, she took it up to 1,500 feet and banked sharply to the right. She made a circle of the hangar area before setting it back onto the tarmac within a foot of her starting point. When she cut the power and removed the helmet, she said, "She handles just like a full-size ship. Unless there's something I'm missing, I could fly the mission tonight."

"It's easy to see you've had many hours of helicopter time. It took me a week of hovering and messing up to do what you just did. So, I agree, no sense hammering the same nail. Let's move on to some cross-country work."

Carlo took Mary Jo inside the flying club's office area and pointed to charts on the wall that indicated the approaches in and out of Urbe. Since the airport was in the northern suburbs of Rome, it would be simple to clear the traffic and get into the open countryside. He walked to the chart of the area just north of Rome and said, "The X-14 battery is capable of two hours of sustained flight, with a payload of 300 or less, flying at a cruise speed of 70 KPH — or about 45 MPH. Do the math, and that would be good for a 90-mile flight. Today, without all of your gear and no VTO system, you could probably double that, but let's stay within the margin of error."

Carlo put his finger on the airport and said, "You'll start here," and he ran his finger along a highway leading north. "You'll reach the intersection of E-85 and S-53, where you'll turn due north and follow the highway until you reach the town of Orte. At Orte, you'll follow SS678 to Viterbo; then, you'll turn north and follow SR2. From your altitude, you should be able to see a large lake to the northeast. SR2 will border the lake until it reaches Bolsena. I'll guide you to a landing spot, and we'll have lunch. Then, we'll follow the same route back to Urbe."

"I assume you'll be following me in the Toyota?"

"Right. We'll be in constant radio contact, and I'll have you in sight for the entire trip. I'll have tools and an extra battery, just in case we need them for the return flight. Don't be offended. I believe you could fly the X-14 back to Alabama, if you wanted to, but I'm protecting my ass here. If something happened and it fell into the wrong hands, I'd have hell to pay."

"Yeah, I can see that," Mary Jo replied. "How far will the round trip be?"

"Close to 70 miles or an hour and a half each way. It's almost 11:00 now, and I'd like to be back before sunset, which, today, will be just before 5:00. Let's program the GPS with the flight info, and we'll be ready to take off."

While Carlo was loading the battery into the truck, Mary Jo took the opportunity to use the bathroom. No sense tempting fate. When she returned, Carlo watched as she strapped in and flipped the battery to "Power On."

"You shouldn't have any trouble following the roads. Try to stay to my left front so I can keep an eye on you. I'll drive slowly enough for you to keep position, and, of course, we have the Bluetooth. If a problem does come up, just set down as close to the highway as you can."

Mary Jo said, "Okay, see you in Bolsena," as she lifted off the tarmac.

EIGHTEEN

AS CARLO DROVE OUT of the airport and turned north on Rte. E85, Mary Jo hovered over the runway and then took up her position slightly ahead and to his left. They kept radio chatter to a minimum, and, when she spotted the lake off to her left, Mary Jo keyed the mike and said, "I've got the lake in sight."

"Okay, it'll take me a couple of minutes to find a landing spot, so climb to a couple of thousand feet and wait until I call you."

Carlo sped up, and he was soon on the southern outskirts of the little town of Bolsena. He took a short street off of the main highway and pulled beside an open field next door to a church and a convent. He keyed his mike and said, "Okay, I think I've found a spot; it's a little east of SR2 near a church."

Mary Jo replied, "Yeah, I've got you in sight; I'll put her down as close to the truck as I can."

Mary Jo set the little craft within 20 yards of Carlo's vehicle and cut the power. As Mary Jo was climbing out of the seat, Carlo walked up and said, "Let's load her into the truck and go get some lunch."

The friends soon had the ship in the bed of the pickup, secured with heavy-duty bungee cords, and Carlo drove toward the lake. He pulled into the parking lot of Trattoria del Moro, where he threw a tarp over the X-14 and led Mary Jo up the steps to an open-air café that was built on pilings above the lake. When they were seated on the open deck looking out over the lake, Mary Jo said, "I have the feeling that you've been here before."

"You're right; it's the perfect destination for a day trip from Rome, and the food is exceptional. Even though it's right on the lake, their specialty is grilled meats. I've never tried the seafood, but it's probably pretty good too."

The two looked at the menu, and Carlo decided on grilled Italian sausage and pasta, while Mary Jo ordered the fried cefalo labbrone. Carlo looked surprised and asked, "Do you have any idea what you just ordered?"

"C'mon, Carlo. Remember, I was stationed in Rome. Yeah, I just ordered fried mullet."

"Mullet. People really eat mullet?"

"I live on Mobile Bay, and mullet is considered a delicacy."

Carlo shook his head. "To each his own. I suppose it's an acquired taste."

The friends ate their lunches, watching the sailboats on the lake, and, finally, Carlo looked at his watch and said, "It's almost 1:30. We probably need to head back." He paid the check, and they descended to the truck, where he pulled the tarp off and folded it. "We might as well launch you right here in the parking lot. You can take off over the lake and follow me back. When we clear town, resume your position to my left and we'll retrace our route back to Urbe."

When the ultralight arrived at Urbe, Mary Jo landed near the club hangar and helped Carlo carry the X-14 back to its spot. Carlo opened the four VTO units and then signaled a man in overalls to come over. "Gino, I'd appreciate it if you'd mount these. The instructions are in the boxes. You may need to fill them with compressed air, as well. We want to try them out in the morning."

"Si, this I will do before I leave."

"Grazie, Gino."

"Prego."

While Carlo talked to the mechanic, Mary Jo called Roberto, who said, "Mary Jo, I was just about to give you a call. We need to meet to go over our plans."

"Yes, Carlo and I are out at Urbe. I just finished a cross-country flight in the X-14, and, tomorrow, we'll work with the VTO units."

"Did you see the photos I sent over?"

"I did, and they're perfect. Have you decided on how we will get to Sardinia?"

"Yes, and that's what I want to meet about."

"Where do you want to meet?"

"We can't do it here; all of this is way off the books. Can you and Carlo meet me at Cacio e Pepe's?"

"That sounds fine; we can take care of dinner while we're there."

"Good. It's 4:45 now, so I'll call Cosimo, reserve the back room, and meet you there."

Carlo pulled in front of Cacio e Pepe's and tossed the Toyota keys to the valet. The young boys looked disappointed until Carlo said, "Don't worry...still got the Jag."

Cosimo met them at the front and took them to a private room in the back of the restaurant. Roberto was sitting at the table sipping a glass of wine, and, when he saw them, he said, "Thank you, Cosimo. We'll need some time to tend to a little business before we eat."

"Si, Generale. Just ring the buzzer when you need something. What can I bring for you and Miss Thibodaux, Signor Baggetti?"

"I think a bottle of whatever Roberto is drinking will be just fine."

The trio made small talk until Cosimo returned with a bottle of wine, two glasses, and antipasto. Once the glasses were filled, Roberto asked, "Mary Jo, did you bring the photos?"

"I did, and the building plans, as well."

Mary Jo pulled a stack of papers from her flight bag and spread them across the white tablecloth. Roberto took a sizeable military map of Sardinia and pinned it to the wall. When everything was in place, he said, "The weather forecast for Christmas Eve is clear skies with a quarter moon, and it will be close to minus five degrees Celsius after midnight. The lack of clouds will be perfect for us because there will be no contrast, so it will be difficult for anyone to see you on your approach."

Mary Jo asked, "How about the wind?"

"10 to 20 KPH, out of the northwest."

"Good, the wind won't be a factor. All that's left is for me to familiarize myself with the VTOs, and we'll be good to go. Once I'm on the roof undetected, the real fun begins."

"We better get you to Sardinia before we get into that," Roberto added.

"Yeah, I assume you have all of that worked out."

"I do. An unmarked helicopter will pick you, Carlo, and the X-14 up from the military side of Urbe and transport you to an abandoned NATO weapons-testing site near Aglientu, a village about four miles northwest of Luogosanto. There's a ridge on the test site that has a clear view of Castle Castellano. Carlo will be able to see the rooftop from that ridge."

Carlo thought for a moment and then said, "Even with the best naval binoculars, I won't be able to see much in detail."

Roberto said, "No, but you will have a surplus device used to sight naval gunfire. It's mounted on a tripod and equipped with night vision. You'll feel like you're on the roof."

Mary Jo interjected: "Okay, so he can see the roof, but, if he detects anything going wrong, there's not much he can do about it."

"This is true, but at least we'll know what happened. You chose to do this alone, and, if things go badly, you'll have to fix it yourself."

"Fair enough. Will the helicopter wait until I get back?"

"That's the plan. If all goes well, they'll take you to Ajaccio afterward and then return Carlo and the X-14 to Urbe."

"Okay, so much for in and out. Now, let's take a look at what I do once I'm on the roof."

Roberto pointed to the photo and said, "I had one of our aerial photo analysts take a look at the roof, and she located two entrance points to the castle: one here," he said, pointing to a small house with a door, "and another here," he said, indicating a trapdoor across the roof. "Matching the photo to the plans suggested that the upright door leads to the main stairwell, and the trapdoor leads to the heating and cooling equipment. Either one would get you into the living area. Once you're in the main stairwell, Don Giuseppe's bedchamber is located here."

Mary Jo followed Roberto's pointer and said, almost to herself, "The bedchamber has three rooms and a large bath area. The door from the hallway opens into a sitting room, and there's a library just to the left. The bedroom and bath are to the right. We'll have to assume he'll be asleep, and, hopefully, with a little too much to drink. If all goes well, I can be in and out in no more than 15 minutes."

Carlo spoke up. "Yeah, I agree. If everything goes as planned, you can do that…but it probably won't, so let's think about just what *can* go wrong."

"The first thing that comes to mind is that he isn't in his room," Roberto offered.

"In that case, I'll have to abort the mission, and we'll have to come up with a plan B after Christmas."

Carlo said, "Okay, but what if he's there in bed with a woman — or a man, for that matter?"

"Then they become collateral damage. Sleeping around has its risks. If he's in the bedchamber, then I'll kill him and anyone else who's with him. If he's not there, I'll abort. Too risky to search for him."

"What if there's a guard in the hall or the chamber?"

"Then there's additional collateral damage. Occupational hazard."

"Damn. I wouldn't want to be in your way. Too easy to be collateral damage," Carlo commented.

"Don't murder any of my friends, and you should be safe."

"I'll keep that in mind," Carlo muttered.

Roberto broke in and added, "Well, that seems to be all we can do for now. We just wait and hope the weather holds. Carlo, have everything ready to go and be on the military side of Urbe at 0400 tomorrow. Now, let's order dinner. Assassination always makes me hungry."

Cosimo and his staff served dinner, and, when the dishes were being cleared, Carlo looked at Roberto and said, "There is something I've been wondering about. I read Mary Jo's 201 file, but there was no mention of her receiving the Military Medal of Honor. How did that come about?"

Mary Jo smiled and replied, "I'm glad to find out that even some things are still secret, even from the CIA and the NAS. There is a top-secret file maintained on all field agents in the 902nd, and it contains information on black ops. Apparently, your clearance wasn't high enough to get it."

Mary Jo continued, "In 1995, I was a 1st lieutenant in the 101st Airborne, working in G-2 at Division. The 101st was slated to take part in the NATO mission to Bosnia, and I was part of an advance team sent to do a recon of events on-site. The war in Bosnia was starting to wind down, and there were rumors of last-minute massacres taking place. NATO attempted to create zones to provide a safe harbor for Muslim refugees, and a Dutch battalion was assigned to protect a safe area in a valley near Srebrenica. Roberto was a major serving with the Italian Special Forces, and he and I wrangled permission to join the Dutch as liaison officers."

Carlo turned to Roberto and asked, "So you were in special ops?"

"Actually, I was serving in the Monte Cervino Regiment at the time."

Mary Jo said, "Don't let him fool you. He was an Olympic downhill skier who joined the Alpine Parachute Regiment. The Monte Cervino is Italy's equivalent of Delta Force."

"Okay, Roberto, what made you decide to join the army?"

"Italian men have a two-year military obligation, and, since I love to ski, after university I decided to join the Alpini so I could continue skiing."

"I see, and you and Mary Jo met each other in Bosnia?"

"Si. I commanded the NATO liaison unit assigned to work with the Dutch peacekeepers. There were four of us: Mary Jo, a French captain, a German lieutenant, and me. The Dutch commander, Lt. Col. Karremans, was less than delighted to have us along but allowed me to roam about freely. Shortly after our arrival, the valley was empowered with Serbian units under the command of General Ratko Mladic. There were several clashes between the Serbs and the Dutch — casualties on both sides — until the Serbs managed to take Srebrenica in July and the Dutch handed over control of the safe zone to the Serbs."

Roberto continued: "The Muslim refugees were left to the mercy of Mladic, and the Dutch began to withdraw from the valley. The four of us in the liaison unit were preparing to leave, as well, when a member of the Bosnian self-defense forces came to our office. He said that all of the Muslim men were being rounded up and moved to a location in the hills outside of town to be executed."

"Did you believe him?"

"Not at first, but Mary Jo and I decided that we had to investigate the claim. I explained to the team that we would be acting entirely on our own, and the Frenchman and the German declined to join us. Mary Jo and I loaded up a radio, a video camera, and our personal weapons and accompanied the man to a ridge overlooking a small clearing filled with men and boys. While we watched, the Serbian army began slaughtering them with machine guns and heavy weapons fire. Even tanks were used, and we had to watch helplessly. We did manage to get some video footage before we were spotted. The first burst of fire caught me in my left leg and killed the guy who was with us. Mary Jo pulled me across her shoulders and carried me over the ridge top. We knew that it wouldn't be long before the Serbs came for us, and Mary Jo decided to call back to the U.S. Command to ask for help. She spoke to an officer serving with a Navy SEAL team aboard a U.S. Aircraft Carrier in the Adriatic. He got our location and asked if we could withdraw to a landing zone about a klick to the west, and Mary Jo agreed."

Roberto continued, "I was unable to walk, and Mary Jo had to carry me while fighting a rearguard action to hold off the Serbs. I passed out before we got to the LZ, and I'll let Mary Jo tell you the rest."

Mary Jo sat quietly for a moment and then said, "I was half carrying and half dragging Roberto, along with both of our weapons and ammo plus the dead Bosnian's AK-47. I made it to a small knoll within sight of the LZ, when I had to stop and dig in. The Serbs realized that there were witnesses to their ethnic cleansing and sent a reinforced company to take us out. I managed to hold them off at first, but, soon, they were bringing up tanks and APCs. They were determined to wipe us out, and, just as I thought the jig was up, a flight of Navy A-4 Skyhawks came roaring in and hit the tanks and APCs. I pulled Roberto across my back and headed to the LZ, just as four Apache gunships hit the Serbian infantry. A Sea Stallion landed, and a SEAL team pulled us in and took off for the carrier."

Mary Jo finished by saying, "Roberto was treated for his injuries and airlifted to Rome, while I was debriefed. The video we shot was pretty damning and later proved instrumental in Mladic's trial at the Hague. The French admiral commanding the NATO task force sacked the U.S. admiral who approved our rescue, and the whole business was classified and swept under the rug."

Carlo thought for a moment and then said, "I was still with the agency and saw that video, and — you're right — it left no doubt about what happened. I had no idea where the footage came from. So we decided the whole thing never happened, and you got no commendation?"

"Yeah, pretty much, but the Italians took a different view and probably overdid the medal thing."

Roberto broke in and said, "I wholly disagree. Not only did Mary Jo save my life, but she also made sure that the evidence of the Serb atrocities made it back. My government was appreciative of both actions."

Carlo said, "Well, as Paul Harvey used to say…now I know the rest of the story."

Roberto began to unpin the map, and Mary Jo gathered the photos and plans. The three of them headed to the front of the restaurant, and, after Cosimo called for their vehicles, Roberto shook Carlo's hand and hugged Mary Jo goodnight.

As Carlo drove toward his home, he turned and said, "I'm glad I asked about Bosnia. Now I understand the close relationship between you and Roberto."

Mary Jo smiled and said, "I'm glad, as well; I want you to understand as much as possible about what drives me because, on Sunday night, my life will be in your hands."

NINETEEN

AFTER A QUICK BREAKFAST on Saturday morning, Carlo and Mary Jo drove back to the flying club at Urbe. When they reached the club's hangar, they saw the X-14 sitting on the tarmac, with the mechanic working on the VTO system. When they walked up, the mechanic wiped his hands and said in broken English, "Buongiorno. The little helicopter is almost ready."

"Grazie, Gino," Carlo replied. "We'll grab a cup of coffee. Just let me know when you're done."

Carlo and Mary Jo walked to the small office in the front of the club hangar and found a handsome lady with salt and pepper hair sitting behind the counter. Carlo smiled and said, "Good morning, Tess. You're out early."

"Si, I want to catch the early-morning thermals."

Carlo walked around the counter and poured two cups of coffee before saying, "Mary Jo, this is Tess Digorni, one of Italy's leading aerospace engineers. Tess, this is my friend Mary Jo Thibodaux. Mary Jo is getting checked out on the little helicopter you've seen me flying."

Tess Digorni looked Mary Jo up and down and then said, "You must be very special to be allowed to fly the X-14. Did you and Carlo work for the same agency?"

Mary Jo's red flags began to wave, and she replied, "No, Carlo worked for the U.S. State Department as a trade attaché while I was stationed in Rome as an army officer. I live in the U.S. now and came for a visit."

A wide smirk creased Tess's tanned face, and she replied, "Miss Thibodaux, in my work I have a very high-security clearance, and I know what Carlo did when he was with the CIA. I'm willing to bet you once held a post in the 902nd. We are all on the same side."

Mary Jo looked at Carlo and arched her eyebrow. Carlo grinned and said, "As Tess said, she has the highest clearance, and she and I have worked together in the past. As far as she's concerned, we were never out here this morning, right Tess?"

"My lips are sealed, but I do want to watch you work with the X-14. I've been dying to see the new VTO system at work. I want to try something similar with a small glider."

Mary Jo looked at the woman and said, "From what you've said, I assume your work is in powerless flight."

"Not all together, but gliders are my first love. When I finished university in Bologna, I did my post-doctoral work in the U.S."

Mary Jo's interest perked up, and she asked, "Where in the U.S.? I have a Civil Engineering degree from Louisiana State University."

"I spent two years researching alongside Dr. August Raspet at Mississippi State University. Dr. Raspet was working on power-assisted lift enhancement for fixed-wing aircraft, especially those used in applying chemicals to crops. We did most of our design work on gliders."

"I'm very familiar with Mississippi State. I ran track at LSU, and we competed against them every year. In fact, I was in Starkville just last fall. My engineering firm is working on a project the university developed in the energy field," Mary Jo replied.

A big grin crossed Tess's face, and she said, "If you went to LSU, then we have something in common: 'Go to Hell, Ole Miss!'"

"Right on," Mary Jo replied. "Go to Hell, Ole Miss!"

Gino, the mechanic, came to the office door and said, "The helicopter, she is ready to fly."

"Grazie, Gino. We'll be right out."

Gino smiled and said, "Prego, and how is the beautiful professor this morning?"

"Very well, Gino…thank you for asking," Tess replied.

Mary Jo smiled at Tess and said, "Seems you have an admirer."

"Yes, Gino has a crush on me, and he is relentless. I try to be kind because he is one of the best aircraft mechanics I've ever seen. Now, let's go see if the VTO system works on the X-14."

Gino had wheeled a large air compressor next to the X-14 and was busy filling the canisters. When he was done, he rolled the compressor to the side, swept his hands across the little ship, and said, "She is ready to fly."

Carlo and the two women walked over and did a visual inspection of the system while Gino stood wiping his hands. Carlo turned to him and said, "Well done. Everything seems to be in working condition. I'll give her a test flight."

Carlo climbed aboard the ship and strapped in. He looked over at Tess and asked, "Tess, do you have a stopwatch?"

"Yes. What can I do?"

"The time it normally takes to start the motor and gain enough lift to clear the ground is 15 seconds, and to gain forward thrust is 25 seconds. With the VTO package, I should be able to launch as soon as the blades are rotating, clear the ground in five seconds, and be moving forward in 15. Would you time me, please?"

"Sure, let me know when to start."

Carlo started the motor, and the rotor blades began a slow rotation. When he hit the VTO switch, there was the sound of compressed air escaping, and the X-14 rose slowly from the tarmac. It reached a height of several hundred feet; the nose dropped; and the ship began to move forward. Tess checked her stopwatch, and it showed 13 seconds.

Carlo circled the field and set the ship back in its takeoff position. He climbed out and said, "Well, Tess, how'd it do?"

"You gained forward thrust in 13 seconds. Is a savings of 12 seconds worth the hassle?"

"It is if someone is shooting at you," Carlo retorted.

Tess smiled and said, "Yes, well, I can see that. When does Mary Jo get to try it out?"

"She's ready to go. Mary Jo, it's not much different from a normal takeoff. You just do it quicker. Take it easy and it'll feel normal."

Gino wheeled the air compressor over and refilled the canisters while Mary Jo strapped into the pilot's seat. When all was ready, she gave the thumbs-up and started the rotors while hitting the VTO button. Mary Jo rose rapidly to several hundred feet, dropped the nose, and moved forward. She brought the ship back in and looked at Tess.

"Sixteen seconds," Tess reported. "Not bad."

Mary Jo made three more test flights and then suggested that the most likely thing that could go wrong would be the loss of thrust before the rotors gained full efficiency. Carlo agreed, and they decided to try a flight and cut the canisters off before full stability had been achieved.

Mary Jo fired the canisters and then hit the "off" switch after rising to less than a hundred feet. The X-14 lost lift, and she had to make an emergency landing. The rotors had gained enough lift to allow a safe landing, but Mary Jo couldn't keep the craft aloft. She climbed out and said, "A similar situation coming off a four-story building would add over 50 feet of altitude. I believe I could regain flight before hitting the ground."

"I agree," Carlo replied. "But let's hope we don't have to face that."

Tess asked, "If you're done with the testing, I'd like to go up while I still have the thermals. Do you need the stopwatch?"

"No, I think we're done for the morning. Have a good flight and I'll see you later."

Tess returned to the office, and Carlo asked Gino to put the X-14 back in the hangar. He and Mary Jo made sure everything was stored properly and then walked to Carlo's pickup.

Mary Jo said, "You know…I'd like to take a look at the castle from the air and have one last meeting with Giovanni before I go in tomorrow night. Why don't we take my plane and go to Corsica?"

"Okay, we need to stay busy, so that sounds good. Give Giovanni a call and make sure he can see us."

Mary Jo used her cell to call Giovanni, and he said that she and Carlo would be met at the airport when they arrived. Mary Jo had the Citation moved to the tarmac, and, after the preflight inspection, she suggested that Carlo do the flying.

Carlo grinned and said, "You know how much I love flying this baby, don't you?"

"Yeah, you really ought to think about buying a Mustang. It has the range to fly all over Europe."

"You know? I really should. What does a Mustang cost these days?"

"I just traded mine to a dealer in Paris, and I got a credit for $1,800,000. I'm sure you could pick one up for that or less."

"Well, it's certainly something to think about."

Carlo took off from Urbe and turned west to overfly the castle and Aglientu, the site of tomorrow's launch. He made one pass at 3,000 feet, with an airspeed of barely 150 MPH. Anyone seeing the plane would assume they were in the landing pattern for La Maddalena's airport. Once they cleared the northern tip of Sardinia, Carlo set a course for Ajaccio.

Antonio met Carlo and Mary Jo and drove them straight to the villa. Giovanni and Jeppe were waiting by the front door, and all went directly to the Don's conference room.

When everyone had a coffee or tea, they all took seats, and Giovanni said, "I'm glad the two of you decided to come this afternoon. I want to hear all about the test flights in the X-14."

Carlo spoke up and said, "Everything went perfectly. Mary Jo is a natural pilot with hundreds of helicopter hours, and she can fly the X-14 as well as anyone. The VTO packages worked as advertised, and Mary Jo shouldn't have a problem tomorrow night if the weather continues to hold. As of an hour ago, we are still expecting clear skies with a quarter moon. The temperature will be frosty, but that really works in our favor."

Mary Jo asked, "Do we have any new intelligence from the castle?"

Giovanni said, "No, and we won't unless there's an emergency. The maid must be very careful and has been instructed to contact us only if there's a problem. Our sources in the village report that provisions are being delivered for a large family dinner after Mass."

"Do you have all the plans in place to hit the Castellanos's commercial holdings during my visit to the castle?"

"Yes. Roberto tells us that you will be in place by the middle of the afternoon tomorrow and that you'll launch the X-14 at 2:00 a.m. We'll hit them once we know that you have safely returned to Aglientu."

Mary Jo thought, "For some reason, I don't want to return to Rome tonight. I can't explain it, but I really don't want to."

Mary Jo looked at Carlo and asked, "Would you have a problem with spending the night here and flying back to Urbe tomorrow in time to meet our helicopter transport?"

Carlo said, "No, all of the gear we need is in my truck at Urbe, and we wouldn't need to go to my home for anything. If Giovanni can lend me a heavy jacket, I'll be fine with staying here tonight."

Giovanni replied, "There's no problem on our end. All of Mary Jo's gear is still in her room, and I've got plenty of jackets and other cold-weather gear. So just plan to spend the night here."

The group discussed the plans for a while; then, Mary Jo asked to be excused. She went to her room, washed her face, took a fleece-lined flight jacket out of the closet, tied a scarf over her hair, and went outside. She walked through the covered walkway to the chapel. Once inside, she dipped her fingers in the font, made the sign of the Cross, and knelt at a prie-dieu. She stood and lit a red candle for Maurice, and then she pulled a rosary from her jacket pocket and began to pray. She made the sign of the Cross and stepped out of the chapel into the crisp December air. The sky was a deep azure blue, and the trees still held the last leaves of autumn. She walked across the chapel grounds to Maurice's gravesite, where the fresh dirt was still mounded over his grave and no headstone had been placed.

Mary Jo stood quietly thinking about Maurice and how much she loved and missed him. While she was standing by the grave, Carlo came looking for her, but, when he saw where she was, he stepped back behind the chapel wall, realizing that lunch could wait until she returned to the villa.

Mary Jo's mind swirled with memories of Maurice until, finally, they were replaced by a calm resolve. She knew then that she was fully prepared to avenge his death. She returned to the villa and found a buffet lunch being served in the small dining room. Suddenly, Mary Jo realized that she was extremely hungry. She prepared a heaping plate and then joined Carlo and Giovanni at the dining table. Carlo noticed that her demeanor had changed. She had been pensive and quiet before, but now she was smiling and almost glowing. Whatever had been bothering her had been put to rest, and she was like the old Mary Jo. Carlo knew now that she'd handle tomorrow's work with her usual efficiency.

Giovanni, too, noticed the change and said, "I know that before I faced a combat situation, I found it helpful to get my mind off of it once all the planning had been done."

Mary Jo looked at Giovanni and said, "I agree. It's easy to overthink the operation and peak too early. I used to find a movie on the eve of action."

"Well, I don't know about a movie, but the children in Ajaccio will have a Christmas pageant this evening. They'll reenact the Nativity, and there will be carols and costumes. We usually try to take our children. It's over in time for dinner. Would you and Carlo like to go with us?"

Mary Jo looked at Carlo, who nodded yes, and she said, "That sounds like just what I need. What time should we be ready?"

"It starts at 6:00 and lasts about an hour and a half. It's held outside on the piazza. There'll be seating provided, but we'll need to dress warmly and bring some blankets."

"Count us in. I think I'll take a long walk up into the hills after lunch, but I'll be back in time to go."

Carlo asked, "Would you care for some company?"

"Sure, that'll be great, if you think you can keep up with me."

"I'm in pretty good shape, but let's not make this a competition. It's a beautiful winter day, and the hills will still retain some of their fall splendor."

"Okay, I'll keep the pace slow enough for you to manage."

The two exited the grounds of the villa through a gate at the back of the property and found a well-used walking path that led up the hill behind the villa. The trail zigzagged back and forth across the face of the hill, and the ascent was gradual. They had just made one of the switchbacks when Mary Jo dropped to her knees and signaled Carlo that there was something wrong. He crawled up and knelt next to her. She whispered, "There are two men tracking us, and they're armed."

Carlo whispered, "Yeah, I saw them just after we started up the trail, but there are three of them, not just two, and I wanted to see how long it'd take you to spot them."

"Damn, Carlo — why didn't you say something? Now we're a mile away, and they've got us pinned down. Are you carrying?"

"Oh, yeah. I've got my Colt .45. How about you?"

"I've got my razor, and that's all I'll need if I can get close enough. You cover my back, and I'll take them out."

"Well, I suppose that would work, but I'm thinking it's really gonna piss Giovanni off if we kill three of his guys."

"Oh, shit! I should have known he'd send escorts. I can't believe you didn't give me a heads-up."

"Far be it from me to advise Shiva on such things, but the thought crosses my mind that you may be losing your edge. I think we should just stick to the original plan and enjoy our walk in the woods."

Mary Jo mumbled something under her breath and headed up the hill. When she and Carlo reached the crest, they paused and admired Ajaccio in the distance, bathed in the soft light of a winter afternoon. The sea sparkled and gleamed in the distance, and they could see the white sails of boats in the bay.

Finally, Mary Jo said, "It's getting late; we better start back."

Carlo agreed, and they began the descent to the villa. Mary Jo noticed that Giovanni's men kept them in a protective pocket until they reached the gate into the villa grounds; then, they just disappeared.

When the hikers entered the back door of the villa, they were met by Antonio, who said, "It is 4:30, and we will leave for town in 30 minutes."

Carlo and Mary Jo went to their rooms to freshen up, and then they joined the rest of the family on the front steps. The whole Capriati family stood waiting as a caravan of SUVs and sedans loaded up. Mary Jo and Carlo joined Giovanni, Nicole, and their boys in one of the SUVs, and soon the whole motorcade was pulling through the villa gate.

Mary Jo tensed as they neared the ambush site, and she noticed armed men, with rifles slung across their shoulders, standing in the fading sunlight. Giovanni was taking no chances. Mary Jo had thought of the possibility of the Castellanos's taking advantage of the holidays to strike again. She thought, "Why not? We're planning to do it."

The caravan pulled into a side street near the piazza and began unloading. Antonio rounded everyone up and led them to a reserved section of bleacher seats with a perfect view of the stage. When they were all seated and snuggled into their blankets, Mary Jo turned to Giovanni and said, "Being Don has some advantages, doesn't it? These are the best seats on the piazza."

"Yes, there is certain respect extended to the Don, and his generous support of the pageant doesn't hurt either."

Soon, the sun faded behind the hills to the east, and a candlelit procession emerged from the church on the other side of the square. The choir began to sing "O Holy Night" as the procession moved to the stage. The carols and pageant lasted for almost an hour, and, when it was done, Antonio loaded everyone back into the cars. By 7:00, they were all back at the villa drinking hot chocolate or something a little stronger.

The main dining room was set up for the adults, and the children were placed in the smaller room. Dinner was served, followed by Zuppa Inglese, layers of cake and fruit in a huge glass bowl, similar to an English trifle. After dessert, the children were sent to bed, and the adults gathered in the living room. A fire crackled in the large fireplace, and a 15-foot Christmas tree stood in the corner.

Brandy and other after-dinner liqueurs were served, and Nicole sat at the grand piano playing Christmas carols while everyone visited. Mary Jo was standing by the fireplace, warming her backside, when Anna Maria, Maurice's oldest sister, came and stood beside her. They listened to Nicole's playing until she took a break, and then Anna Marie said, "Mary Jo, you're now a part of this family, and we all know that you plan to avenge Maurice. Every one of us would like to go with you and help you kill the murdering bastard. Our hopes and prayers will be with you tomorrow. Please, return safely to your family home."

Mary Jo felt a lump in her throat and didn't reply for a moment. Then, she said, "Anna Marie, you have no idea how much that means to me. All of the family will be with me tomorrow, and I can promise you that Giuseppe Castellano will not live to see Christmas morning."

Anna Marie said, "That will be the best Christmas present we could receive." She hugged Mary Jo and rejoined her husband on the sofa.

Mary Jo swept the room with her eyes, taking one last long look at Maurice's family, and then she decided that she had better try to get a good night's sleep. She would need to be on top of her game tomorrow night.

TWENTY

MARY JO AWOKE just after sunrise and realized that it was Christmas Eve. She did her morning ritual and dressed in a clean flight suit. When she walked into the kitchen, Jeppe was sitting at the table holding a hot mug of tea. He smiled when she came in and said, "Mary Jo, please, come and join me. Cook is just taking some fresh croissants from the oven."

Mary Jo could smell the aroma of the baking croissants, along with the smell of freshly brewing coffee. She sat down and said, "Jeppe, you're up early this morning."

"Sadly, it's my usual hour. When you reach my age, you are lucky if the sun is up when you are. You are young enough to sleep till ten o'clock. Are you troubled by tonight?"

"Not really. In fact, I've pretty much made my mental preparations, and I'm ready to get on with it."

"When I was a younger man, I had skills much like your own. I could slip in, cut a throat, and be gone by the time the victim realized he was dead. I can remember the sense of everything being in slow motion when it came time for action."

"I know exactly what you mean. All of the senses are intensified, colors brighter, sounds and smells more distinct. That's when the animal brain takes over, and you can sense danger before it appears," Mary Jo added.

"Indeed, once the planning is done, then one has to improvise. The plan rarely works as drawn up. I always viewed this as an opportunity, not a problem. Some of my best work happened when I was improvising."

Mary Jo sat quietly thinking about what Jeppe was telling her. She realized it was his way of giving her a pep talk. She smiled and said, "Jeppe, thank you for your concern, but this won't be my first rodeo, and I'm at ease with it."

"Well, as they say in theatre, break a leg. I'm about to take a ride around the villa grounds. Want to go along?"

"Sure…let me have one of these hot croissants and refill my coffee mug."

Jeppe led Mary Jo to the former stables behind the villa and pressed an opener to raise the garage doors. There, in a space that once housed 50 or more horses and their various carriages and carts, sat all of the estate's motor vehicles. Jeppe flipped on the lights and walked over to a green John Deere Gator. Jeppe climbed into the driver's seat, and Mary Jo got in the passenger side. He cranked the engine, and they rolled into the crisp winter morning, just as full daylight lit the countryside.

Jeppe took the path to the back of the estate near the gate that she and Carlo had used on their walk. Jeppe turned to the left and drove parallel to the brick wall, carefully checking for signs of any disturbance. Mary Jo realized that he, too, was worried about a preemptive strike by the Castellanos.

It took almost 20 minutes to make the entire circuit around the fence, and, when the two returned to the garage, Jeppe said, "Thank you for coming with me. I wanted another set of eyes. We are close to dealing the Castellanos a devastating blow, and it would be easy to get complacent. I didn't see anything to indicate a problem, did you?"

"No, all seemed to be fine, but I'd keep vigilant if I were you. Giuseppe Castellano is no fool, and he has proven he can hit us on our turf."

"We are doing everything we can to prevent a surprise attack. Giovanni has sent out foot patrols in all directions, and, so far, they've found no sign of trouble. Why don't we join everyone for breakfast?"

"I thought we'd eaten breakfast."

"Don't be silly. A couple of croissants cannot be considered breakfast. There's a buffet laid out in the small dining room. It should be filling up about now."

When the two walked into the dining room, Mary Jo saw Carlo sitting next to Giovanni in deep conversation. When they saw Mary Jo, they broke off their talk and began eating their breakfast. Mary Jo filled a plate at the buffet and joined them. She took a seat and said, "I'm not interrupting anything, am I?"

"Not at all," Giovanni replied. "We were just going over the last-minute details."

"I assume all is in order then?"

"As far as one can make plans it is. There is always the unanticipated consequences of one's actions that can throw a monkey wrench into the gears," Giovanni said.

"I've learned over the years that to worry about that is pointless. What's going to happen is going to happen. It's how you handle the consequences that decides success or failure. I have pretty good instincts for the unexpected, and I have always been able to, as Jeppe just suggested, turn a problem into an opportunity."

"My, we're confident this morning," Carlo commented.

"We all know the definition of confidence. It's that warm, fuzzy feeling you get just before you screw up. I'm not confident so much as prepared. Big difference."

"Touché," Carlo replied.

Giovanni decided to change the subject and said, "Mary Jo, what are your plans after tonight is over?"

"I haven't given it much thought, but I suppose I'll return to Mobile and spend some time adjusting to the reality of Maurice's death. My engineering firm is swamped with work, and I'll need to get a handle on where we are."

"I hope you know that you'll always have a home here on Corsica with your family. I know you will have to stop in Paris and pick up your clothes, so feel free to use the apartment for as long as you like."

"Thanks, I'll sleep there for the evening before I head out over the Atlantic, but I think I'll just stay the one night."

They all chatted for a while until Mary Jo said, "Carlo, it's time for us to return to Rome. We don't want to keep Roberto's guys waiting."

"I'm ready when you are," Carlo replied.

Giovanni said that Antonio would take them to the airport. Then, Giovanni stood and said, "I'll say goodbye now. I'm going to run some last-minute errands, so I won't be here when you leave."

Mary Jo stood, hugged him, and replied, "Until we meet tomorrow morning again…Merry Christmas."

"Merry Christmas," Giovanni said. He then shook Carlo's hand and left the dining room.

Mary Jo looked at Carlo and said, "Okay, cowboy, let's round 'em up and head 'em out."

Carlo flew the short hop back to Urbe and taxied to the private aviation terminal. Mary Jo gave instructions to the ground crew, and they walked to Carlo's pickup. On the way to the flying club, she handed Carlo a folded piece of paper and said, "This is just in case things don't work out tonight."

Carlo opened the note and read: "To whom it may concern, I, Mary Jo Thibodaux, do bequeath my Cessna Citation CJ4, Tail Number N98476, to my good friend Carlo Baggetti. Mary Jo Thibodaux, December 24, 2011."

Carlo refolded the note, handed it back to her, and said, "We won't be needing this."

"Probably not, but, just in the event we do, I've sent a copy to Emile Dalhousie to be attached to my will. It's a done deal, and you might as well accept it. She's all yours if I die before you do."

Carlo didn't reply, and soon they pulled up to the flying club hangar. Carlo parked by the back door and pressed the remote to open it. When the door opened, Gino walked out and said, "I have checked the little bird out, and all is ready. The battery has a full charge, and the VTO canisters are fully loaded. She is ready to fly."

"Grazie, Gino. If you will help get it loaded on my truck, we'll leave and let you get back to your day job."

The three of them loaded the X-14 into the bed of the pickup and secured it with bungee cords. Then, Carlo and Mary Jo drove out of the civilian airport and took a narrow road that led to the military side. They approached a guardhouse with an MP standing outside. When they stopped and handed the MP the note from Roberto, he said, "You will follow this road until it intersects with Gentile Road; then, turn left. You will come to a deserted building, and you are to wait there. You will be picked up at 1400 hours."

Carlo thanked the MP and followed the directions until they were stopped in front of an old WWII Quonset hut. There were no vehicles to be seen, and the front door of the hut clattered back and forth with the wind. Carlo looked at Mary Jo and said, "I guess we wait until our ride shows up."

Just before two, Carlo and Mary Jo heard the rotating blades of an extremely large helicopter coming in for a landing in the parking lot. An Augusta A-101 transport helicopter landed in a cloud of dust. The pilot shut the single rotor down, and the sound of powerful turbines began to fade. An officer dressed in battle fatigues descended from the interior and jogged toward them. He extended his hand and said, "Signor Baggetti?"

Carlo shook the officer's hand and replied, "Si, and this is Lieutenant Colonel Thibodaux. We're to be your guests this afternoon."

The officer didn't offer his name but said, "Is that the little helicopter in the bed of that truck?"

"Si, it is," Carlo said.

"Shall we load it aboard?"

Carlo drove the truck around to the tail of the helicopter, and a loading ramp opened. Four men, all wearing battle dress, came down the ramp and helped Carlo bring the X-14 inside. Mary Jo took her duffel bag from the truck, slung it over her shoulders, and followed Carlo up the ramp. The four men and the officer took seats along the starboard side, and Carlo and Mary Jo sat opposite them.

The turbines began to howl, and soon the ship dipped its nose and headed to Sardinia. When the island was in sight, the pilot overflew the strait separating Sardinia from Corsica and then flew out over the sea before reversing his course. He set the big ship down on the flat top of a large hill with some deserted buildings. When the blades quit turning, the ramp came down, and the four men began unloading the X-14, along with a stack of wooden crates.

The helicopter crew began to tie down the ship, and the officer came over and said, "Colonel Thibodaux, I am Lieutenant Max Von Thalen of the French Foreign Legion, and I have Sergeant Major Klause with me. He and my men will assist with the helicopter and the ship's rangefinder; then, we must move into position before nightfall."

Mary Jo turned to Carlo and said, "Is there something you need to share with me?"

"Yes, Giovanni and I agreed not to tell you while you had a chance to screw things up. Lieutenant Von Thalen and his men served with Maurice in the Legion, and they volunteered to support our mission tonight. You will never see them unless something goes wrong and you need them. They will be in place just outside the walls of the castle."

Mary Jo decided to accept the reality of the situation and stifled her natural instinct to raise hell about it. Instead, she extended her hand and said, "I'm glad to meet you, Lieutenant, and I appreciate your help. I assume you have been fully briefed on tonight's mission?"

"Yes, I believe we have. We will be stationed just outside the walls directly on the path of your flight in and out. We will act only if you have a problem."

"How will you know that I need help?"

"Monsieur Baggetti will be on our radio net, watching with the naval rangefinder."

"Then I guess we'd better get it unpacked and set up," Mary Jo replied.

While Carlo and Mary Jo began to ready the X-14, the Legionnaires set up the rangefinder on its tripod. The sun began to approach the western horizon, and the wind picked up, with a definite chill. Once the rangefinder was ready, Carlo focused it on the castle roof and said, "Come take a look. I feel like I'm on the roof."

Mary Jo peered into the rangefinder and made a slight adjustment. Carlo was right — she could see details that weren't visible in the aerial photos. She did a complete circuit of the rooftop and said, "Damn, this thing is amazing. I can see the brands of the heating and air-conditioning equipment. You won't have a problem covering my back."

"We've decided not to intervene if you don't return to the rooftop. We'll assume that you have been discovered and are either dead or are a captive. If the helicopter is undiscovered, we'll attempt a rooftop mission to recover it."

"Let's hope you don't have to deal with any of that."

Lieutenant Von Thalen gathered his men, wished Mary Jo good luck, and trooped down toward the castle with his fellow soldiers. Night came all at once, and the temperature dropped below freezing. Carlo suggested that they wait in the helicopter until time to launch the X-14. At least it was out of the wind.

Mary Jo looked around the interior of the A-101 and noticed a serial tag indicating a manufacturing date of 1964. She pointed it out to Carlo and said, "Do you realize that this bird is older than you and I?"

"Can't say that I have given it any thought."

"Well, there must be a story, and I'm going to ask the crew about it."

Mary Jo stood and knocked on the cabin door, which was opened by a young man in a flight suit. He wore no insignia or rank. She smiled and said, "Pardon me, but I noticed that this ship was built in 1964, and it seems to be in pristine condition. How can that be?"

The young man smiled and replied, "Si, she is getting on in age. She is a one of a kind. This is the only one in existence."

"You mean that all of her sister ships have been scrapped?"

"No, there are no sister ships. This is the preproduction prototype that never went into production. We keep her in flying condition at the Augusta company museum. Today, she is on loan to the Air Force; she is the only helicopter large enough to handle all of the gear and people."

"You know, I was sort of surprised to see the single rotor on a ship this big. I would have expected multiple rotors."

"Si, all of the modern ships have them, but she still can outperform many of the new ships. You seem to be familiar with helicopters. Do you fly?"

"I do. I own a Bell Jet Ranger and a Cessna Citation. If we had the time, I'd try to beg a shot at this old bird."

"Maybe sometime you can visit our museum at Cascina Costa. With your connections, I suspect you could wrangle a flight. I'd like to try out the little machine we just unloaded."

"I might be able to arrange that. Let's talk when I return."

Mary Jo closed the cabin door and returned to her seat. Carlo was napping, and she let him snooze. When her watch showed 1:30, Mary Jo nudged him and suggested that they get ready to launch. Carlo went to the rangefinder and turned on the night-vision device, and he could see the target gleaming in dull green. He hit the radio's "Send" button twice, and there was a return of two clicks, indicating that Von Thalen's team was in position and all was quiet.

Mary Jo changed into her all-black jumpsuit and jacket. She blackened her face and pulled the ski mask into place. She put the helmet on and tested her radio. Carlo reported that all was working properly. She strapped her equipment bag to the frame of the helicopter and made sure her Colt .45 and her razor were in place. She turned to Carlo and said, "I'm as ready as I'll ever be. Wish me luck."

Carlo reached out, wrapped Mary Jo in a bear hug, and said, "You be damn sure you come back in one piece. We still have some unfinished business to discuss."

"You can count on it," Mary Jo replied. She snapped the visor of her helmet into place and boarded the X-14. Pulling the safety straps tight, Mary Jo flipped on the motor and gently lifted into the dark winter sky.

TWENTY-ONE

MARY JO GUIDED THE X-14 to about 500 feet before dipping the nose and heading toward the castle. The winter cold crept into her flight suit, despite the insulated underwear and down jacket. The sky was filled with millions of stars, and her night vision was so sharp that she could quickly make out features on the ground.

Maneuvering the X-14 to the south, Mary Jo lined up the castle for a dead-on approach to the north. There were lights scattered over several floors of the building, but she couldn't see the east side where the Don's suite was located. She hovered over the castle and slowly began her descent. Her eyes swept back and forth across the rooftop, and all appeared quiet. She set the little helicopter down in the open space that she had seen on the aerial photos and then cut the power. The rotors spun to a stop, and she unstrapped and gingerly climbed onto the roof. She pulled her equipment bag over her shoulder and stood perfectly still until she tuned into the rhythm of her surroundings. She could see the HVAC equipment, along with the door leading to the interior. She crept up to the door and tried the doorknob. It was locked.

Mary Jo looked carefully at the lock, reached into the bag, and removed a small meter that was sensitive to electrical current. She held it to the doorjamb and watched the dial as she moved the meter over the full perimeter of the door. The meter registered current at two points, indicating that the door was alarmed. She decided to try to pick the lock, just in case she needed a quick escape route. She removed a set of lock picks, and, as quietly as possible, she worked two of the picks into the lock and felt the tumblers engage. The lock clicked open. She replaced the picks and removed the lock; then, she moved to the trapdoor leading to the equipment room and did the same test.

There was no current registered, so Mary Jo lifted the door. It made a small creak as she pulled it open, and she paused and held it ajar while listening attentively. Once she was sure that no one had heard the noise, she slipped into the dark equipment room. She gently lowered the door back in place and stood quietly in the dark until she had regained her night vision.

One of the heater units switched on, and Mary Jo used its low-level noise to move across the room to the door leading into the central part of the castle. She paused while reviewing the layout of the castle in her head and knew that she would enter a hallway on the opposite side of the castle from the Don's suite. She ran the meter around the doorjamb and found there was no current, so she carefully cracked the door about an inch. She removed a small dental mirror from the bag and poked it into the hallway. Searching in both directions, Mary Jo saw no sign of life. There was a dim light in the hall coming from a night-light in a wall socket. She eased along the wall, pulled the light from its socket, and unscrewed the bulb. The hallway became totally dark, and she replaced the deadlight in the socket. She glanced at the radium dial on her watch and saw 2:13. She was 13 minutes into the mission.

Mary Jo crept along the hallway until she came to a corner with another night-light glowing. She removed the bulb and moved to the next turn. Using the dental mirror, she checked around the corner, and all was clear. Soon, Mary Jo stood next to the suite door, where, again, she used the meter to check for current. There was none.

Before trying the doorknob, Mary Jo placed a small flexible cable under the door and swept the room with the tiny camera embedded in the cable. The vision-enhancing camera showed the living room of the Don's suite in bright green light, like the images from night-vision goggles. On the wall to her right, Mary Jo could see a fireplace with glowing embers. There was a draped window on the far wall and the door to the bedroom on the left. She withdrew the cable and then tried the door. It was locked, so she quietly used the key from the maid. The doorknob made a click, and the door unlocked. Gently, Mary Jo pushed it open, stepped into the room, and quietly eased the door closed. She stood for a full minute, listening for sounds of life and getting the exact layout of the furniture fixed in her mind. Then, she moved to the bedroom door, which stood ajar.

The bedroom had no light, and the thick drapes were closed. Mary Jo could see the outline of the big four-poster bed but couldn't see if there was anyone in it. She took her night-vision goggles from her bag, placed them on her head, and turned the switch on. The room was bathed in the eerie green glow, and she could see a pile of sheets and blankets, but no one in the bed.

There was the sound of a toilet flushing, and the bathroom door opened, allowing light to pour into the bedroom. The bright light from the bathroom flashed, and Mary Jo snatched the goggles off just as a naked Giuseppe Castellano came walking into the room. Mary Jo was bathed in the yellow light from the bathroom, and she and Castellano saw each other at the same moment.

Castellano reacted first and dove across the bed, reaching for the night table — but, before he could find his weapon, Mary Jo leaped on his back. She grabbed his long, black hair, pulled his head back, and slit his throat from ear to ear.

Arterial blood gushed against the headboard and splattered the wall. In his death struggle, Castellano knocked the bedside phone to the floor, and Mary Jo could hear a dial tone.

Mary Jo made herself stop to take stock of the situation. She checked her watch. It was 2:28. Carefully, she wiped the razor on the bedsheet and returned it to her pocket. She found the goggles and placed them in her bag. She was reaching for the telephone when she heard an agitated voice say, "Don Giuseppe, is anything wrong?"

Mary Jo turned and left the bedroom just as an alarm began to sound. She raced to the door leading to the roof, figuring its signal would be redundant, and stepped out onto the rooftop. The grounds were bathed in high-powered lights, and she could hear dogs barking frantically. She raced to the X-14 and hit the power switch while she was simultaneously strapping in. The rotor blades were just beginning to rotate when she hit the VTO button, and the ship rose with a gush of compressed air.

There is a point in the flight of a flushed pheasant when its vertical takeoff is switched to forward flight. The bird is nearly stationary at that exact point. Mary Jo was still rising when the rooftop went ablaze with lights, and two men burst through the door. They caught her at that crucial moment before she dipped the nose and started forward, and a burst of automatic rifle fire ripped into the rotor housing.

A blast of adrenaline pumped into Mary Jo's system, and everything went into slow motion. She flipped on the radio in her helmet and said, "Carlo, can you see what's happening?"

Before Carlo could answer, Mary Jo dipped the nose and pushed the rotors forward, just as the motor came apart above her head. The X-14 maintained its forward motion but began to lose altitude, and she made a quick calculation of her glide pattern, realizing that she would never make it over the castle wall. Once reconciled to crashing inside the wall, Mary

Jo began looking for a defensible landing site. She chose a line of trees and bushes against the back wall and guided the dying ship in that direction.

The helicopter dipped below the level of the roof, just as a high-powered searchlight started to probe, looking for Mary Jo. The rotors were now turning without power, and she had lost all lift. Mary Jo just managed to clear the top of the bushes and set down hard about 20 feet from the castle's outer wall. The landing fractured one of the steel skids, and Mary Jo hung in her harness at an angle. She hit the quick release and dropped to the ground.

Mary Jo could hear men shouting, dogs barking, and the scream of the castle's alarm shrieking in the predawn cold. She managed to drag the wrecked X-14 behind the hedges, and she heard Carlo on the radio calling her name. Mary Jo checked her position in relation to the castle and saw a group of lights forming up to begin a search for her. She keyed the mike and said, "How 'bout it, Carlo…do you see that?"

"Yeah, I know approximately your position, but I can no longer see you. I've sent a message to the Legion team. They should be headed your way."

"Well, they better get a move on. Half of Sardinia is gearing up to find me. I wish I'd thought to bring something a little heavier than Giovanni's .45. I can probably hold them off for a minute or two, but, with the dogs, they'll be on me quickly. I need to get busy — over and out."

Mary Jo took up a firing position just inside the tree line and waited for things to develop. She could see a group of men with dogs on leashes moving in her direction. Rather than reveal her exact location, she decided to hold her fire until they were closer and then take a few out before changing positions. Mary Jo hated to leave the X-14 behind, but there was nothing she could do about it now.

Mary Jo unslung her equipment bag and removed a small grappling hook attached to a length of nylon rope and stuck it in her jacket pocket. The men and dogs were now within pistol range, but she decided to leave the dog handlers alone and concentrate her fire on the others. She didn't need a pack of German Shepherds clawing at her. Mary Jo took careful aim and got off six shots before rolling to her left and scrambling further along the wall.

Three of the men fell in Mary Jo's first volley, and everyone else dropped to the ground. The bushes where she'd been when she fired were being shredded by automatic fire, and she could see three men begin a flanking maneuver, trying to cut off her movement along the wall. The men were well trained and started to fire and maneuver. It would only be minutes before she was faced with overwhelming firepower.

Mary Jo decided that it was time to leave and flung the little grappling hook over the wall, pulling the nylon rope tight. She scrambled over the top and dropped to the ground beside the wall. She tensed as her animal brain sensed danger. Before she could react, one of the Legionnaires reached out and touched her arm. "We'll take it from here," he whispered and handed her a topo map. He turned on a penlight and pointed out an area, about a kilometer away, marked in black crayon. He pointed north and said, "This is the emergency LZ for extraction. Go there and wait until we join you. Now that you're safe, our mission is to recover the helicopter. The big helicopter will pick us up there. If we're not there in 10 minutes, they'll leave without us."

"Bullshit! I'll stay with you while you try to recover the X-14. At least I'll give you one more gun."

The Legion officer saw that it would be useless to argue with her and handed her his Uzi and four clips of ammunition. Then, he disappeared into the night.

Mary Jo eased into the woods until she found a downed log and crouched behind it, eyeballing the wall. She keyed her mike and said, "Carlo, do you read?"

"Yes, are you safe?"

"For the time being. The Legion team is attempting to recover the X-14, and I'm covering their backs."

"I don't suppose you'd consider moving to the LZ?"

"No, I can't leave until these guys are with me."

"I figured. We're all packed and moving to the LZ. Let me know when you begin to pull out."

"10-4," Mary Jo answered and turned off the radio.

There was a long burst of automatic weapons fire, followed by a loud explosion. The fire continued in short controlled bursts and additional blasts. Mary Jo thought, "Damn, somebody has heavy weapons. I hope those guys can manage to get out before the Castellanos bring in the armor."

The firing began to die down to single shots as if someone was finishing off the wounded. Mary Jo had just about decided to withdraw to the LZ, when she saw five men running along the wall toward her. Four were carrying the X-14, and the officer signaled for her to join them. Mary Jo keyed her radio and said, "We're headed to the LZ."

"10-4," Carlo replied. "We'll meet you there."

It took less than 10 minutes to reach the LZ, with the four men taking turns with the X-14. The big Augusta was waiting in the clearing with its ramp down. The officer ordered the men to quickly load the X-14 and board the ship, while he and Mary Jo provided defensive cover. When the men were safely aboard, they sprinted up the ramp, and the pilot began to take off as the ramp was closing.

Carlo smiled when he saw Mary Jo and said, "That wasn't quite the exit we had planned."

Mary Jo removed her helmet, let her tresses fall to her shoulders, and then replied, "Yeah, it got a little hairy toward the end. I couldn't believe the Castellanos had heavy weapons."

Lieutenant Von Thalen laughed and said, "Oh, they didn't. You heard our RPGs. They decided to make a hasty retreat after a couple of rounds."

"I should have guessed," Mary Jo said. "Maurice once said that the Legion was like the Boy Scouts — always prepared. By the way, I'm delighted you guys showed up. This is the third time my butt's been saved by the Legion."

The lieutenant said, "Glad to be here. Maurice would have loved it."

Carlo touched Mary Jo's arm and said, "I hesitate to bring it up, but was Don Giuseppe among the casualties?"

"He's dead as a doornail."

"Yeah! Merry Christmas, Maurice!"

Mary Jo looked out over the ocean and could see the sun peeping over the Italian mainland. She looked at her watch and saw that it was 6:15 on Christmas morning. The Augusta landed at the Ajaccio airport, and Carlo said, "Giovanni is waiting for you inside the terminal. I'll go back to Urbe and take care of the X-14. When you decide to come get your plane, we can have a farewell dinner at Cacio e Pepe."

Mary Jo nodded in agreement and then asked, "What about Lieutenant Von Thalen and his men?"

"Their ride is waiting on them over there," Carlo answered, pointing to a twin-engine jet, with French Air Force markings, sitting on the tarmac.

Mary Jo looked at Von Thalen and said, "Thank you again."

The lieutenant smiled and said, "No problem. We were never here. General Capriati mentioned that you might want to visit our museum one day, and I'd be delighted to be your guide."

"Maybe one day. I wish you and your men fair winds and good fortune in the future."

"Yes, Colonel, it was a pleasure serving with you."

The ramp lowered, and Mary Jo and the Legionnaires deplaned. They jogged toward the jet, and Mary Jo walked into the terminal building. A beaming Giovanni was waiting in the lobby, and he swept her up in his arms and twirled her around.

Giovanni set Mary Jo down and said, "We've been monitoring the Castellanos's radio net all night long, and they have not had a Merry Christmas. It seems that a large force of commandos hit the castle in an unsuccessful attempt to breach their defenses. It seems Don Giuseppe died a hero's death while leading the defense. Also, unknown forces sank four of their largest freighters and destroyed their facilities in Marseilles, Genoa, and Tripoli. All in all, a bad night for them."

"Do you think we have their attention?"

"I'd say that we do. We received a message from their new Don, Dano Castellano, requesting a meeting later this afternoon. Of course, we extended our condolences and agreed to meet with him."

Giovanni led Mary Jo to one of the SUVs, and they left the airport with two more in front and two bringing up the rear, all filled with heavily armed men. Mary Jo said, "I see you're taking no chances between now and the meeting."

"No. I know what I would do in their place, and I don't want to let our guard down until we have a formal peace."

"So you think all of this might end by tonight?"

"One can only hope. We damaged the Castellanos last night — at least to the point that the new Don will need time to reorganize his holdings. I'd like to think we could end the feud all together, but this is Corsica and Sardinia, and our families have been at this for several hundred years."

"Will I be allowed to attend the meeting?"

"I think not. We don't want the Castellanos figuring out your role. Their arm of revenge might reach to Alabama. I'll fill you in as soon as the meeting ends. Let's get you back to the villa and let you grab a few hours' sleep. I know you've been up all night."

"I'm all for that. I feel myself coming down from the high, and I can probably sleep all day."

"Would you like some breakfast before you go to bed?"

"No, I'd like a hot bath and a soft pillow."

The caravan stopped at the front of the villa, and there was a welcoming committee waiting on the steps. All of the family and most of the staff began clapping as soon as Mary Jo climbed out of the SUV. Giovanni took her arm and said, "How does it feel to be a living family legend?"

"Right now, I'm numb. After a bath and a nap, I might be able to answer that."

Mary Jo was hugged and kissed and slapped on the back, until Giovanni cleared the way for her. Soon, Mary Jo was soaking in a steaming hot bath, and, when the water began to cool, she dried off and slipped between newly ironed sheets.

TWENTY-TWO

MARY JO AWOKE TO THE SMELL of freshly brewed coffee wafting through the room. She looked at her watch on the bedside table and thought, "Damn, it's after 6:00. I must have slept all afternoon. I guess the cooks are making coffee for the meeting. I think I'll go down and see if they can put together a little something for me to eat. I'm starving."

Mary Jo climbed out of bed and noticed her flight suit and long underwear scattered on the floor. She scooped them up and threw them on the bed. Then, she pulled jeans and a pullover from her flight bag. She ran a comb through her hair and took the stairs to the first floor. She was walking to the kitchen, when she passed the small dining room and saw Giovanni, Jeppe, and Don Ernesto sitting at the table eating and laughing.

When the men saw Mary Jo at the door, they all stood, and Don Ernesto said, "Mary Jo, my child, come and join us. This is a great day for the Capriati family."

Mary Jo caught the aroma of food coming from the buffet and replied, "Give me a chance to get a plate, and I'll be right over."

The buffet was loaded with dishes of hot food, and Mary Jo piled her plate high. Giovanni rose and held a seat for her, and she sat between Jeppe and the Don. A servant poured Mary Jo a hot cup of coffee, and she asked, "What are we celebrating? I thought that would come after Don Dano's visit tonight."

Jeppe laughed and said, "That was last night, my dear. I'm afraid you slept through it."

Mary Jo looked confused and then asked, "How can that be? It's not even 7:00 yet."

Don Ernesto smiled and said, "Yes, of course, you are right, but it's nearly 7:00 *in the morning*. After you've finished your breakfast, Giovanni and Jeppe will give you a firsthand account of the meeting with our friend Don Dano."

Mary Jo thought, "No wonder the buffet has all of this breakfast food. I can't believe I slept for over 20 hours."

Giovanni grinned and said, "Do you feel rested?"

"I've never done this! Even after the most dangerous mission, I was always able to recover almost instantly. I feel like such a baby."

"Well, you indeed slept like one," Giovanni teased.

"I don't want to push you too much, but I'd be interested in anything you feel comfortable telling us about Don Giuseppe's demise," Don Ernesto said.

Mary Jo took them through the events that led up to her crash-landing and then said, "I suppose you know all about the rescue by Lieutenant Von Thalen. He seemed to know Giovanni's family connection."

"Yes, we've all seen the after-action report," Giovanni replied. "Now, let me take you through our meeting with Dano last night. It went far better than we'd hoped. First, he came alone, which was an indication of trust that didn't go unnoticed. He insisted on telling us what the Sardinian police would release as the official account of Christmas Eve."

Giovanni continued: "It will be announced today that a force of terrorists from Africa mounted an attack on all of the Castellanos's holdings, including an attempt to capture the castle. The attack on the castle was repelled, but Don

Giuseppe was killed in the defense. There will be no mention of a helicopter or of an assassin."

Mary Jo asked, "Why is Dano being so cooperative?"

"He realizes that Don Giuseppe initiated the hostilities between our families after years of peace, and he wants to restore the trust and cooperation. He is willing to let what has happened bring an end to the hostilities and for everyone to start anew."

"Do you trust what he says?"

"As much as one may trust a Sardinian. I like the policy of your President Reagan: 'Trust but verify.'"

"Well, in this regard, we can rely on the old saying, 'All's well that ends well.' It doesn't bring Maurice back, but at least he didn't die unavenged, and some good came out of his death," Mary Jo replied.

Giovanni said, "Yes, and now I suppose we can all return to our normal lives. My leave is about done, and Paulo and Jean must also return to their responsibilities. We'll be leaving on the Bombardier later today, and we'll be glad to drop you off in Rome, or you can stay here with Jeppe and the Don for as long as you like."

"I think I need to get back to Mobile to try to restart my life. I'll take you up on the ride to Urbe this afternoon."

"We'll be leaving the villa at 10:00 if you can be ready."

"No problem. All I have is my flight bag to pack. I'll give Carlo a call and get him to meet me."

Jeppe took her hand and said, "Mary Jo, you have a home and a family here in Ajaccio. We hope you will come and visit from time to time, and I want you to know that all of us have a great deal of respect and affection for you."

"Thank you, Jeppe. You can depend on seeing me often in the future. I'll stop over in Paris for a night on my way home. Can you let Louie and Portia know to expect me?"

"Of course. Just give them a call before you are arriving, and you can stay as long as you like."

"I'll only stay for a night. I want to say goodbye to my friend Collette and her husband before I leave for the States, but then I'll be on my way."

Everyone finished breakfast and left Jeppe and Mary Jo at the table. When they were alone, Jeppe said, "I would like to ask a question about Don Giuseppe, if it won't make you uncomfortable."

"Of course. What would you like to know?"

"Do you have any misgivings about killing him?"

"None whatsoever. He murdered the man I love, and I'm only sorry I couldn't look him in the eye while he died."

"It's been years since I've had to kill, and sometimes I wonder why I don't feel any remorse over the death of my victims, but I feel nothing. Others tell of recurring nightmares and long bouts of depression resulting from taking a human life, but I cannot relate."

Mary Jo thought for a moment and said, "The only explanation I can offer is what a friend of mine who lives in Texas once said when I asked him the same question. He said, 'Hell no. The son of a bitch deserved killing.' As far as I am concerned, Don Giuseppe fell well within that category of victim."

Jeppe sat in silence for a while and then said, "When you put it like that, all of my victims qualified, as well."

"Then, good riddance, and don't look back. We're warriors, Jeppe, and killing comes with the territory. I can't say I enjoy it, but sometimes it's necessary."

Mary Jo hugged Jeppe and then climbed the stairs to her room. She sat by the window, called Carlo, and asked him to meet her at Urbe. He agreed, and she packed her flight bag, slipped into her jacket, and carried the bag and her funeral outfit to the front steps. Giovanni and his brothers and their families were loading a small mountain of baggage into four black SUVs. Jean took Mary Jo's bags and placed them in one of the vans, and she climbed in with his kids.

The heavily guarded caravan stopped at the Capriati hangar and began to offload all of their bags. Ground crewmen loaded a cart and placed the luggage into the Bombardier CRJ parked on the tarmac. Jean suggested that, since Mary Jo only had the one piece of luggage and the garment bag, she carry them on for the short flight to Rome.

The Capriati jet landed near the terminal at Urbe. Mary Jo told everyone goodbye and carried her bags down the stairway. Carlo was waiting on the steps of the terminal and was holding two cups of coffee. He leaned down, kissed her cheek, and handed her the coffee. They watched as the Capriati Bombardier took off and disappeared into the cloudless sky.

Finally, Carlo said, "Have you decided what you're going to do?"

"Yeah, I'm flying to Paris in the morning and on to the States Thursday. Are we still planning on dinner at Cacio e Pepe?"

"Yes, we have reservations at 8:00, and I took the liberty of inviting Roberto to join us."

"Good. I was going to suggest that we invite him. He really stuck his neck out for me."

"He indeed did, and I suspect he'd do it again. Do you need to do anything to prepare for your flight to Paris?"

"I just need to let operations know I'll need my plane. I'll file a flight plan in the morning. Give me a minute and we'll be good to go."

When Carlo had put Mary Jo's bags into the trunk of the Jag, they pulled up on the freeway leading into Rome. He said, "I thought we'd drop by my house and let you freshen up; then, I'd like to take you to my favorite spots in Rome."

"That sounds good. I would like to change clothes. Will we return to your house before dinner?"

"Yes, it gets dark so early this time of year, so we'll have a couple of hours before dinner. How are you holding up?"

"If you're referring to killing that bastard, I'm just fine. If you're talking about Maurice, I really don't know."

"I guess I meant both."

The two rode in silence until Carlo pulled into the circular drive in front of his home. He gave her bags to Malcolm, who escorted Mary Jo to the guest room. She stripped out of her jeans and pulled on a pair of wool slacks and a turtleneck sweater. She gave her hair a quick brush and put on some fresh lipstick. When she came down, Carlo was sitting by the fire with Johnny Mathis crooning about roasting chestnuts.

Carlo stood when Mary Jo came in and said, "I'm having a glass of wine. Would you like one?"

"Sure. It sounds a lot like Christmas. This is the first American Christmas song I've heard since I've been here."

"Yeah, you had an unusual Christmas…that's for certain."

Mary Jo took the glass of wine, closed her eyes, and listened to Johnny. Finally, she said, "I never had a chance to ask if you were able to salvage the X-14. Were you?"

"There was really very little damage. Gino was able to repair the broken skid, and she's as good as new. I'll give her a test flight next week, just to be sure."

"I'm glad the guys were able to get her out. I suspected that they were there to be sure she returned home."

"That was their secondary mission. Your safety came first. Fortunately, both were accomplished."

Mary Jo raised her wine glass and said, "To the Legion."

Carlo followed suit and answered, "To the Legion."

The friends sipped their wine and listened to the music, until Carlo said, "It's about time to leave. We'll have lunch at La Tavernaccia in Trastevere here on the Left Bank. It's close to the spot I mentioned earlier."

Mary Jo took the last sip of wine and said, "Good. It's pretty chilly, so let me grab my jacket and I'll be ready to go."

Carlo told Malcolm that they would return before dinner but that they'd be dining out. Carlo started the Jag to let it warm up, and, when the two got in, the interior was comfortable.

Carlo drove on the surface streets through quiet neighborhoods until he turned on to Via degli Stradivari and then up to the parking valet at La Tavernaccia. The small, intimate ristorante was about half full, and the two friends were seated by a crackling fire. Carlo looked at the menu and said, "This is one of my regular places. Their specialty is rigatoni, but every dish is a culinary delight."

They both ordered one of the rigatoni dishes, and Carlo chose a red wine to accompany the hearty plates of pasta. During the meal, they talked about the attack on the Castellanos and the Capriatis, and Carlo shared with Mary Jo his affection for the family. Finally, Carlo looked at his watch and said, "The light should be just about right. It's time to go see one of the wonders of Rome."

"I can't wait. I thought I'd seen them all while I was based here."

"Have you ever been to the Janiculum Hill?"

"No, I don't think so. Is it one of Rome's seven hills?"

"No. It lies outside the Tiber, but it's the second highest hill in the area."

"What makes it so special? Does it have ruins or monuments?"

"Like all of Rome, there are ruins on the hill, but that's not what makes it worth experiencing."

"Well, what does?"

"You'll see."

Carlo and Mary Jo left the restaurant and drove up on a hill high above the Tiber. There were cars and tour buses packing the parking lot, but Carlo finally found a parking place and held Mary Jo's door open while she got out. He took her by the arm and guided her to an observation point overlooking the heart of Rome. When Mary Jo reached the stone wall, she stood stunned. The sun setting in the west cast a warm, soft light over the city, creating the perfect painting. She gasped and said, "My heavens! I've never seen such perfect lighting. Rome looks like an impressionist painting."

Carlo smiled and asked, "Magnificent, isn't it? As I said, this is my favorite spot in all of Rome."

"I can certainly see why. Do you bring all of your dinner dates up here?"

"No, this is very personal to me. I come here when I'm worried about something. I wanted to share it with you."

Mary Jo looked at Carlo. She could see the love in his eyes and decided not to tease him any further. Instead, she changed the subject and said, "I can see at least a hundred easels set up along the wall. I wonder if anyone ever catches the lighting just right?"

"Many have tried, but I haven't seen one yet who caught it perfectly. The light only lasts for less than an hour before the sun sinks below the horizon. It's inspired not only artists but composers, as well. It's said that Respighi stood on this very spot and wrote the third movement of his 'Pines of Rome.'"

Mary Jo drew in a deep breath. "You can smell the pine trees. This is truly a magical place. Just think about how many people have marveled over it in the last 3,000 years. You can almost feel all of them in the air up here."

"This hill has seen a lot of history, no doubt about that," Carlo added.

The sun was dipping toward the sea, and the magic light had faded. The wind picked up, and leaves and pine needles were swirling at the couple's feet. Carlo pulled Mary Jo close and wrapped his arm around her. She cozied up to him to shelter from the wind and said, "Carlo, thank you for sharing this with me. I can see why it's your favorite spot."

"Now it can be our favorite spot," Carlo answered. On the way back to his house, they rode in silence.

When they reached Carlo's home, Mary Jo said that she'd like a shower before dinner and went straight to her room. After her shower, she stood in front of the full-length mirror and held up her little black dress. She'd planned to look nice for dinner, but, since it was freezing and she had no suitable coat, she decided to go back to the slacks and sweater plan.

Once she'd dressed and done her hair, Mary Jo came down to the living room, where there was a crackling fire. Carlo was sitting holding a drink, and he said, "I'm having a scotch. Would you like a Jack Daniel's?"

"I believe I would. Make mine neat."

The two arrived at the restaurant and found Roberto waiting when Cosimo led them to the private room. Roberto stood, hugged Mary Jo, and shook Carlo's hand. Then, he raised his wine glass and said, "Well, we all meet again, and everyone remains safe and sound."

Carlo replied, "To the successful completion of another mission, thanks, in a great part, to your support."

The friends all sat down, and Roberto poured the wine. Cosimo brought antipasto and said that he had prepared a special dinner in honor of the occasion. Everyone agreed to go with his suggestion, and, when it came, it was delicious. After the plates were cleared and the brandy served, Carlo said, "I'd like to propose a toast to Sergeant Maurice Lebeaux of the French Foreign Legion."

The trio raised their glasses and said, "To Sergeant Lebeaux."

Roberto asked Mary Jo what she planned to do, and she told him that, after a short visit to Paris, she was flying back to Mobile.

"Carlo and I hoped you'd stay in Rome for a while."

"I'd love to, but I've got a business to run, and we're extremely busy at the moment, but I'll be coming back as much as I can."

The evening wound down, and it was after 11:00 when Mary Jo and Carlo returned to Carlo's home. When they were back in the den, Carlo stirred the fire to life and asked, "Is there anything I can get you?"

Mary Jo smiled and said, "I have to fly in the morning, and I've had enough to drink, but there is something I want."

"Just name it."

"I want to fall asleep with you tonight. No hanky-panky. I just need you to hold me while I dream."

Carlo took Mary Jo's hand and led her to the master suite.

TWENTY-THREE

CARLO WAS STILL ASLEEP when Mary Jo awoke. She was curled in his arms, and he was gently snoring. She ducked under his arm, slipped out of bed, and looked at the bedside clock. It was 6:45. Mary Jo went to the bathroom, showered, and dried her hair. She slipped on a clean flight suit and her boots, tiptoed out of the room, and descended the stairs.

Mary Jo could hear Malcolm rattling around in the kitchen and found him looking into the oven. She asked, "What smells so good?"

Malcolm turned with a smile and said, "Thought I'd make hot brioche for your last breakfast with us. There's coffee on the counter, if you'd like some."

Mary Jo poured a cup and sat at the breakfast nook looking out on the bright winter morning. The trees had lost most of their leaves, and there was a white frost covering the ground. "Should be a great day to fly," she thought.

Malcolm brought a plate of the freshly baked brioche to the table, and Mary Jo was buttering one when Carlo came into the warm kitchen dressed in corduroys and a turtleneck sweater. He poured a cup of coffee, sat down across from her, and said, "I don't know about you, but I slept like a baby."

"Yeah, me too."

"We have plenty of time to sort it out, but I suspect you'll let me know when and if you're ready to move forward."

"I will. I just need some time to get my head straight."

"One thing that I'd like you to think about is the possibility of our working together. I think we'd make a great team," Carlo added.

"I do too, and I think that would be a good starting point."

The two finished breakfast, and Malcolm loaded all of Mary Jo's bags and boxes into the Jag. The couple drove to Urbe, making small talk as they moved through the early morning traffic. Carlo parked the car in the private terminal and helped Mary Jo carry her bags to the lobby. When they were inside, he took her hand and said, "I think you know how much I love you, but we move on your terms and in your time. Now, I'm going to leave before I say something stupid."

Mary Jo reached up, kissed Carlo gently on the lips, and said, "Thank you, Carlo. Thank you for your love, and thank you for giving me some time and space."

Carlo gave Mary Jo one last hug, and, without saying anything further, he turned and left the building. Mary Jo watched until the Jag had pulled away, and then she signaled for a porter to help with her baggage. Soon, she was flying into the rising sun.

www.ingramcontent.com/pod-product-compliance
Lightning Source LLC
Chambersburg PA
CBHW050509260626
47157CB00004B/1250